MW01127475

The Sun Daughter's Gift

By Eva Finley

Chapbook Press

Schuler Books
2660 28th Street SE
Grand Rapids, MI 49512
(616) 942-7330
www.schulerbooks.com

The Sun Daughter's Gift

ISBN 13: 9781948237529

Library of Congress Control Number: 2020917873

Printed in the United States by Chapbook Press.

CHAPTER 1

In the future...

Claretta hit the flashlight against her left hand as she tried to remember what Kamyra told her. Thanks to her, she was able to escape and if light could be created and her past self-listened, everyone could be saved. *They,* however, would do everything possible to stop her. Soaked, Claretta continued to run in the cold night air, as the darkness around her moved. Up ahead, a single lamppost stood in an empty parking lot. She ran to the artificial light and like Kamyra instructed, she took several deep breaths to slow her heart beat.

With her mind now clear, she swiped her hand across the air, smiling when pure light flowed from it. As the shadows started to catch up to her, Claretta tossed the wet letter she'd been holding onto, into the light, praying it would reach her younger self in time.

CHAPTER 2

In the past...

"Claretta, check the mail before you go!" Her mother yelled from the kitchen, three weeks ago.

"But I'm already late meeting Audi," 13-year-old Claretta replied with her hand on the doorknob.

"Then a few more minutes won't kill you!"

Claretta rolled her dark brown eyes and tossed her floral patterned purse on the closest couch.

Taking only her keys and her cell phone from their apartment on the 16th floor to the elevator, *Audi's going to kill me*, Claretta thought as she reached the main floor.

On the way back up, Claretta flipped through the latest edition of *Girls' Life Magazine* before rifling through the mail. When she did a letter addressed to her caught her eye. Even stranger than Claretta having mailed it too herself; there wasn't an envelope. It was just a folded piece of paper with her name written across in sloppy cursive. *Ding*, the elevator rang as it opened to her floor but Claretta didn't he it. Her mind was focused on the cursive letters that spelled her name. The sound of the doors closing freed Claretta from her trance and she quickly stuck out a hand to make them open again.

This has got to be a joke. I didn't write a letter to myself. How it even get in the mail like this, Claretta thought as she reached her apartment. In a hurry to get going, she placed the other mail on the coffee table and shoved the letter in her purse.

Fifteen minutes later, Claretta got off the city bus in her hometown of Quincy, Ohio. When the bus moved on and the traffic slowed down, she walked two blocks down to the KFC on the left. Once through the glass doors, she spotted Audi in a booth near the exit.

"You're late," Audi said. She smiled glancing over her right shoulder where her long brown hair with golden highlights was draped.

"Sorry," Claretta said as she sat across from her best friend. "I got your letter in the mail. Very funny making it seem like I mailed it to myself."

"I didn't mail you a letter," Audi said her brows furrowed as she stirred a mound of mashed potatoes and gravy.

Claretta placed the letter on the table and slid it towards Audi. She hoped her friend would confess it *was* just a joke once she saw it but Audi remained silent. After a few more seconds passed, Claretta got up to join the growing line at the counter.

While waiting in line behind a woman with two young kids, movement to the left caught Claretta's attention. She stopped gathering her long natural hair into a low ponytail and searched the wall by the exit near the drive-thru. *I could've sworn I saw a shadow move;* Claretta thought but now saw nothing of the sort. *It was probably just someone's shadow.*

Chicken Little combo, with an extra side of wedges on her tray,

3

Claretta made her way back to the booth.

"Huh," Claretta gasped as she stumbled forward, catching he Coke before it fell off the tray. She looked at the tiled floor to find what tripped her but nothing was there. When a shadow moved unde: a table diagonally across from her, Claretta brushed it off as a trick o the light.

"Did you read this yet?" Audi asked, glancing towards the ceiling corner at the booth behind Claretta. There was no movement. They were safe, for now.

"Talk about invasion of privacy," Claretta joked. "What if it was a love letter?"

"Then we would've spent the next half hour going over ever₃ detail."

"True and no, I didn't," Claretta said, taking another look at i

"Read it, please," Audi said, all joking aside. *To my younger self, the dark isn't safe. Don't trust the shadows, they fear the light. Y. must USE YOUR POWERS to beat them. Claretta, from the future*

"Are you sure you didn't send this?" Claretta asked after having read it twice. The handwriting on the inside was even worse than her name. The lines raised up and down, half overlapping a wor here and there and some of the letters were unfinished.

"I promise, I didn't," Audi said. She looked toward the corne ceiling again.

"What do you keep looking at?" Claretta asked looking over her shoulder.

"We should go!"

Claretta reluctantly left her uneaten food and went with Audi who rushed her out the door clearly afraid of something.

Audi grabbed Claretta's hand and dragged her down the sidewalk the way Claretta had came. Customers grumbled as they waited outside a full diner, whose line spilled onto the sidewalk. The late afternoon Sun was hot but it was worth waiting for the best pasta in town. The bell to the gift shop two doors down from it dinged, as she led them to a city bus, whose out of service sign light had come on. Audi continued to glance over her shoulder, as the overweight driver and its passengers exited the bus.

Using the distraction to her advantage, Audi pushed Claretta onto it, while the driver led the disgruntled passengers to the next bus stop.

"Yes, I know, it's an inconvenience," they heard the driver say to an older woman with a large purse, "but another bus is on its way."

The smell of sweat and fried food filled their noses as they stayed crouched in the aisle. When the voices were no higher than a whisper, the bus gave a violent shake.

"What the...I think someone just hit the bus," Claretta said, moving towards the back door in her crouched position.

"Don't get out! Not yet!" Audi said, grabbing Claretta's arm.

With Claretta by her side, Audi placed both hands on the floor.

"What are you doing?" Claretta asked.

Audi ignored her question and focused on her task. She took a

5

deep breath and slowly released it from her lips as pure light flowed through her body to her hands. A few moments later, the bus was fill a bright golden color, as Audi checked for shadows inside. Satisfied with her search, the bus returned to normal.

"What just happened?" Claretta asked.

"Do you remember what I told you a couple months ago, about who I am?

"Not the whole Sun's daughter thing again?"

"You still remained my friend, even though, you didn't believ me."

"I just thought it was a joke you kept trying to pull."

"Well, it's not. You *need* to take this letter seriously though. *You* wrote it to yourself from the future."

"Yeah right. I was probably half asleep, trying to write mysel reminder for something."

Audi stared at Claretta, desperately, wanting her to believe he as the bus shook again. She didn't have much time but knew she had give Quincy a chance.

"I want to give you something for being such a good friend. You may not fully understand its' importance now but you'll need it.'

"Okay," Claretta said slowly.

"Give me your hands!" Audi instructed as the bus shook for ; third time.

Claretta looked at her eyebrows raised. "What's going on out there?" She looked out the window at the street and the sidewalk but there were no cars on either side of them. Across from a Toyota parallel parked four spots down, two men in their 20's stood in the shadows of a hardware store's archway. Every few seconds, they would glance over at the bus from beneath their matching baseball caps. They appeared to be in no hurry as others walked around them into the shop. *What are they up too?*

"Claretta Marie Arbogast, give me your hands and trust me."

"I hate when you use my full name." Claretta mumbled, giving in to Audi's demand.

Audi just smiled.

"Close your eyes!" Audi instructed. Once Claretta's eyes were closed, she did the same thing. "Let your breathing match mine. If your heart is ever beating fast, you have to slow it down and clear your mind, no matter what's going on around you."

When Claretta's breathing matched hers, Audi created pure light but this time not as a weapon. A gold colored light came from her palms and fingertips and washed over Claretta's brown skin. Audi knew transferring her power would leave her defenseless but she knew the Shadow People were coming for her. If Claretta, at least, had the power to create pure light, then their city had a chance. "For the Sun's children," Audi whispered when Claretta's entire body stopped glowing.

Not liking what they saw, the two men pulled their caps down and moved from the safety of the shadows. The shorter man gave a low growl as they stepped into the Sun, rubbing their arms in an attempt to soothe the pain caused by the Sun's rays. Though getting struck by pure light was a quick way to turn them to ashes, the longe: they remained in the light, the worse the pain got. Seeing them approach, Audi grabbed Claretta's hand once again and ran to the fro: of the bus.

"Tell me, what's going on." Claretta said as they ran down th sidewalk. The two men followed behind.

"You now have the power to create light. It's not normal ligh though; it's pure sunlight, pure light as we call it." Audi talked fast as they continued to run, trying to reach the next stop as a bus passed by them. "The more you practice, the better you'll be. Remember what I told you over the years and *trust* the letter."

The bus started to pull away before they could reach it, but Audi didn't slow down. "Keep running!" She yelled at Claretta as the two men started to catch up. She pounded on the side of the bus until stopped, its front end sticking out into the street. The new driver opened the door with an annoyed look on his face. As soon as they were both inside, he closed the door and sped off, leaving the two me behind.

"Whatever you do, don't trust the shadows." Audi whispered from their seats near the back, as the bus came to a stop outside Claretta's apartment building.

"I haven't been afraid of the dark since I was little, you know that." Claretta said walking to the back door of the bus.

"The world is going to need the light when it goes dark. Goo(

luck," Audi said ignoring the weird looks from those around her.

Screeching tires made Claretta turn away from the doors of her apartment building. *That's the same car that was parked behind us,* she thought. She looked at the Toyota until it turned the corner following the city bus.

With her cell phone out, Claretta walked past the mail boxes on her left to the elevator on her right. She was so busy updating her Facebook and tweeting that she didn't notice a shadow had moved into the elevator and exit with her moments later.

The shadow brushed across the ceiling of the 22nd floor and into apartment 32.

Unaware she'd been followed; Claretta unlocked the door, letting herself and the shadow in. Having some time alone until her parents returned from the store, Claretta went to her room and took the letter out again. She decided to humor her friend and compared the writing in the letter to her own; it was an exact match.

That's impossible, Claretta thought. *I didn't mail anything to myself.* She flipped the letter over and stared at her name. *Someone must've bribed the mailman to let them sneak this in when he was delivering the mail.*

Claretta bit her thumbnail as she sat on her bed with the letter in her lap. She read it again and decided to try and create pure light. *Why not?* She thought. Claretta closed her eyes and with everything that had gone on today, it took her several minutes to clear her mind.

A warm feeling rushed through her body and when she opened

her eyes a golden light radiated two inches from her hands. It lasted í a few seconds before her hands returned to normal. Claretta tried it again this time with her eyes open. A small glow started from the palms of her hands and got brighter as it spread to her fingertips until the golden light radiated from her hands once again. Claretta moved her glowing hands around. As she did, the shadow across from her slithered on the yellow wall.

Claretta gasped and the light vanished with her concentration

The shadow remained still and watched as Claretta created pure light once again. This time she did something the shadow wasn' expecting. With glowing hands, Claretta walked to where she saw the shadow move. It tried to stay put but refused to be turned to ash. To say, it felt like it was on fire would be an understatement. You were burned from the outside to your very soul.

Claretta screamed shielding her face as the shadow moved towards her. The shadow retreated for now and Claretta surprisingly followed it out her room and out the apartment. She stood in the doorway watching it slither down the hall.

After slamming the door shut, Claretta turned on everything from lamps to ceiling lights. Once she was able to calm down, she remembered what the letter said and decided to walk to the store 8 blocks from the apartment.

CHAPTER 3

In the future...

"Stay away from me!" Claretta yelled as the shadows swarmed her. Her heart pounded in her chest as though she'd just run a mile. She tried to create pure light again but nothing happened. *I should've listened to Audi,* crossed her mind as it had every day since she was captured.

A minute later, the shadows parted to reveal the a Shadow Person standing before her. Claretta hated when they appeared in their true form. It was bad enough when they shifted to a shadow but this was even worse. Their true form was like looking at a person's shadow standing in front of you while the edges of their silhouette made her think of smoke blowing in the wind. Somehow, they were a shade darker than a starless night in an open field with black eye sockets she dared not look in. Since they took over Quincy, there was no longer any need for them to take on human features.

Claretta tried to back away from the Shadow Person but the shadows kept her in place. Grabbing her around the waist, the Shadow Person pulled her to him, and stuck a needle in the side of her neck. He continued to hold Claretta as her legs gave out, and her eyes closed.

Hours later, Claretta awoke with her back against a wall, facing in what she assumed to be the direction of the door. *I hope there aren't any shadows in here,* she thought, searching the familiar darkness for any movement.

11

"Hello! Is anyone there?" Claretta shouted but no one answered. When she first arrived, she was placed in a room with Kamyra. After the stunt they pulled, she wasn't surprised to find herself away from the others. She knew the letter had to be sent but Claretta hated being alone. The dark silence that surrounded her was deafening and she was beyond tired of humming and singing to herself off key. At least with Kamyra, she had someone else with her.

Tired of sitting still, Claretta got up and felt her way around the cement room. It was about the size of a small pod and completely bare. When she returned to sitting against the wall, the door across from her opened and closed. It continued to do so for the next 20 minutes. Claretta and the Sun's daughters hated when the Shadow People played with their "*trophies*" or "*toys*" as they were called. Sometimes they hid in the room only to scare them or push them around later. Other times, no one was there at all.

"What do you want?" Claretta yelled.

"How did you escape?" A male voice asked from beside her.

Claretta looked to her left, where a Shadow Person sat beside her.

"Ahhhhh!" Claretta screamed as she scooted away from him. *How long has he been sitting there?*

The Shadow Person laughed at the girl's fear. He'd been there since the beginning, watching her eyes widen as the door opened and closed and her frantic search for any movement in the dark.

"Who are you? Claretta asked from the corner. "Are you the

one in charge here?"

"I'm the second in command here. You don't want to meet our leader again."

Again? When did I ever meet their leader?

"You *will* answer my question though."

"I followed the moonlight. You may have killed the Sun but the moon still shines bright."

"Moonlight doesn't matter to me. What does is *you* creating pure light. Now, why would you be doing that?"

Claretta remained silent but the Shadow Person was determined to get an answer. In just three steps, he pulled Claretta off the ground by her arm.

"What did I say about answering me?" He said an inch from her face.

Eyes on the ground, Claretta answered him. "Kamyra thought that if I could create pure light, I'd be able to escape and bring back help," she lied once again.

"Show me."

The Shadow Person let go of her arm and stepped what he hoped was a safe distance away. Claretta held out her hands and closed her eyes. Between the Shadow Person staring at her and the fear of what would happen if she succeeded, Claretta was barely able to make her hands glow.

The Shadow Person laughed at her sad attempt.

"If anyone catches you trying to create pure light again, you *will* regret it," the Shadow Person left her with a warning as he exited the room.

CHAPTER 4

In the past...

Both arms loaded with bags from Sundial Market, Claretta carried the solar lights home. In her haste to get more light, she'd forgotten about the pools of shadows among the houses, trees, and cars that seemed to crowd the small dirt road. As though taunting her, the thin trees branches, whose shadows stretched across the road, shook in her direction. *I don't remember there being this many shadows,* Claretta thought after she jumped for a third time.

Once home, Claretta set the solar lights in the yard outside her apartment building, praying the other tenants or landlord wouldn't take them down. While they soaked up sunlight, Claretta sat on a bench outside the door, until the shadows chased her inside. That evening when her parents got home, they found every light in their three-bedroom apartment on and solar lights everywhere. They turned off some of the lights as they walked down the hall to Claretta's room. Opening the door, they found every inch of their daughter's room, filled with every version of solar light she could find.

Mr. and Mrs. Arbogast looked at each other, then their daughter who sat on her bed reading a book.

"You're too old to still be afraid of the dark," her father said, remembering she used to leave the lights on when she was younger.

"I'm not afraid," Claretta said. *Well, at least, not as much until now,* she thought.

"If you want to keep a few on in your room that's fine but the rest need to go," her mother said looking around again.

"Fine," Claretta sighed, closing her book. She walked past her parents to the kitchen for a garbage bag then proceeded to clear the kitchen and living room.

Having finished, Claretta returned to her room and dumped the bag on her closet floor. *I can't believe this is happening to me*, she thought, thinking about what happened at KFC. *No, this can't be real What Audi did on the bus had to be some sort of magic trick.* Picking up her cellphone, Claretta called Audi. It just rang and rang, eventually, going to voice mail. After trying two more times with no response, she threw the phone on her bed.

Claretta tried calling her friend several times throughout the day but still received no response. As she got in bed that night, she tried one last time making sure to leave a message for Audi to call her

The next morning, Claretta groaned as sunlight shined through her curtains. Nonetheless, she welcomed it. The moment sleep came her; it had been snatched away by the shadows scratching at her window or tapping at her bedroom door. Though the solar lights failed to reach every corner of her room, they kept the shadows out for now

Kicking back the sheets, Claretta rolled to the edge of her bed and pulled part of the curtain aside to let in more light. Sitting up, her eyes searched the dark spaces. Seeing no movement, a breath that had been held captive escaped as a sigh of relief and Claretta got out of bed.

She walked down the hall to find her dad in his pajamas standing in front of the refrigerator door. He held it open with his right hand and had a cup of coffee in his left.

"Where's mom?" Claretta asked.

"The hospital called her in early," he said taking a sip of his coffee. He stared back into the fridge as though it would tell him what to cook. "What should I make us for breakfast?"

"You're going to make breakfast?" Claretta asked skeptically. Her dad was good at cooking a lot of things but breakfast wasn't one of them.

"Maybe we should go get something to eat instead. Breakfast toasters?"

"Sounds great. I'll go get them," Claretta offered wanting to get some fresh air.

"Did you sleep okay last night?" Her dad asked as Claretta turned back to her room.

"Yeah, dad!"

"Are you sure? Because that was a lot of...."

"I'm fine. I was just joking around," Claretta lied.

"Okay," her father said, dropping the subject.

Meanwhile, not far from there, 14-year-old, Daijon Cooper, sat at a table with his friends at the Sonic Drive-In. The weather was surprisingly warm for 9:30 am but Daijon hadn't noticed. He was worried about his little sister, Audi who he hadn't seen since the day she met up with Claretta. Not paying attention, he knocked his Cherry

17

Vanilla Dr. Pepper off the table and onto his black jeans.

"Shit," Daijon mumbled. When he looked up to grab a napkin he spotted Claretta standing at the patio menu board in jeans and a floral tank top. *I'll protect her,* Daijon thought remembering the last promise he'd made to Audi. She was the only person who knew his secret, even though, his father told him to tell no one until the time was right. Unlike his sisters, he couldn't create pure light but what he *could* do might be enough to save them.

"Hey, I'll be right back," Daijon said to the dark-haired guy sitting next to him while looking at Claretta.

"Bring more fries back with you," Mark looked up at him the followed his gaze. "Oh, I see. She's cute."

"That's my little sister's best friend," Daijon said giving Mark a playful punch on the shoulder. He had to agree though; she was cute As he walked over to her, his friends made kissing noises and laughed

"Hey," Daijon said standing next to her.

Claretta looked at the laughing boys then at Daijon. "Hey," she said. "Haven't seen you in awhile." She took a good look at her best friend's brother. He was a year older than them and lived with their d while Audi and her sisters stayed with their mom. Well, except Prima who was in college. He had chocolate brown eyes and naturally curly hair with golden blonde highlights that he and his siblings swore was natural. Oh and he was cute. Realizing she was staring, Claretta returned her attention to the board.

"Same here," Daijon said. "Hope my sister is not getting you

18

into any trouble."

"I'm thinking it's too late for that."

Daijon just looked at her, not sure what she meant by that but it didn't sound good. Audi told him she was going to do something stupid but wouldn't tell him what it was. All she said was to protect Claretta.

"Can't decide what to get?" Daijon asked as Claretta continued to stare at the menu board.

"I was going to get a breakfast toaster for me and my dad but now I'm thinking about french toast sticks."

Daijon couldn't help but laugh at the cute way Claretta tilted her head as she contemplated her choices. "You could always get both and you and your dad can share."

"Sounds good to me," Claretta smiled finally pushing the red button to order.

While she waited, they talked about classes and summer vacation. Neither of them brought up the Shadow People or Audi.

When the food came, she waved goodbye to Daijon and walked to the bus stop. Just as it pulled up, Claretta heard a low chuckle come from behind her. Looking over her shoulder, she expected to see a person but no one was there. Hearing it again, her eyes went to the trees behind her. The branches started to sway but Claretta wasn't sure if it was because of the light breeze or if shadows were cloaked in the trees leaves. She thought about going back to the restaurant as Daijon returned to his friends but, thankfully, the bus arrived and she didn't have to find out what was lurking nearby.

19

Sitting on his bike down the street from Claretta's apartment, Daijon stayed out of sight as he watched her walk into the building. I had no intention of going in until he saw a man in workout clothes following her. To anyone else, he was an average guy going into a building but Daijon knew better. He was the only male born to the Su and while he may not have his sister's powers, he could distinguish a human from a Shadow Person. When they took on human features, h could see the dark smoky aura that surrounded them. It didn't matter where they hid in shadow form. Even if it was another person's shadow, he'd still be able to see them.

Hopping off his bike, Daijon ran towards the building.

"What are you doing?" Claretta shouted just as she was abou to push the elevator button. "Get off him!"

Daijon had jumped on the Shadow Persons back and now struggled to keep the 6-foot man pinned to the ground. "Run!" He shouted looking up at Claretta. The man rolled from beneath him, elbowing Daijon in the chest. When the man went after Claretta, whc stood frozen by the elevators, Daijon grabbed his arm. This time, the man was ready.

"Run!" Daijon managed to yell again before he was slammec against the mail boxes.

Claretta pushed the button over and over trying to get the elevator to move quicker. The man punched Daijon in the side and gripped the boy's neck with both hands. Remembering what his dad taught him, Daijon brought his hands over the man's arms to the top his wrist. Using all his strength, he knocked the man's hands away and kicked him in the groin. "No, take the stairs," Daijon said dodging the man's hands as they attempted to reach for him while he was bent over.

As soon as Claretta hit the second step, another Shadow Person came through the door. Changing to shadow form, he went after her while Daijon continued fighting. In the stairwell, Claretta tried to relax in order to create pure light but was too scared to clear her mind. Making it to the 7th floor, she needed a break but the shadow that followed her stretched itself up the stairs. Her moment of rest ended too soon when Claretta saw the shadow's hand stretch around the corner. She pushed off the wall she'd been leaning on and opened the door to the 7th floor.

Back on the main floor, Daijon managed to lure the Shadow Person outside. Once the man was locked out, he took the stairs looking for any signs of Claretta. He found the door to the 7th floor open and when he went into the hall; he found Claretta and the shadow.

Claretta backed away from it as Daijon tried to get her attention. TV's, shouting and the sounds of kids playing could be heard coming from behind the other tenant's doors. Trying not to disturb anyone, Daijon got Claretta's attentions by waving a solar light he took from the yard. The shadow saw what Daijon was trying to do and went after him first.

"Claretta," Daijon said tossing her the solar light before the shadow knocked him back into the stairwell.

21

She glanced at it, not sure of what to do.

The shadow expanded, covering the ceiling, floor and both walls. Claretta was running out of room when Daijon appeared back the stairwell door.

The hallway grew darker as the shadow got closer. All her fea of the dark when she was little started to resurface but she had never imagined anything like this. Claretta tried to relax as she held the sol: light with both hands. Closing her eyes, she pretended it was just a dream and she was safe in her bed hiding beneath the covers. As her heartbeat slowed, the color emitting from the solar light turned a golden color and started to glow. It was weak but when the shadow saw Claretta put the pure light into the solar light; it retreated.

When it was over, Claretta just stood there with such a light touch on the solar light that it fell from her hands. Glass sprinkled around her in chunks as the white clear ball on top of the solar light I the ground.

"Come on, let's go," Daijon said guiding Claretta to the stairwell and away from the broken glass that still held pure light.

Claretta broke from her daze and led Daijon to her apartment.

"We have a lot to talk about," Daijon said handing her the bag from Sonic that she'd dropped.

Claretta simply nodded her head and opened the door.

"Hey dad," Claretta called as she rounded the corner to the living room. She found him sitting on the loveseat that sat parallel to the TV. "Is it okay if Daijon hangs out here for a while?"

"Who?" Her father asked looking up from the paper and over his right shoulder. He'd shed the pajamas and now wore jeans and a solid black tee-shirt; his feet remained bare.

"Daijon Cooper, Audi's older brother," Claretta said taking half the sandwich and a few French toast sticks before handing him the bag.

Her father looked at the boy with golden streaked hair. "We haven't seen you around here in a while."

"I've been keeping myself occupied," Daijon smiled shoving his hands in his pockets.

"So, can he stay?"

"That's fine," her father replied retrieving his half of the sandwich from the bag's depths.

"We're just gonna go watch a movie in my room," Claretta said.

"Don't forget, door open!" her father yelled down the hall at her. Daijon chuckled and followed behind Claretta who tried to hide her blush.

The first thing Daijon noticed when entering her room was the solar lights. They were on the dresser, hanging from the mirror, and spilling out the open closet.

"So, you finally believe her," Daijon referred to his sister as he played with the string solar lights on the full-length mirror in the far corner.

"Kind of hard not to now," Claretta replied sitting on her bed

23

next to the window.

"Then let's begin," Daijon said turning on her TV and anythi:
else that would be a distraction.

"You've got to learn to ignore everything around you and focu
on the pure light *inside* you in order to create it," Daijon chastised afi
yet another failed attempt. He looked at her from across the room,
where he leaned against the closed bedroom door. "Out of all her
friends, why did Audi chose you to save our sisters and this city?"

"Out of the few of us she told, I'm the only one that remaine
her friend," Claretta replied from the other side of the bed. "No matt
how many times she told me, I still didn't believe she was one of the
Sun's daughters. I thought she was playing a joke."

"Yeah, my sisters is big on loyalty and she trusts you."

"How does she expect me to fight the Shadow People? I mea
look at me."

Daijon looked Claretta up and down making her slightly
uneasy. He grinned seeing nothing wrong with her. "You just need to
practice."

"Oh, there's also the letter," Claretta said momentarily
forgetting all about it.

"What letter?"

Claretta walked to the closet and reached into her favorite pai
of boots. Tucked inside, next to a small solar light was the letter.
Daijon's left eyebrow raised in question as he walked over to her.

"What?" Claretta replied seeing his expression. "I was keepii

24

it safe."

Daijon had to read it twice to decipher the sloppy writing. "Is this how it came to you?"

Claretta nodded.

"It appears my sisters learned how to send letters through time." He saw the confused look on Claretta's face and explained further. "When I was younger, Audi told me they had experimented with sending letters through light. Kamyra wondered if they could control not only where the letters came out but *when* they came out. Tell me something, if you hadn't gotten this letter, would you have believed Audi?"

"No not until she gave me her powers."

"The only thing, I can think of, is your future self needed to change something around this time. That's the main reason my sisters tried it; to get out of trouble. In order to protect Quincy, you have to be able to transfer pure light into a lamp post. These have a symbol of the Sun on them."

"How's that going to help save your sisters?"

"As far as I know, all my sisters have been caught by the Shadow People. Putting pure light into the lamp post will keep Quincy safe until they're free. If our mother dies, we and those lights are all that's left to protect everyone."

It was around lunchtime when Claretta's dad called her from the kitchen.

"Mr. McGregor, from the third floor, just called!" He yelled from his bedroom. "I'm going to pick up the tools he borrowed. It shouldn't take too long. If you need anything, Mrs. Stern, is just a couple doors down and keep that door open."

Claretta opened it just as her dad stepped into the hallway leading to the bedrooms. He looked at his daughter, then the boy standing behind her. "Don't worry, dad, I'll be fine," she said before h could say anything else. She walked him to the door and locked the deadbolt behind him.

"You want something to eat?" Claretta asked Daijon.

"Sure," Daijon replied surprised she hadn't kicked him out ye He'd been hard on her pushing her to create pure light but she just scowled at him and kept at it.

Upon entering the kitchen, Daijon couldn't help but laugh as Claretta pushed the refrigerator door closed with her foot. He continued to watch her as she struggled to balance everything.

Lettuce, tomatoes, mustard, pickles, cheese, and three kinds c sandwich meat toppled from her arms onto the kitchen table.

"You could've helped," Claretta said when she realized Daijc had been there the entire time.

"And miss your balancing act," he laughed walking over to t bread box. Grabbing a loaf, he placed it next to the other items. "There, now I've done my part."

Claretta rolled her eyes but couldn't help but laugh.

Just then, there was a knock at the door.

Leaving Daijon to start making his sandwich, Claretta walkec to the door and looked out the peephole. A woman, in her early 30's with short hair stood in the hallway, staring at the peephole as though she could see Claretta. Not knowing who she was Claretta backed away from the door assuming the woman would just leave.

The moment she walked away; the knocking continued.

"Who's at the door?" Daijon asked walking around the wall that led to the kitchen.

"There's some woman there but I don't know who she is," Claretta whispered.

Daijon walked past her and looked out.

"What's wrong?" Claretta asked when Daijon quickly backed away.

"She's a Shadow Person."

"How do you know that?"

"Shadow People have a dark smoky aura around them that only I can see."

"She can't get in, can she?" Claretta asked moving to stand by Daijon near the hallway.

"As long as there's no opening at the bottom or a..." Daijon trailed off noticing the slight gap near the top of the door.

As soon as the words left his lips, a shadow squeezed through it. Remembering the solar lights in her room, Claretta turned to retrieve one but was blocked by the shadow hanging halfway off the ceiling. It dropped to the floor making no sound and advanced on them.

"Now would be a good time to create pure light," Daijon said, moving in front of her.

Claretta looked over his shoulder as the shadow got closer.

"Ignore it," Daijon said taking his eyes off the shadow to look back at her.

Claretta took a few deep breaths and looked at her hands. The golden color of pure light came and went from them like the caution light at a traffic stop. "It's not working."

When the shadow returned to the ceiling, they tried to make it to Claretta's room but stopped when a black round object the size of a golf ball fell from the ceiling.

"What is that?" Claretta asked.

"Shadow orb. They look harmless but can be sharp like razor or hard like a baseball."

Claretta and Daijon dodged the shadow orbs that continued to fall from the ceiling.

"Keep it down up there!" An angry voice yelled from below.

Running into the living room, they slid under the coffee table. They huddled close together with their backs on the ground and knee slightly bent.

"How's that light coming?" Daijon asked as another shadow orb hit the table.

"Um..." Claretta replied her hands barely glowing.

"You might want to hurry because the shadow will get tired of playing with us and your dad will be back at any moment."

28

Claretta slid from under the table and Daijon followed. The shadow fell from the ceiling and stood a few feet away. Closing her eyes, Claretta held her palms in front of her facing the Shadow Person. Focusing on the light, she meant to send a pure light orb at the shadow from both hands but succeeded in only producing one. It was enough though. Not expecting the girl to be able to use her powers, the shadow barely dodged it in time. Still, it took a step forward but retreated when Claretta's other palm started to glow. Not willing to risk it, the Shadow Person threw another shadow orb. While the children were distracted, it turned back into shadow form and slithered back through the crack in the door.

"Good job. See, I knew you could do it." Daijon said after checking the peephole for any movement.

"Thanks, but what am I supposed to tell my parents about the scratches on the table and floor?" Claretta asked.

"Well, thankfully, the carpet's dark and the shadow orb made a clean cut so maybe they won't notice. As for the table, we could try to cover it with something."

Claretta thought for a moment then remembered the lace table runner her mother kept on the top shelf of the living room closet. She grabbed a stool and though it was far from being centered; it at least covered the scratches. When her dad finally returned moments later, Claretta and Daijon were back in the kitchen making their sandwiches as though nothing had happened.

Hours later, Claretta was finally able to put pure light into one of the solar lights that no longer glowed. She held the small staff away from her surprised by what she had done.

"Until you can control pure light better and learn to fight with it, you can use the solar staff," Daijon explained. "It'll work on a Shadow Person no matter what form they take. If you ever find yourself trapped in the dark, wave it. Any shadow trying to hide would rather move than be burned."

"What are we burning?" her mother asked. She'd just gotten home from a long day and wanted to check on her daughter.

"I was just telling Claretta about the last candle my dad burned," Daijon replied.

"Hello, Daijon, nice to have you around again," Mrs. Arboga said. "Claretta, can you run to the gas station and get a two pack of light bulbs for the dining room. Dinner's about to start and I'd hate for us to sit in a half-lit room."

"Sure. Can Daijon stay for dinner?" Claretta asked realizing they'd been working most of the day.

"I'm sure his father would like to see him at some point today but if it's okay with him, then yes. It'll be ready in an hour."

On their way to the gas station, Claretta and Daijon came across an empty parking lot that belonged to an insurance company. The sun had already set and there were shadows everywhere but there was nothing they could do about that. They stood at the edge of the parking lot while Daijon surveyed the area; his grip firm on the solar light he'd taken from Claretta's room.

"We could go around but we could still run into Shadow People." Daijon said taking note of the lamp post in the parking lot.

On their return from the gas station, it was darker out. Needing to get back to the safety of the apartment building, Daijon and Claretta were forced to take the shortcut through the parking lot again. This time, the only light was coming from the distant lamp post and that of the emergency light right inside the building.

"We're not alone," Daijon told Claretta. "Put more pure light in the staffs."

Claretta looked at him confused.

"Trust me, it'll fit."

The Shadow People in the parking lot began to move; no longer needing to hide. Claretta could only see the darkness that continued to get darker while Daijon could see the Shadow People becoming one with the night. For him, it was like seeing a person in the afternoon light.

"Claretta!" Daijon shouted as she stood there unmoving. "Claretta, focus!"

Claretta's eyes darted everywhere barely able to see.

"Don't search for them just focus on the staff."

She lowered her eyes and cleared her mind trying to create pure light in one hand while holding the staff in the other. When the pure light was the right size, she placed it on the glass of the solar light and lightly pushed.

31

"Don't worry, it won't come out. Only someone with the pow of pure light can remove it from an object," Daijon said.

As he and Claretta started moving through the parking lot, a shadow rose from the ground and stood before them in its true form. Daijon took a step back and placed himself between it and Claretta then quickly thrust forward with his staff. The Shadow Person shattered the emergency light with its hollow shout.

Claretta swung her staff around with both hands and jumped when she heard a shriek. That's when she noticed the Shadow Person move for the first time. *They're darker than the darkness around ther. How is that even possible,* Claretta thought.

"How good can you throw?" Daijon whispered.

"Why?" Claretta asked nervously.

"Because getting across here depends on it."

Claretta continued swinging at shadows while Daijon thought his plan through. Afraid of the moving darkness around her, she took step forward to run but Daijon grabbed her arm pulling her closer to him.

"I'll tell you where to throw and you're going to have to trust me," Daijon whispered in her ear.

"Okay," Claretta whispered in the same nervous tone that had more to do with the Shadow People than being close to Daijon.

Daijon turned Claretta's shoulders to the left a little then pointed to an old lamp post in front of her. Trying to calm the panic inside her, Claretta managed to create an orb of pure light, and then threw it with such precision you would think she'd done this before. She lightly flinched when the light reached the glass. Instead of breaking, it consumed the pure light letting it feel every crevice.

"My mother made lamp post like these. How and when I'm not sure but I know this symbol means that it will hold the pure light you and my sisters make," Daijon explained pointing to the sun symbol on the pole as he pushed Claretta towards it. "If I'm unable to find her symbol, I know to look for the sun shaped glass."

Standing in the light that now formed a circle around the base of the lamppost, Claretta was able to see better. Shadow People waited for them on the edge of the light but they had no choice but to venture into the darkness to get home.

"There's another lamp post by the edge of the street." Daijon whispered.

Claretta saw the one he was referring to. The Shadow People danced in delight as Claretta neared the lights edge. An orb of pure light started to form in her hands when a Shadow Person came up to her. It gave a deep hollow shout that almost sounded like race cars on a track but deeper and much scarier.

The ball dissipated but Claretta tried again attempting to ignore the Shadow Person before her. When it got in her face, Claretta lifted the orb of pure light to her mouth and lightly blew on it. Particles of pure light brushed off the top towards the Shadow Person. It gave another hollow shout loud enough that it was bound to wake up someone in the houses nearby.

"Claretta," Daijon said.

She tore her eyes from the burn marks on the Shadow Person's face and threw the orb at the lamp post. Making it there safely, Daijo decided to try something. It was there only chance.

"Put three orbs of pure light in the staff," Daijon said.

Claretta did as she was told.

With each orb added, the staff grew brighter. Eyes on the Shadow People, Daijon whispered in Claretta's ear exactly what to do She then held the staff closer to the bottom and raised it above her head. Hitting the concrete, the orb shattered as golden light shot forward and to the sides creating a path of pure light. Now one solar staff down, they ran and didn't stop until they made it back to Claretta's apartment.

When they walked through the door, her parents looked at the with furrowed eyes wondering why they were out of breath. Not wanting to believe what just happened; there was no way she could t her parents. Claretta told them they raced part of the way home. Not seeing anything physically wrong with the two young teens, her mother let the matter go. After dinner, when Claretta offered to walk Daijon down, he refused; it was safer if she stayed in the apartment with the solar lights.

"You need to start training to fight the Shadow People," he said when her parents were no longer in earshot, "and we need to star lighting the lamp post."

"Fine," Claretta mumbled too exhausted from the day's even

34

to really care at the moment. "I'll see you later." She closed the door and went straight to her room, falling asleep in the clothes she'd worn that day.

CHAPTER 5

In the future...

"You're not going out there!" Mr. Cooper loudly whispered to Daijon not wanting to frighten the others. He pulled his son towards the stairs. Lee, a junior at his high school, waited by the door while they talked.

"We're running out of supplies and more people keep showing up," Daijon replied.

"I don't want to lose you too."

"I can't just sit here and do nothing anymore."

It was the morning of the third day since the Sun died and the world was covered in darkness. The Shadow People were taking over Quincy and would soon move onto other towns unless they were stopped. There had always been Shadow People in Quincy but his mother and sisters kept them in line. In the last few weeks, though, their numbers had grown as they put their plan into action. One by one, his sisters had gone missing and Claretta refused to use the powers Audi had given her.

"It's not safe," Mr. Cooper said.

"You've been training me my entire life in case something like this happened," Daijon replied.

"Are they going with you?" Mr. Cooper nodded towards the other teens gathering by the door.

"We're just going to grab what we need and come right back."

Mr. Cooper looked at his son then his makeshift team by the door. They were just kids around the same age as his daughters. They had no hidden abilities to take on what they were about to be faced with but like his son; they wanted to help.

"Make sure you come back," Mr. Cooper said giving Daijon a hug then a slight push to the door.

"I will."

Daijon led Lee and the others to the red Saturn that sat behind his dad's car in the driveway. Lee's two door pickup wasn't big enough for the five of them so Parker offered the use of his car.

"If anybody wants to back out, now's the time," Daijon said, looking at each of them.

He knew that Lee was in and Parker let him use his car. Andrew, a senior, the oldest of the group, wasn't going to let the younger kids go out alone. There were adults at the farmhouse but they were either too scared to come or wanted to stay with their families. His dad wanted to come but he couldn't leave their unexpected guest alone. The last member of the group was a 15-year-old girl named Autumn, who'd shown up by herself the day after the Sun died. Her dad was on a business trip and wouldn't be home for another two days. When she heard talk of the Shadow People avoiding the house with the solar lights, she figured it was the safest place to be.

"Alright then, let's go," Daijon said getting into the passenger seat.

It was a little after nine in the morning as they rode the dark streets to the Walmart less than an hour away. Street lamps that lined the roads were the only source of light outside. Homes and other businesses still had electricity but it had no damaging effect on the Shadow People.

The teens rode in silence watching for any signs of Shadow People that may be lurking nearby. Hidden beneath blankets on the floor were the solar lights Daijon had taken from the yard. The last thing they wanted to do was attract any unwanted attention but the Shadow People knew what he could do. If they ran into trouble, it wa the only thing that could keep them safe.

As they continued to ride, Daijon thought back to when he las saw Claretta. He did his best to persuade her to use the powers Audi had given her but she refused. Now Claretta believed her after being chased on the street and attacked at home by the Shadow People; she was too scared. She believed they would leave her alone if she did nothing but she was wrong. Not long after the attack in her apartmen the Shadow People came and took her. Claretta had no idea how to u her powers but it didn't matter to them; they weren't going to take an chances.

When they finally reached Walmart, Daijon went over the pla one last time.

"We split in two groups, grab what we need and get back to the car. You see anything that looks weird, leave the area. If someone tries to fight you for an item, let them have it, it's not worth getting hurt over. Most important, if you see a Shadow Person you run and get back to the car. Only fight them if you have no other choice. Parker is going to wait in the car, in case, we need a quick getaway. We've got one hour."

"What about the solar lights?" Lee asked. "We can't just walk into the store with them."

Looking around, Daijon noticed two empty shopping carts three spots down from them. "I've got an idea."

With Autumn's help, he pushed both carts to the passenger's side. They removed the solar lights from the blankets and placed two in each cart. Removing their jackets, they draped them over the solar lights hiding them from view. As they reached the entrance, they noticed two police officers standing just inside the doors. Every news station showed footage and pictures of the Sun vanishing though no one knew what really happened. A few hours later, when it set in that the Sun was really gone; riots broke out at several grocery stores. People swarmed the stores for food and any other light source they could find. Daijon knew it was a matter of time before people tried to take the solar lights from the farm but at the moment; he had no plans to prevent it.

Entering on the food side, Autumn and Andrew ventured towards the home and sports section while Daijon and Lee shopped for food. Looking around, Daijon was surprised to see the usual number of workers present. Across the city, people had been calling off because they were afraid to leave their homes. A few even quit their jobs.

The sounds of children running through the aisles and orders being placed for meat were absent from the chaos that used to fill Walmart. Now, people kept their distance from one another and children no longer joined their parents while shopping. In fact, Daijon was the youngest person there.

"I never thought I'd wish I lived in a small town," Lee said grabbing packs of the largest chicken breast they could find.

"Why?" Daijon asked as he put the fourth pack of toilet pape on the bottom of the cart.

"Seriously. My mom managed to drag me here in the mornin a few times and it is *not* this quiet. At least, if it were a small town, everybody would know each other and you could tell who didn't belong. Here, you can't tell if someone's a Shadow Person or if they'r just someone who lives in town you haven't met yet."

"Trust me, seeing them isn't any better, especially, because I don't have my sister's powers."

"Yeah, I'm still trying to wrap my head around all that."

As they continued to fill their cart, Daijon noticed a man and woman had started following them. At first, he thought it was a coincidence, I mean, who doesn't need toilet paper but then he *kept* seeing them. He and Lee had been zigzagging around the food department remembering things that weren't on the list and this was the fifth time the couple crossed their path.

"We're being followed," Daijon told Lee as they headed to th front. "The couple behind us."

Lee casually looked to his left grabbing a bag of fries from the freezer section. As he dropped it in the cart, his eyes wandered to where the solar lights lay surrounded by food. "Are they Shadow People?"

"Yeah," Daijon whispered. "Did you see any shadows on the way here?"

"Everything is casting a shadow," Lee replied, "but no, I haven't seen *those* particular shadows."

As they left the aisle, the couple continued to follow them but kept their distance. *What are they up to,* Daijon wondered?

After they finished paying, Daijon and Lee waited up front. It was 10 minutes until the hour was up and they hadn't heard from Autumn or Andrew.

"Have Parker pull around and take the stuff out. I'm going to see what's going on," Daijon instructed. No longer caring if anyone saw it, Daijon took his solar light from the cart and held it at his side.

That's when his phone rang.

"Daijon, we need your help!" Autumn said among the shouts in the background.

"Where are you?" Daijon asked.

"By the light bulbs!"

"I'm coming."

"I'm coming with you." Lee said.

"No, take the stuff to the car then wait near the entrance on the home side. We may need help getting out."

Going their separate ways, Daijon ran past the registers. As he neared the other side of the store, the shouts got louder. People left their carts behind as they ran past him running from the Shadow People. He rounded the corner past the blenders and that's when he saw it. A Shadow Person in its true form came from the aisle Autumn called him from.

"Autumn, Andrew, where are you!" Daijon shouted.

"We're still down here!" Autumn cried.

Not waiting for the police, who were probably dealing with the crowd heading their way, Daijon charged towards the Shadow Person He stopped when it looked his way. "What do you think you're going to do with that toy," the Shadow Person said. Its deep voice, the only indicator that he was male.

"Come closer and you'll find out," Daijon replied.

Only a few people stood nearby as Daijon and the Shadow Person began to fight. If he was lucky, he'd be able to defeat him, and grab Autumn and Andrew before the police, or more Shadow People arrived.

The Shadow Person threw two shadow orbs at Daijon, then changed to shadow form. Daijon dodged the first one, and then blocked the other. As soon as the shadow orb touched the solar light, turned to ash. Daijon looked around for the Shadow Person but couldn't find him. Slithering out from the shadows of a nearby shelf, he tripped the boy. Unable to catch himself, Daijon fell into the display of children's toys and hit his arm on the stand. Rolling onto his back, he struck the shadow on the ground.

While the Shadow Person howled and returned to his true form, Daijon hid behind a larger display. It had yet to be filled with any product but was big enough for him to crouch down behind. When the Shadow Person came for him in shadow form, he was ready. When it slithered across the floor, Daijon struck the ground inches from it returning it to true form once again.

Using the display to his advantage, Daijon jumped onto it with the solar light stretched out before him. When the Shadow Person was close enough, he jumped off sliding the solar light down its entire form. Daijon then backed away looking at the Shadow Person. It wasn't a pure light orb but he'd done enough damage to slowly turn him to ash.

Having defeated the Shadow Person, Daijon went to help Autumn and Andrew. When he reached them, Andrew was on the ground and Autumn stood before him fighting off a Shadow Person in true form. She swung the solar light back and forth landing a blow here and there but it still didn't back down.

"Hey, over here!" Daijon yelled distracting it.

When it turned to face him, Autumn placed the solar light on its left side and kept it there. The Shadow Person yelled as ash fell from it. Seeing it was outnumbered, the Shadow Person retreated.

"What happened to him?" Daijon asked looking at the blood dripping down the side of Andrew's leg.

"The Shadow Person...it threw this black thing. I don't know what it was," Autumn said.

"It's a shadow orb," Daijon explained. "Come on, we have to go."

Daijon and Autumn stood on either side of Andrew and together lifted him off the ground.

"What happened to him?" One of the officers that guarded th entrance asked as they rounded the corner.

"We were attacked by a Shadow Person," Daijon said. "You know those things they've been showing on the news."

"You kids get out of here and go straight home," the officer told them.

Planning to do just that they continued to help Andrew limp t the exit. When they arrived, Daijon looked for Lee but couldn't find him. *He should've been here by now,* Daijon thought *and where's the other officer?* He remembered only passing one. He got his answer when a shadow orb crashed through the glass sliding doors.

Leaving Autumn with Andrew inside by the carts, Daijon walked into the darkness with his solar light not sure of what he'd fin

The white glow from the Walmart parking lights was the only other light Daijon had to find his friends. Around him, people ran to their cars to escape the chaos. He started to take out his phone when saw a flash of golden light out the corner of his eye. Parker, who'd driven around to pick up Lee, was parked in the fire lane between the grocery and home entrances. Lee stood by the trunk, next to their nov empty cart, fighting the woman that had been following them earlier.

44

Parker stood with the car running and the driver's door open. He thrust the solar light forward trying to keep the man away from the vehicle.

Taking a step forward, Daijon noticed a few people watching the fight in the distance. To them, it looked like teenagers fighting adults. It may have even looked like Parker and Lee were trying to steal the couple's car; they were the ones fighting back.

"Guys, we need to go now!" Daijon shouted when he spotted the flash of police car lights from the street. Unless the Shadow People changed to one of their other forms, he was going to have a hard time proving who the couple were to the police.

With the police drawing closer, the couple backed away from the car. As soon as Lee closed the back door, Parker put the car in reverse and backed up to the grocery entrance. Daijon stood watch outside as Lee helped get Andrew into the back seat. They'd only got half of what they came for but he was just glad they all made it out in one piece. Just as they pulled away, the cop reached the front and Daijon's phone rang.

"Hello," he said too busy making sure they weren't being followed to look at the caller ID.

"I need you to come get me," a female voice said.

Taking his eyes off the road, Daijon looked down at his phone where Audi's name appeared on the screen.

CHAPTER 6

In the past...

By her locker at school the next day, Claretta talked to her friend, Anise, thankful to be doing something normal. As she waved another friend that passed them, a shadow moved on the ground by a classroom on her left. Claretta jumped nearly bumping into the perso behind her.

"Are you okay?" Anise asked looking over her shoulder in th same direction as Claretta.

"Yeah, I thought there was a bug on my arm," Claretta lied.

"I don't see anything," Anise said. "Anyway, we should get going. If we're late to English class, Ms. Hoover will give us detentic and we'll miss the pool party."

"Only she would give detention on the last day," Claretta said as they passed the classroom where the shadow had been.

With the solar staff at home and not being able to use her powers at school, she wished Daijon was nearby. He'd told her there were no Shadow People at her school but that didn't make Claretta fe any better. She knew they could appear anywhere. Every time she entered a room, her eyes couldn't help but go straight to the shadows.

When the bell rang ending their third to last period that Frida afternoon, Claretta couldn't have been happier. To celebrate their last year of middle school, the eighth graders got to spend their last two periods at the public pool. While she was excited, she was also nervous because another middle school would be there as well. With everything that had been going on lately, Claretta forgot about it so she sent Daijon a text asking if he could be there.

Later at the pool, Claretta and her friends were having a great time. It was a cloudless afternoon and the sun shined bright making it warm enough to go swimming but not too hot where you'd fry sitting on a lawn chair. They splashed around in the pool for a bit then talked about their vacation plans with their chairs pushed close together. Everything was going fine until Claretta got back in the pool.

They'd just began a game of water volleyball when Claretta thought she saw a shadow. It moved quickly from the shallow end to the darkness of the deep end. Thinking she was mistaken, Claretta kept playing. *There it is again,* she thought as Anise served for the other team. Believing Claretta would do nothing with the others around, the shadow sliced through the water with ease towards her. Claretta rushed to the edge of the pool and pushed herself out.

The other girls looked at her confused. "Where are you going?" Anise asked.

"I'll be back in a sec just going to the bathroom," Claretta said, "keep playing." Not sure of what would happen, she didn't want anyone following her. *Daijon, where are you?*

Their gym bags were still on the wooden benches near the back when Claretta entered the changing room. Nothing seemed to have been bothered and there was no noise coming from the showers or locker area. After checking the nearby shadows, she ventured further into the room.

"Hey Claretta, tired of playing already?" A girl asked as she came around the last row of lockers by the left wall. She appeared to be her age but much taller with long brown hair.

"Just came to use the bathroom," Claretta said standing by the bags. She didn't know the girl and assumed she went to the other school that was there. *Wait, how does she know my name?* "I'm sorry don't remember you from school."

"I don't go to school."

"You know what, I don't really need to go after all," Claretta said backing away as the girl smiled and walked towards her.

Claretta turned to run but found the way blocked by the shadow from the pool. With her solar staff at home, she had nothing but her hands to rely on. Holding them up towards the shadow, she acted like she was going to create pure light but instead ran for the door. The shadow caught up with her two rows down and wrapped around Claretta's legs. She fell to the tile floor landing hard on her le: shoulder. The shadow kept a firm grip on the Claretta as it traveled u her body. Pain shot down her arm as she twisted around and sent a quick burst of pure light at the shadow. It shrieked and slithered up ai over the wall leading to the showers.

Claretta pushed herself off the floor with her good arm and continued past the showers for the door. Before she could make it, th girl blocked her path.

"You've caused us enough trouble. It's time you joined the others."

The girl charged at Claretta throwing her against the wall to the showers. Before she could use her hands to burn the girl, the shadow came down and pinned her wrists above her. Moving quickly, it tied her wrists together with a brown rope whose other end was secured around a shower head on the other side of the wall. Claretta tried to slip one of her hands free but the rope was too tight and the tugging made her shoulder hurt even more.

Satisfied that Claretta couldn't move, the girl pulled a small syringe out of a purse Claretta hadn't noticed before.

"What is that?" Claretta asked as she tried to think of another way to free herself.

"Just something that will keep you asleep so the shadow can carry you with no trouble."

"People are going to notice a Shadow Person carrying me."

The girl smiled. "It'll be kind of hard to see you trapped in the shadow."

Trapped in a shadow. Seriously, how am I supposed to beat that? Not realizing what she was doing, Claretta created a small force field around her out of pure light. It only extended two inches in front of her but it was enough to keep her safe.

"Impressive but tell me," the girl said, "how long can you keep it up. I doubt you'll last as long as the party."

It was more than likely no one was going to come in before

she lost control of the force field and Claretta knew she wouldn't be able to hold it for long. The girl walked right up to it and tapped it wi the syringe. It wasn't completely solid and she could probably wear it down with something bigger but going through it herself was not an option.

Neither of them got to see how long it would hold up though, because just then Daijon came into the girl's changing room. He'd jus gotten to class when he received Claretta's text, even though, it was t last day; sneaking out wasn't any easier. When he arrived at the pool, he searched for Claretta but didn't see her anywhere. It wasn't until he asked one of her friends that he discovered where she was. As much he wanted to run to her, he had to wait until no one was looking befo he could sneak into the girl's changing room.

"Get away from her!" Daijon shouted by the closed door.

Hearing his voice, Claretta lost control and the force field broke. Its pieces sliced the girl's skin leaving her with burn marks. While the girl and the shadow were distracted, Daijon ran into the showers and untied Claretta. Removing the rope from her wrists, she managed to make it to Daijon before the shadow could get her. As soon as she stepped outside, Claretta rejoined her friends trying to pretend like nothing happened. Not ready to get back in the water, sh suggested they grab something to eat.

"Do you want anything?" Claretta asked Daijon as her friend got out the pool.

"Sure, I'll have a hot dog."

As Claretta walked to the concession stand with her friends, she looked over her shoulder to make sure Daijon was still there.

"Don't worry, I'll be here when you get back," Daijon said with a reassuring smile.

"What's that all about?" Anise asked looking between the two.

"It's nothing," Claretta replied.

After they'd gone back to school, Daijon waited with Claretta for her mom to arrive. When she did, Claretta asked if Daijon could come over. Thinking it was strange to invite just him over; her mother looked around for the boy's sister. Before she could say anything, Claretta jumped in with the excuse they'd came up with.

"Daijon came to hang out but he didn't realize their mom picked Audi up for a doctor's appointment." Claretta explained.

"You'd be safer if you stayed at the ranch house," Daijon whispered next to Claretta in the back seat of her mom's Impala.

"I've got all those solar lights," Claretta replied as her mother hummed along to the radio.

"They didn't stop the shadow from getting inside your apartment."

"I took care of it."

"Barely," he sighed. "Look, having a few solar lights in your apartment and a few out front that won't stay lit or go missing, won't be enough."

"Maybe if I stop using my powers, the Shadow People will leave me alone."

51

"And what about Quincy?"

He has a point, Claretta thought. *I can't just abandon the city.* "Fine, I won't stop using my powers."

As Daijon followed Claretta and her mother through the apartment building, the presence of several shadows unnerved him. The Shadow People knew Claretta had Audi's powers and that he had powers of his own. Claretta was still new to her powers so the Shado People had the upper hand but they remained still for now. *They're up to something,* Daijon thought.

When they got to Claretta's room, he understood why they were there and Claretta believed he was right about her not being saf Every solar light that she had brought was destroyed and her room w trashed. Claretta locked the door so her parents wouldn't see the mess and with Daijon's help, they got everything cleaned up.

"Okay, I'll go to the ranch house," Claretta agreed as she hid the bag of broken solar lights in her closet. "We've just got to get my parents to say yes."

Twenty minutes later, Daijon came out Claretta's room sayin; his dad was on the way to pick him up.

"Hey mom, can I stay over at Daijon's house this weekend?" Claretta asked her mom who'd started to prepare dinner. Her dad was at work and she knew if her mom said yes, he was more likely to as well. "Audi and her older sisters are going to be there and they decid to have a girl's night in. They wanted to know if I could come over."

"I've already started making dinner and I thought maybe we

could have our own girl's night since your father will be working late."

"Mom, please. It's rare that all her sisters are home on a Friday. Can we have movie night another time?"

Claretta's mom looked at her pleading daughter and smiled. "Okay. Just be home by Sunday."

"Thank you." Claretta hugged her mom then went to pack her bag.

By the time she was done, Daijon's dad was waiting for them outside.

The ride to the ranch house was bathed in the kind of silence that wasn't meant to be disturbed. Daijon sat up front with his dad while Claretta sat in the back with her legs curled beneath her and her head against the window lost in her own thoughts. Her eyes were closed and her lips turned down at what lay ahead for her now.

They drove further and further away from the city and closer to the country. When they neared the ranch house that was just on the edge of town, Daijon turned in his seat and nudge Claretta.

"You're going to want to see this," Daijon said.

Claretta's eyes grew wide and a smile appeared on her face at the sight before her. Light was the first thing she saw. There was so much of it; you could barely even tell there was a house there until you were on top of it. To anyone else, it was an unnatural color light that seemed to be coming from the ground but Claretta knew better. It was the golden color of pure light coming from the hundreds of solar lights that lined the perimeter three to four feet in. They were about two feet tall with little brass spirals that formed a cage around the glass ball th held the light. It was unlike any solar lights she'd ever seen.

"The Sun, my wife, built this house to protect Daijon and me Daijon's dad said as he pulled into the long driveway. "She always thought it was odd that only the girls could create pure light. We all used to live together in the city but something happened and by the time Audi turned two, it was too dangerous to remain together."

After they parked the car in the driveway, Claretta followed th others into the house. Off to the right was a large living room filled with black leather furniture that formed a half circle around a stone fireplace set into the wooden walls. To the left of that was a kitchen that separated itself from the living room with a small wall that connected to the counter. Beneath it stood three black barstools. The rest of the area which would normally house a dining room table was sparring area. Large black mats covered the floor leading to a mirror that claimed the wall near the stairs.

Daijon lead her up a dark brown staircase that wrapped past th front door and faced the living room. He took her to the room across from his; the one that would've been Audi's. His other sisters had rooms as well and hopefully, one day they'd get to stay in them.

Once Claretta was settled in, he took her to the sparring area. They walked over to the glass doors that led to back of the house where the barn was located and looked out.

"That's a lot of solar lights," Claretta said looking at the light in the distance.

"There's also a couple on the roof," Daijon chuckled. "Wait here a second." Since there was still some light out, Daijon thought they should try and enjoy it. "I've got a surprise," he said coming back over to Claretta.

"What's that?" Claretta turned to face him.

"We're going riding."

Claretta smiled for the second time since the incident at the pool making Daijon smile as well. She hadn't been horseback riding since summer camp last year when she fell in love with it. Daijon slid open the glass door then held his hand out to her. Claretta looked at the oncoming darkness a bit worried but took his hand anyway.

When both horses were saddled and ready to go, Daijon showed her the rest of their property. It got darker the farther they ventured from the house but not completely dark. Every now and then, they rode past a nine-foot-tall solar light.

"Where did your mom get all the solar lights?" Claretta asked on the ride back. She'd thought only the front yard had that many but it turned out the entire property's perimeter had the same amount of lights.

"I'm honestly not sure. I haven't seen any like them in the stores," Daijon said. "Maybe she made them."

That night after dinner, Daijon trained with his dad on the sparring mat. Though his father was an accountant, he was a skilled fighter in hand to hand combat. Something he used to do in his spare time, he'd said when Daijon asked where he learned it. He was six feet tall with a thin but muscular build like his son. Though his hair held none of the golden highlights like the rest of his family, it was still a beautiful chestnut color. As Daijon began to train, Claretta watched from a bar stool. His father wasn't harsh in his teaching but he wasn't taking it easy on him either. From the half grin on his face, Claretta could see Daijon seemed to enjoy what she discovered was their nightly routine.

When the two of them were done, Mr. Cooper motioned Claretta forward. Shoes off, she walked slowly onto the mat not sure of what to do. Waving her forward, he walked her through some basic self-defense moves. An hour later, Mr. Cooper left the mat to take a quick shower and get some work done. Thinking she too was done, Claretta started to follow him but Daijon told her to stay there.

"Now, it's time for your light training," Daijon said solar staff in hand. "It's not only important to be able to create pure light; you have to learn to fight with it. All my sisters know how."

Claretta just stared at him.

"Go get your staff."

Sighing, Claretta reluctantly went to retrieve it, and then returned to the mat. Daijon motioned for her to raise it.

"Until you get better with your powers, you're most likely going to have the staff solar light with you," Daijon reminded her. "OK, act like you're using the staff to block an attack."

Daijon raised his staff like he was going to hit her while Claretta held her staff horizontal above her head.

"Great, now do that again except put pure light into it while you raise it."

Claretta lowered the staff then began to raise it with one hand.

"Now with both hands on the staff, direct the pure light through your body. You're not only going to put pure light into the ball at the end but in the entire staff."

Claretta sighed yet again.

"That's it," Daijon said when she finally got it. With her solar staff still raised, Daijon lowered his fast. When the two connected, pure light sparked out towards his face. "That can do some real damage. Now, let's try something else."

Daijon took Claretta outside and at first; they stood close to the glass doors. "I want you to create a large ball of pure light, break it into smaller lights, and distribute it into the solar lights."

"Seriously, you want me to try this. That's a big step up from putting light in a staff," Claretta said.

"I still want you to try it."

Claretta stepped away from the door and looked at the five solar lights Daijon had spread out a few feet away. Taking a deep breath, she created a small orb of pure light between her hands. As it got larger, her hands grew further apart. When she attempted separating smaller pieces, her hands were shaking and within moments the entire thing burst. As the remains of the orb drifted to the ground, a shadow screamed and turned to ash off to their left. While they were preoccupied, it had tried to navigate the slivers of shadow between the solar lights.

"We should go back in," Daijon suggested, "we can try again later."

"Okay," Claretta said. She looked at the solar lights to her right just past the barn as she followed Daijon. Claretta couldn't see i but just outside the perimeter, a Shadow Person paced back and forth watching them.

With the training for the day done, they retired to their rooms Hours later, Claretta fell off the bed that belonged to her best friend tangled in a blanket and sheet. It was not the shadows that kept her awake tonight for she was safe in the large ranch house. It was the mere thought of having to fight them that robbed her body of much needed sleep. Claretta sighed as she got off the floor and back into be silently wishing she never showed Audi the letter. *There's no going back now,* she thought as she snuggled under the covers once again, praying sleep would come.

The next morning, Claretta was awaken by the deafening sou of church bells going off in her ears. She covered them trying to drov out the sound but that didn't matter because now someone was shakir her. *This is the most vivid dream I've ever had,* Claretta thought as sh rolled towards the wall.

"It'll be a cup of water next if you don't get up," Daijon threatened.

Claretta rolled back over and opened one eye. Seeing Daijon standing there in shorts and a fitted workout shirt, she sat up in the

58

bed. "What are you doing?"

"*We* are going to train," Daijon told her. "Well, *you* need to train; I'll be supervising. The less dependent you become of the staff, the better."

Claretta grabbed the plastic alarm clock from his hands and looked at the time. It was six in the morning. "Yeah, that's not going to happen. Do you see what time it is?" Claretta gave him back the alarm clock; buried herself back under the warmth of the blankets and tried to go back to sleep. Less than two minutes later, Claretta coughed and wiped at the water on her face.

"I warned you," Daijon said not bothering to hide his laughter.

Twenty minutes later, Claretta joined him downstairs in shorts and a tee shirt. "I hate you right now," she laughed. "I still can't believe you poured water on me."

After training, they showered then met each other back downstairs where a breakfast of Belgian waffles awaited them. Today's plan was simple enough; fill the lamp posts with pure light and collect as many solar powered items as they could. If something were to happen to the Sun, the solar items should buy them a few hours to devise a plan.

"How can everyone not know about the Shadow People yet?" Claretta asked.

"It's not something that's easy to explain. I didn't believe it at first either. It's more like something you have to see," Mr. Cooper said.

Claretta understood what he meant though on a different level.

She couldn't imagine how he felt when his wife told him about how special the girls were and who she was.

After breakfast, Daijon and Claretta rode their bikes to the Dollar Tree where the twins, Kamyra and Klarissa Cooper, worked. / soon as they arrived, a girl with short blond hair in a green shirt stopped him.

"Where are your sisters? No one's heard from them in days.] had to cover both their shifts," the girl said clearly irritated.

"I live with our dad so I couldn't tell you," Daijon lied alread knowing the Shadow People had taken them.

The girl went back to work and left them to fill two reusable bags with solar lights of various kinds. As they were leaving, Daijon noticed a sun shaped light on top of a lamp post they'd passed in the parking lot.

"What are you doing?" Claretta asked realizing Daijon wasn' behind her.

"We might as well get started," Daijon said leaning his bike against the post and putting his bags down.

"With what?" Claretta asked looking around the parking lot wondering what they could possibly do out here.

Daijon pointed to his mother's symbol and then the sun shape light at the top.

"Okay but I can't exactly toss a ball of light up there," Claret said looking at the people returning to their cars.

"You don't need to. All you have to do is send it up."

Claretta looked up at the intimidating height of the lamp post.

"The sooner you stop being afraid of the power, the easier it'll be to use."

"What do you expect?" Claretta started to shout then lowered her voice when an older couple gave them sideway glances. "I didn't even believe any of this was real until the other day and now I've got these powers. I didn't know Audi was going to transfer her powers when she asked for my hands."

"This is new to me too," Daijon said with a hint of frustration. "I didn't know my sisters could transfer powers."

They stood leaning against the lamp post with the bags at their feet. Around them, people walked to and from the shops in the plaza or to their vehicles that waited to take them to their next destination.

"So, how do I do this?" Claretta asked.

A few seconds later. Claretta walked to the side of the post so her back faced the stores and placed both hands on it. Remembering what she did last night, she let the pure light flow through her. It transferred from her hand and into the lamp post with ease. With her hands still in place, Claretta sent it to the top where it filled the glass.

Having succeeded, Daijon suggested they go to the elementary school next. When they arrived, Daijon looked at his watch then at the sky checking how much time they had before night fall.

"If the Shadow People have your sisters, how are we supposed to light the entire town if the Sun dies?" Claretta asked.

"Nothing is going to happen," Daijon said like he was trying

61

to reassure himself more than her.

"If something does?"

Daijon remained quiet for a second. "Pray, we find my sisters before then."

Walking closer to the building, Daijon pointed to the lamp po out front. "This one and three others form a barrier around the school

Claretta looked at the lamp post that stood near the flagpole. "How do you even know where all these lamp posts are? I mean, the light may be shaped like the Sun but seriously."

"My mom gave my dad a map with their locations on it wher was younger. Once I memorized it, he burned it so the Shadow Peopl wouldn't get it."

Just as Claretta made her way to the lamp post, the tree branches across the street started to sway. This wouldn't have been a problem except there was no wind.

"You're going to have to light them all at once," Daijon said the trees continued to sway.

"How?"

After quick instructions, Claretta placed both hands on the ground took a deep breath then let the light flow from her and seep into the grass and dirt. She watched as the blades of grass lit up all around them. When the swaying of the tree branches grew more intense, they both ran up the wide school steps only to find the doors locked.

"Make an orb small enough to fit in the lock," Daijon said.

"What?"

"Hurry up," Daijon replied as the tree branches became still.

A few shadows now slid along the concrete that wasn't covered in pure light. Claretta looked over her shoulder with wide eyes at the shadows coming towards them. Faster than she'd ever had before; a small orb was created and placed into the keyhole.

"Now concentrate only on the orb and make it expand," Daijon instructed.

Claretta nodded squatting down until she was eye level with the keyhole. She concentrated on the pure light that constantly flowed through her body while her mind rifled through the pure light around her until she found the right source. Inside the lock, the orb expanded until the lock broke.

Once inside, Daijon called his dad to come pick them up. Claretta walked over to the windows that lined part of the hall and looked outside; the shadows were still coming.

"Daijon," Claretta said.

Daijon held up a finger as he tried to listen to his dad.

Not sure what to do, Claretta put her hand on the glass and even though, it wasn't solar power ribbons of pure light snaked through it. Finishing his call at the same time she finished the windows, Daijon asked her what was wrong.

"They're still coming," Claretta said pointing to the shadows sliding up the building away from the grass. *Why haven't they attacked yet?*

"That's not possible unless..." Daijon ran to a classroom situated in the back of the school. Claretta followed him.

"I missed one," she said wide eyed.

They hurried back to the front of the school.

Claretta ran to the rooms closest to them and put pure light in the glass on the doors while Daijon ran to secure the door at the othe: end of the hall. He made it halfway down the hallway when the door burst open and a couple of Shadow People in true form strode throug Standing by the foot of the wall between the front doors and the glas: windows, Claretta waited for Daijon to reach her. The moment he dic she clapped her hands together making the glass shatter. Shards of pu light pierced the Shadow People's skin that now fell away as ash.

Shadow People that had clung to the building came through t] now broken windows and shifted to their true form. Joining the other they walked towards the two children. Having lost control of the ligh when she broke the windows, the glass that crunched under the Shadow People's feet no longer held pure light.

"Lift and light the glass," Daijon whispered still looking straight ahead, "but you're going to have to be quick."

There's no way I can light them all at once, Claretta thought but tried anyway. Five strands of light escaped her fingers and made their way into the shards of glass closest to them. Using her other hand, she flicked her wrist sending the glass upward slicing into the Shadow People in front. Thankfully, a car honked outside and they didn't have to worry if she could do it again. Running outside before the Shadow People could recover, they climbed into Mr. Cooper's car and sped towards home.

Shaken up by the day's events, Claretta stayed in Audi's room the remainder of the day. "I'm not hungry. I just want to be alone," she said hours later when Daijon brought her a plate of food.

Later that night, Claretta's stomach growled awaking her from a nap that had been hard to fall into. Desperate to satisfy her hunger, she looked at the solar lights scattered around the room. Daijon and his father stared at her when she requested to have some but thankfully, they didn't question her. When Claretta's stomach growled again, she sighed and got up but not before checking under the bed. Just as she hoped, the solar lights she'd put there earlier were still in place.

Making it to the doorway, she stopped and searched for any movement in the hall. Her breathing got faster when she looked at the darkness before her. *What am I supposed to tell my parents Sunday? I can't go home,* Claretta thought as she stepped into the hallway. With the large solar light on the roof, Daijon and his father saw no need to have any more around the house. This, however, was no help to Claretta whose fear of the dark had returned.

Grabbing her solar staff that lay against the wall, just inside the door, she filled it with more pure light. With the solar staff before her, Claretta stepped into the darkness and made her way to the stairs. Daijon having woken to the sound of footsteps opened his door to investigate. He saw Claretta at the top of the stairs just standing there with a solar staff. Saying nothing, he continued to watch her from a distance. As Claretta slowly descended the stairs, Daijon moved further down the hall. Reaching the bottom, Claretta fell onto the ste as she backed away from a shadow. Ignoring the pain in her elbow, h hand frantically searched the foyer wall for the light switch she knew was close by. When the light came on, Claretta retrieved the staff fro the floor by the stairs and searched for the shadow. She gave a sigh o relief when she discovered the shadow belonged to a plant that stood next to the glass door.

Daijon wanted to leave the shadows of the staircase in which he hid to reassure her there were no Shadow People in the house but didn't. He wasn't sure what was going on but wanted to see what she' do next.

Claretta turned the TV on low then curled up in the corner of the couch with a box of Cheerios. Daijon was about to return to his room when he saw her do something he wasn't expecting. Claretta gc up to get a drink but instead walked over to the mat where the rest of the solar lights laid; the others being in her room. Daijon crept down the stairs to the darkness of the foyer and hid by the small wall near the stairs where he continued to watch.

With the solar lights spread out in front of her, Claretta sat ar began putting light into each of them hoping the extra practice would do her some good. While filling the last light, Claretta looked over to the glass doors. She pulled back the curtain and saw the solar lights were working just fine. Thinking back to the school, she tried putting light into the glass but didn't make it shatter. Instead, she placed her index finger on the glass and pulled out a strand of pure light. *Wow,* Daijon thought, *I definitely didn't teach her that.*

Seeing that she was okay and glad that she was improving, Daijon went back to his room and left Claretta to practicing; where she returned to bed an hour later.

CHAPTER 7

In the future...

Audi left the privacy of the closet with her phone in her back pocket. It was one of the few places the Shadow People wouldn't hea her. It was also the first time she'd talked to anyone besides her moth since giving Claretta her powers. The closet door frame rattled and a loud bang filled her room as Audi slammed the door closed. Thinking about Claretta still made her angry but she didn't want to be. She kne what was at risk when she gave Claretta her powers but at the time sl was left with no choice. Daijon tried to explain what happened with Claretta over the phone but he felt there was more to it than what he' been told.

With a heavy sigh, Audi left her room and went to her mother Standing in the doorway, her eyes searched the room landing on a seafoam green patchwork blanket on the rocking chair. It instantly reminded her of the last time she saw her mom.

"Audi, thank God one of my daughters is safe," her mother had said as Audi ran through the door slamming it behind her.

That was close; I didn't think I'd make it, Audi thought huggin her mom.

"What happened to your powers?" her mom asked no longei able to sense the pure light in her youngest daughter.

"I gave them to Claretta. I'm so sorry but they were coming for me and I didn't think I would escape. I figured if Daijon helped her, she might be able to beat them."

BANG! BANG! Came the loud knock at the door.

Stepping away from Audi, the Sun had walked forward until she was inches from the door. With one outstretched hand, she sent a large orb of pure light through the door at the Shadow People on the other side. Their screams lasted for a second before turning their entire bodies to ash. They should have known by now not to attack the house at night when the Sun was always home.

"Come with me," her mother had said leading Audi to her bedroom. The Sun picked up the seafoam green blanket on the rocking chair before going the window. "Daijon told you about his powers?"

"Yes, but only after I told him my plan," Audi replied.

The Sun just nodded her head as she scanned the darkness outside "When morning comes, I must leave," she said putting the blanket down with sad eyes. "No matter what happens, if you stay in the house, the Shadow People won't be able to get you."

"But..."

"Please try. For as long as you can, don't leave the house."

"Okay."

That night they tried to pretend that everything was normal. They snuggled together on the couch, watched their favorite movies, and eating junk until they felt they'd explode. Audi tried to stay awake the entire night but her eyes betrayed her. When morning came, she awoke to find herself alone on the couch and the Sun in the sky.

Wiping away a tear that slid down her face, Audi walked dow the back staircase that led to the kitchen. She'd been stuck in that house alone ever since that day and while she liked having time to herself; this was a bit too much. Scanning the large selection of cerea Audi grabbed a box of Fruity Pebbles. Holding the box horizontal wi the name facing her, she placed a ceramic bowl on top with a spoon and glass sitting in the bowl. Balancing this in one hand, she ignored the banging on the kitchen window and went to the fridge. With orange juice hooked on her index finger and the milk on her middle t pinkie, Audi used her foot to close the door. With four kids living at home by themselves most of the day, their mom made sure the fridge and cabinets were fully stocked.

As Audi placed her food on the coffee table, the living room windows began to rattle. "You're not getting in!" She yelled.

After putting the milk back and the empty orange juice jug in the trash, Audi turned on a movie and snuggled into the corner of the couch with the bowl in her lap. Golden light cascaded down from the ceiling lights above her and every other room in the house. A Wrinkl in Time became background noise as Audi thought back to when she woke up that next day.

They'd had so much fun laughing, pretending for a few hours that nothing was wrong. That's when she noticed the letter among la: night's feast. It told her to stay in the house and not to leave even if tl lights went out. It also told her to look in the closet. She didn't know

70

what she meant by that until she looked up and realized the lights were a golden color. What surprised her was the box of gifts left for her in the living room closet.

She was brought back to the present when the windows stopped rattling and a strange noise came from out front. Not wanting to alert the Shadow People to what the closet hid, Audi went to the downstairs bathroom. Closing the door, she was careful unscrewing a light bulb then turned the other back on. Holding its base, she walked to the front door and gripped the handle. Audi's heart beat fast against her chest as she continued to stare at the door.

Taking a deep breath, Audi opened the door and stepped back. A Shadow Person in true form stood just beyond the threshold. It moved as though to take a step forward but stopped when she held up the light bulb. It stared at her with narrow eyes then he smirked and stepped aside. Behind him, kneeling in the grass was another Shadow Person. *What is he doing?* Audi thought until she realized where it was standing. Eyes wide, she closed the door and ran to the kitchen. Placing the glowing bulb onto a dry towel by the sink, Audi turned the hot water on but nothing came out. *They're trying to draw me out,* she thought.

As soon as she turned the faucet off, the power went out. Audi went to the fridge scanning what was inside. Besides the milk, there was nothing but food. In the pantry, she found one jug of water the twins used to make tea. With the Shadow People watching the house, there was no way to get any more water and the milk would spoil in a matter of hours. If Daijon didn't come for her soon, she'd either die from dehydration, or be forced to leave the house.

CHAPTER 8

In the past...

On Sunday, Daijon and Claretta rose early for their morning training session and to continue their collection of solar lights. When they got to Walgreens, they discovered someone had just brought them all. Worried, Daijon called his dad.

"Have you brought any solar lights?"

"No," his father said.

Daijon was afraid of that.

"Couldn't we get some of our friends to help?" Claretta asked as they left the store wondering why they had to collect them alone.

"I doubt they'd believe us and we'd be putting them in danger. Only my sisters can help," Daijon said. "We have to protect the city until we can find them. We should take a break and rethink our strategy."

Twenty minutes later, Claretta and Daijon pulled their bikes up to Mr. Peltz's Fro Yo Shop.

"Frozen yogurt, really?" Claretta said as she followed him inside pulling on the bottom of her blush colored tee-shirt.

"What," Daijon said putting his phone back into the side pocket of his dark cargo shorts. "Just because things suck now."

Claretta looked at him with a raised eyebrow. "Okay, really suck doesn't mean we can't enjoy something good."

Smiling, Claretta grabbed a cup; filled it with vanilla then car the toppings. She started with crushed Oreo's and as soon as she put the spoon back, Daijon was already putting gummy worms on top. Claretta looked up at him across the counter.

"They're your favorite," was all he said before finishing his then waiting for her at the register so he could pay.

Claretta couldn't help but smile as she watched him walk awa pleased that he remembered.

"What happened back there?" Claretta asked as they sat on tl shop's patio. "Why'd you ask your dad if he brought any solar lights?

"I think Shadow People are behind it," Daijon explained taking a bite of his chocolate Fro Yo. "It's too much of a coincidence that the moment we start collecting them, the stores are wiped clean. Maybe we should hit the small stores like Dollar General first. If Shadow People are trying to stop us from getting them, they'll probably go to the stores with the highest quantity."

"Wouldn't it burn them as soon as they stepped outside with them?"

"Not if they bagged them in something so the light couldn't reach it. Besides, some are willing to take that risk."

"That sounds great and all but how are we going to carry them?" Claretta asked from the chair across from him. "Backpacks will only hold so many."

"Remember how your future self-sent you a letter through

light?"

"Yeah," Claretta said slowly.

"If you learned to do that, you could send them to my house."

"Yeah, come up with another plan. I doubt I'll be doing that anytime soon," Claretta said leaning back in her chair with her legs stretched out beneath her jeans shorts.

Claretta buried a gummy worm under the Oreo crumbs with her spoon and into the Fro Yo. Scooping them back out, she noticed shadows moving on the walls near the patio entrance. People around them ignored the movement from the corner of their eyes; they thought they imagined them. Claretta remembered when she used to do that and part of her wished she could join them in their shared ignorance, but she was too deep in to turn back now.

"Daijon," Claretta whispered trying not to draw attention to them. "Shadows to your right."

Daijon searched the people and their shadows. Two tables over, a shadow detached from a young woman's shadow knocking over the chair across from her. She looked up confused but just dismissed it, assuming she kicked it by accident.

"We have to go, now," Daijon said putting his unfinished yogurt on the table as the shadow came their way.

Above them, dark clouds threatened to burst open but Daijon hadn't notice them gathering. He'd been too busy watching Claretta play with her yogurt.

As they were leaving, Daijon's phone rang; it was his dad. Mr.

Cooper noticed the dark clouds out and that his son wasn't home yet.

"Can you come get us?" Daijon asked as they mounted their bikes.

"They're not going to let me leave," Mr. Cooper said.

He had gone out to his car when he called but when it reached the solar lights at the edge of the driveway, he saw several Shadow People standing on the other side.

"We're on our own," Daijon told Claretta, "and we're not goi to make it before it rains."

"Is that bad, the rain I mean?"

"When a raindrop hits the ground, the shadows can hide in th dark spot they leave behind. Especially if the Sun doesn't dry it up first. When the grounds completely wet, they can go anywhere."

Daijon and Claretta sped down the side of the road on their mountain bikes as the clouds above got darker blocking the Sun. As the teens turned onto a two-lane road, drops of rain came down. Claretta looked up for a second and saw shadows darting through the clouds following them high above. Around them, the cars continued ; their normal speed not the least bit worried when it started to drizzle.

Up ahead, the street widened providing a middle lane for cars to turn. "Get into the turning lane," Daijon said as he saw several shadows coming at them from ahead.

When the path was clear, they both swerved into the middle lane that ran for several blocks. The shadows came at them from all sides trying to knock them off their bikes. Pure light orbs soared through the air as Claretta struggled to keep her bike straight. Thankfully the orbs would only harm a Shadow Person.

"We have to get off!" Claretta shouted seeing Daijon was having the same problems she was.

The rain got thicker and the only way to be heard was to yell. Car headlights came on to light the way through the darkness but it wasn't the kind of light they desperately needed. Claretta reached over her shoulder for the bag as she walked toward Daijon. It wasn't until she came away empty handed that she remembered Daijon had both of the solar staffs.

By now, every part of Claretta was soaking wet and she had to shield her eyes just to see. She ran a few feet but almost got hit by an oncoming car attempting to turn. The driver honked his horn at her as she stumbled backwards. Wondering how she avoided becoming roadkill, she turned around realizing someone had her shirt. A Shadow Person in true form lowered its hand, its dark form looming over her. Hands together, she tried hitting it with a pure light orb but the Shadow Person knocked her down.

"Why!" Claretta shouted. The Shadow Person looked down at her with black eye sockets. It pointed in the direction Daijon stood in then left her on the ground. Claretta now understood why it had saved her. It wanted her to watch as they killed Daijon.

Up ahead, Shadow People in true form stood and watched as Daijon tried fighting off the shadows. Holding both solar staffs in his hands, he searched the dark for his next target. Since Claretta could create pure light, he carried his and Claretta's in the one shoulder bag slung across his back. That and she needed to learn to not rely on it. Now looking at the constant movement of the darkness before him, Daijon doubted he and Claretta would provide no more than entertainment for the Shadow People.

Around them, several cars pulled over waiting for the blindin rain to stop but the Shadow People could care less. They used the puddles and the parked cars to their advantage.

The best Daijon could do was attack any dark shadow that came his way. He swung a staff striking a shadow. As he did, another knocked him off his feet. Recovering quickly, he squatted low to the ground and spun around in a circle with the solar staffs sticking out. They swooshed in the water hurting any shadows that might be hidin A few shadows in puddles nearby leaped out and surrounded Daijon. His grip tightened on the solar staffs as he looked at the dark human shaped figures. His gaze then turned to Claretta pleading for assistance.

Claretta moved forward attempting to help but was stopped b another Shadow Person blocking her path. *I've had enough of this,* sh thought. With a hand behind her back, Claretta created an orb of pure light and threw it at the Shadow Person. The shadows ignored their fallen comrades and moved closer to Daijon. He thrust the solar staff out at one of them but when it fell another simply took its place.

If the shadows can travel through the water, then maybe so cc light, Claretta thought. Relying on her instincts, Claretta squatted

78

down and let the pure light seep from her outstretched fingertips. Ribbons of light moved not only through the puddles but six feet up into the raindrops that continued to fall. The Shadow People opened their empty mouths but were in too much pain to even scream.

Daijon looked at the lit-up shadows with wide eyes. All around him, raindrops shone with pure light. *That's insane,* he thought.

Claretta, with one hand still in the water, waved for Daijon to join her. With caution, he stepped between the shadows trapped in the air by the light and ran towards Claretta. They watched as the pure light continued to wrap around every Shadow Person burning them until nothing but ash was left.

"Are you kids okay?" A man from one of the nearby cars asked. The rain was still heavy and to those nearby, the Shadow People almost looked like smoke clouds and the pure light like lightning. "Someone call 911!" The man shouted after hearing no reply from the kids.

Hearing the sirens blare in the distance, Daijon and Claretta knew they had to get out of there. With his dad unable to pick them up, Claretta had no choice but to call her parents. Realizing where they were, Daijon led them to a nearby park where they hid inside the tunnel of the jungle gym. Not long after, Claretta's parents arrived and they were not happy.

"Claretta Arbogast, you had better start explaining what's going on right now!" Her father demanded as they slid into the back seats. "I'm dropping Daijon off then we're going home to have a long talk."

"We can't go home," Claretta protested, "it's not safe. Daijon house is the only place we can go."

"Our home has kept you safe for 13 years, there's nothing wrong with it."

Claretta glanced at Daijon who nodded his head.

"Shadow People are after us, dad. We'd be lucky to make it inside the building."

"Honey, shadows don't attack people," her mother said from the passenger's seat.

Before she could say anything else, a shadow slammed into tl windshield.

"These do," Claretta said grabbing the door as the car swerved.

"Did we hit something?" Her mother asked looking through the rain as the windshield wipers moved back and forth at the highest speed.

"Please don't stop," Daijon said when Claretta's dad started t pull over and slow down.

Taking off her seatbelt, Claretta rolled down her window worried about the shadows more than the rain coming in. Sitting on her knees with her head and shoulder in the rain, Claretta threw pure light orbs at the shadows coming from behind. All the while trying to explain everything to her parents.

When they arrived at Daijon's house, they were faced with

another problem. The solar lights were still fully functional but just outside the lights; several Shadow People in true form awaited them.

"Honey, stop the car," Claretta's mother said. Mr. Arbogast pulled over to the side of the road leaving about a ten-foot gap between them and the shadows. "What is that?"

"Shadow People. Stay in the car," Claretta said opening the door.

It wasn't until the Shadow People moved towards the car that her parents saw what had been terrorizing their daughter.

"Young lady, you are not going out there," her father ordered.

"Mr. Arbogast, she's the only one who can stop them," Daijon said.

Mr. Arbogast turned in his seat and looked at the boy with narrowed eyes then gave his daughter a worried look. Before he could say anything, Claretta got out the car and stood by the open door already creating pure light behind her back. It was barely raining by now but there was enough water to do what she needed.

"I guess your friends didn't tell you what happened earlier. Oh wait that would be hard to do as piles of ash," Claretta taunted taking advantage of the rain once again.

The Shadow People ignored her taunting as they continued forward. Freckle sized pure light orbs floated into the sky behind her and became one with the raindrops. 50 or more droplets hung immobilized a few feet in the air before her while others still came down. Claretta's heartbeat increased as her left foot slid back a step;

her body screaming for her to run. *Just a little closer,* she thought, staying in place. When the last Shadow Person stood under the golde rain, she let them fall. "Go, go, go," she told her dad when she hoppe back in the car.

Mr. Arbogast stepped on the gas and didn't stop until they we safe on the other side of the solar lights.

Mr. Cooper, who had watched everything from the doorway, opened the door wide welcoming his new guest.

"What's going on," Mr. Arbogast demanded the moment he reached Mr. Cooper.

"I can explain all that but its best we get inside," Mr. Cooper said ushering Claretta's parents in.

Once inside, Mr. Cooper showed Claretta's parents where the could stay until it was safe to go home. He also told them it would be best if they called off work and didn't go anywhere without him.

While the adults talked, Daijon and Claretta dried themselves off and changed into pajamas. Everyone was tired but with the Shade People regrouping just outside the solar lights, no one was doing muc sleeping.

Later that evening, everyone was downstairs having a late dir when Daijon thought he heard someone scream his name. He looked around and saw his dad in the recliner, Claretta's parents were on the sectional and Claretta was on the stool next to him at the counter.

"Daijon!" Someone screamed again.

"Who is that?" Claretta asked.

Daijon ran to the glass doors and looked out into the night. He couldn't believe what he was seeing; Audi was running towards the house.

"Claretta!" Daijon shouted getting everyone's attention, "It's Audi!"

Claretta ran over to him and looked out. Not sure what she was going to do yet, Claretta put her hand on the door and stepped outside before her parents could stop her.

Off to the right, a car sped through the grass back to the road. It maintained its speed as it approached the Shadow People who let it pass untouched. Their eyes were set on a better target. Audi ran towards them some distance behind the barn but past the last large solar light.

They watched as a shadow rode the darkness to a height that passed the house then shot back down. As it passed through the light, it turned to ash but it was when the ashes blew away that everyone received a surprise; another shadow was left behind unharmed.

"Now what?" Daijon asked from beside her not having a solution for once.

Claretta walked until she had a good view of not only the solar lights to her left but also the one on the roof. "I've got this," she said thinking back to what she did in the locker room.

Angling her body, she stretched her right hand towards the roof and the other hand stretched to the solar lights on her left. Closing her eyes, she quickly searched for the pure light on the other side of the house and out front. When her eyes opened, the air around them grew brighter as Claretta took strands of pure light from each of the solar lights. She weaved them through the air until they connected to the o on the roof in an arch. Once they were in place, she turned her back t the house and raised her hands to her sides at shoulder height; palms faced outward.

Claretta waited in that position looking in Audi's direction. More shadows sacrificed themselves so another could try and capture the Sun's last daughter. *Closer,* Claretta thought. When Audi was in t desired spot, Claretta flattened the strands of pure light then created a circle with her arms still up. She guided the pure light past the barn until her palms faced her. When she finished, they were now in a dom shaped force field and the other shadows joined their comrade on the ground as ash. Audi fell to the ground a few feet from the force field' edge breathing hard. Daijon ran to his sister side. Helping her stand, they both looked at the force field and the ashes of the shadow's remains.

"How did you do that?" Daijon asked following Claretta bac inside.

"Mr. Cooper told us where your powers came from," her mother said, standing at the edge of the living room. "I can't believe this is happening. Why did you hide it from us?"

"Because all of this is happening," Claretta replied motioning outback and to the front with her hands. "I didn't want anyone getting hurt."

Claretta looked at her mother then her father who still hadn't spoken. *What was I supposed to tell them? I couldn't just say, hey Shadow People are trying to take over the Earth and I must use my powers to stop them. They'd have thought I was crazy.*

"Well that explains why the apartment was filled with solar lights," Mr. Arbogast said. "I thought you were still afraid of the dark."

I am, Claretta thought. "Do you…"

"This is a lot to take in at one time," Mr. Arbogast interrupted, "but if it helps our daughter then we'll do what we need to."

Claretta stood there in silence looking at her father who answered her unfinished question and her mother who nodded in agreement.

"How did you do that?" Daijon asked again breaking the silence.

"I sort of did the same thing around myself in the pool changing room before you came in," Claretta said. "I just tried to do that again but on a bigger scale."

"That's impressive," Audi said. "We've never tried anything like that before."

"How did you get here? I thought they caught you?" Claretta asked.

"It's a long story. Let's just say I stayed in the one place the Shadow People wouldn't look for a Sun's daughter; the dark," Audi explained.

"Audi, you're finally here," Mr. Cooper said. He hadn't

stopped looking at his youngest daughter since she arrived. While Daijon had seen the girls away from the house, it'd been years since his dad had seen them. Just like the Sun hadn't seen her only son. At the time, it was safer for them all that way. The children weren't even allowed at each other's houses. They were taking no chances hiding Daijon's secret.

"Hi dad," Audi said walking past the others and into her father's waiting arms. He embraced her as he shed silent tears.

"We have much to talk about," Mr. Cooper said.

"Later, I promise. Right now, Claretta needs to continue training." Audi looked at Claretta.

"She has been training," Daijon protested, "thanks to me and dad."

"I guess that explains the force field," Audi said.

"That was more like luck," Claretta said.

"What are you talking about?" Audi asked.

"We should talk," Claretta said.

Following her upstairs, they gathered in Daijon's room while the adults remained in the living room.

"So what's this about the force field being luck?" Audi asked sitting next to Daijon on his bed.

"Your powers aren't exactly easy to use," Claretta said from her seat at Daijon's desk.

"I told you how to create pure light."

"I didn't know you were going to give me your powers. I

86

definitely wasn't expecting to fight Shadow People."

"There wasn't exactly time to tell you everything," Audi laughed. "I was just trying to protect the city."

"We've trained and she's done some amazing things," Daijon said before their conversation led to an argument, "but it's like something's still holding her back."

Audi and Daijon looked at Claretta waiting for her to tell them what was keeping her from reaching her full potential. After a few moments of silence, Claretta finally gave in.

"I'm still afraid of the dark," Claretta said head bowed embarrassed. "Sometimes it's not that bad, but other times..."

"I didn't know that," Audi said shocked. "How come you never told me?"

"I didn't want anyone to know," Claretta said looking at her. "I thought I was over it but then I started fighting Shadow People."

"You can't show the Shadow People any fear. They *will* use it against you," Audi said.

"So now what?" Claretta asked.

"Continue to light the lamp posts and try to find the others," Daijon replied.

"Then we need to continue my training."

They talked and trained hard that night knowing time was running out. With Audi escaping their clutches and not having her powers, the Shadow People would be doubling their efforts. To make matters worse, according to Audi, the Sun could no longer come home at night. There had been too many recent attacks at home so she was forced to hide in the glow of a night star.

Now exhausted and covered in sweat, Audi, Daijon, and Claretta laid on the sparring mats. The thick curtains had been drawn across the glass doors and a fire that had once warmed the entire rool now lay quiet and still. Tonight's practice had gone surprisingly well.

"You've got the basics down, " Audi said getting up, "but if you don't let go of your fears, your powers may fail you when you need them most." She held her hand out to Claretta helping her up as Daijon switched on a light.

"I've been wondering since I left if you ever got another lette from your future self?" Audi asked as they sat on the stools with bottles of water.

"No," Claretta said. "Maybe my future self was caught."

"It's possible," Audi said looking towards the stairs. "I'm goi to go talk to dad before bed. I'll see you guys in the morning."

Daijon and Claretta decided to call it a night as well and followed her up.

CHAPTER 9

Still in the past...

The next day, Audi, Daijon, and Claretta continued putting light around Quincy. After lighting the last lamppost at the school, they rode their bikes to the public library. The entire time Daijon kept checking his watch and looking at the sky.

"I thought so," Daijon said as they stopped by the library's back entrance.

"What are you talking about and why do you keep looking at your watch?" Audi asked.

He looked up from his watch and pointed at the sky. "You clearly haven't noticed but it's getting darker."

Audi and Claretta both looked up. Golden strands broke away from the Sun like a piece of hair falling from a person's head while thick strands shot out towards dark shadow filled clouds that neared it. It was too early for the Sun to be setting, and those were *not* rain clouds. To anyone else looking up, they'd think it was a scientific phenomenon but *they* knew better.

Too busy looking at the Sun; they didn't notice the Shadow Person closing in on them.

"We have to go," Daijon said pulling on the girl's arms.

Confused, both girls looked over their shoulder and scanned

the car filled parking lot. That's when they saw a man in his early 30' in jeans and a dark shirt running towards them. Bringing up the rear, Claretta managed to close the library door before they were caught. I rattled as Claretta and the Shadow Person pushed on it at the same time. Claretta's feet slid as the door opened a crack. The Shadow Person overpowered her but Claretta was not easily defeated for she poured pure light into the handle forcing him to let go. The Shadow Person stood on the other side glaring at her as she not only covered the door in pure light but also sealed the cracks with it as will. Claret grinned back as he walked away.

"It's time we let people know what's going on," Claretta said "They can decide for themselves if they want to believe you but we have to do something."

"Fine," Daijon agreed.

Scanning the cluster of computers near the reference books, h led them to the last available computer. The plan was for each of their to post something on every social media site they were on. While she waited for Daijon to finish, Claretta looked around and saw a one-year-old boy on his mother's hip. He pointed and struggled to get dov while his mother tried to talk to the woman at the counter. Claretta looked at where the child pointed and saw a shadow move in the corner.

"What is it, honey? I don't see anything," the child's mother said turning her head around.

Kids can see them better than adults can, Claretta realized.

"Did you post something yet?" Claretta asked.

"Just to Facebook, why?" Daijon asked.

"That'll have to work," Claretta looked over her shoulder again. "Shadows are inside."

Daijon unplugged his phone from the computer and shoved the adapter into his backpack. Trying not to attract any unwanted attention, they walked to the front door at a quick pace. As they neared the small street at the front of the library, it was now darker than when they arrived. By the time, they walked halfway across the intersection, the day had turned to night and it was only two in the afternoon.

All around them cars stopped in the streets as the sky changed in a matter of seconds. Claretta, Audi, and Daijon walked to center of the intersection to get a better view of the sky. Looking up, they saw shadows had now blocked the Sun.

Car headlights were soon turned on but not even the brightest among them could break through the unnatural darkness. Though the sky had already grown dark, the intersection continued to grow darker as shadows filled the space around the three teens. Forming a triangle, they stood back to back with their solar staffs as they awaited the Shadow Peoples next move.

"On your right!" Daijon shouted.

Claretta turned and fired a shot of pure light from the end of her staff hitting a Shadow Person right in the chest. Panicked shouts could be heard coming from all directions in the darkness. No one knew what was going on. All they could see was light flying through

91

the air and turning to dust when it hit a car or tree. Other times, they saw the light stop as though it hit something in midair but they weren sure what it was.

The fight wasn't going well but before they could get captured Claretta created a large ball of pure light. The same kind she failed to do the first night at the ranch. When her hands spread to the width of her shoulder, due to the balls increasing size, she threw it into the sky Separating smaller balls from it, Claretta sent them flying through the darkness like drones until the large one was no more.

All around them, phones clicked, and flashes went off as people took pictures and recorded what was going on. Before the darkness completely receded, Claretta and the others managed to slip away through the commotion.

"I'm sure the Shadow People will be waiting outside the ranc but I know where we can go instead," Audi said leading the way.

The day went in and out of darkness as Daijon and Claretta followed Audi and evaded the Shadow People. Reporters were havin a field day trying to get interviews and footage of what was transpiring. They had no idea what they thought was a scientific anomaly was the Sun fighting to save them.

Still not sure where they were going, Claretta and Daijon climbed onto the city bus after Audi taking three seats in the back row They were away from the windows and the aisle was in front of then in case, they had to make a quick escape. Every time a new passenge got on, Daijon searched for the smoky aura that would give away wh they were. When they'd first gotten on the bus, he thought their solar staffs would be a problem but the driver said nothing. They'd done so much fighting; he'd forgotten that to everyone else they were *just* solar lights.

"A college," Claretta said as the bus stopped outside Hamilton Hall an hour later.

"There are too many people here," Daijon said as they got off. "Do you even know where you're going?"

"It'll be fine, just follow me," Audi said. Her oldest sister, Prima was eighteen and the only one that didn't live at home. She wanted the full college experience so she moved into a dorm on campus.

Daijon relaxed a bit when he saw the Sun was no longer covered in darkness but he still remained alert. Though summer classes were taking place, the campus was still full of students. Unable to check everyone, Daijon focused on those in long sleeves wearing hats that walked too close or stared too long. Claretta tried to calm her nerves after their last fight. *Thankfully, they didn't use shadow orbs,* Claretta thought as they approached the doors of McGregor Hall.

As they entered, florescent light guided them to the dining hall that was situated under the student dorms. Before they could eat, they had to wait in a growing line that stood before a table that held a register. Behind it sat a tall college guy in jeans and a green tee-shirt that said McGregor Hall Dining in black letters above his heart. A white cord trailed from his iPod that sat next to the register by the wall to his left ear. The other remained hanging so he could still hear what was going on around him. Claretta watched as he looked for his next song paying no attention to the student ID's he swiped.

"What are doing?" Daijon asked grabbing his sister's arm and pulling her away from the line. Claretta followed them. "They're not going to let a bunch of kids in there."

Audi rolled her eye. "Trust me, it won't be a problem."

Audi shook off his arm and got back in line. Daijon looked to Claretta for help but she just shrugged and followed Audi. *This better work,* Daijon thought as he joined them. When they reached the register, Claretta and Daijon were shocked when the guy drew his eye away from his iPod and smiled at them.

"Annoying your sister again," they guy said looking at Audi.

"I wasn't trying to James," Audi replied. "I guess it didn't hel that I brought my brother and best friend with me this time." She pointed to Daijon and Audi. "You know how she gets when she's studying."

"Yeah, I do," James laughed. He looked around making sure no one else was behind them and that his boss wasn't around before I let the three kids slip through without paying.

"Thanks, James."

"Anytime. Tell Prima, I still need help with Chemistry when you see her."

"I will."

Claretta, Audi, and Daijon walked through another set of glas doors and into a large room filled with wooden round tables. The smell of roasted potatoes, baked goods, and other delicious foods wafted from the buffets all around the room. They each grabbed a plate and made their way across the tile floor to the various sections. Once their plates were filled, they chose a corner table near an emergency exit, in case, they had to flee.

"So, what was that all about back there?" Claretta asked.

"Oh that," Audi shrugged as though it were no big deal. "I always ate here when I visited Prima. It helps that James has a crush on her. He doesn't need help with Chemistry; *he* tutors other students."

Claretta couldn't help but laugh. They were quiet after that enjoying their food and the peace that surrounded them for the time being. It seemed all they'd done lately was run from one place to another. Daijon hadn't seen any Shadow People yet and they hadn't been followed. All he could do was assume they saw no reason to return to campus since they already had Prima.

When they finished eating, there were fewer students roaming around campus.

"We should light some of the lamp post here while most of the students are in class," Audi suggested as they came across one.

"I don't think that's a good idea," Daijon advised. "The Shadow People don't know where we are and I think we should keep it that way for now."

"He's right," Claretta agreed. "As soon as I light one, they'll know we're here."

Having agreed upon that they decided to hide out in the librar until nightfall.

"How are we going to get in?" Claretta asked when they walked up to Smithdale, the all freshmen dorm, that evening.

"Must you guys question everything," Audi said holding up Prima's college ID card. Prima had forgotten it and her dorm room ke the last time she came home to visit. She'd found it on the laundry room floor and was going to return it. When Prima didn't answer her phone and no one had seen her, Audi knew she'd been taken by the Shadow People.

"That's great and all but I'm sure someone will notice if I sta overnight," Daijon said.

"Go around the back, the third window from the corner," Au said as they neared the building. "Don't get caught," she teased.

Audi and Claretta walked up to the building like it was perfectly normal for two 13-year-olds to be on a college campus. Au swiped Prima's ID and the single door clicked open as if saying yes, you belong.

"Hi Audi," Rachel, the RA said. "Where's Prima, we haven't seen her in a while?"

"She went out of town last minute with our mom for a few days. She said me and a friend could stay one night."

"I really shouldn't with Prima not being here," Rachel said, "but ok, just one night and don't leave this floor. You know the rest o the rules."

"What?" Audi asked seeing the look on Claretta's face. "Like I said, I've been here before and she's Prima's best friend."

Once inside Prima's private room, Audi turned on the light and went over and helped her brother through the window. As soon as he was through, Claretta put light into the window so nothing could get in. She then sent an orb of pure light around the room and into the shadows. There was no open space at the bottom of the door and thankfully, the only way in was with a key.

While Claretta did that, Audi looked around her sister's room. Prima's Chemistry book and notes covered every inch of the desk. Inside the microwave that sat on top of the mini fridge was a bag of popcorn yet to be cooked. Audi took survey of the rest of the room and that's when she noticed it; cuts half an inch deep in the cement wall by the door. *Shadow orbs,* Audi thought, running her fingers down them. *How could no one have heard this?*

When they were sure it was void of shadows, they settled in for the night.

Just before they drifted off to sleep, Daijon remembered something he saw on the map his mother left him.

"There were five spots blacked out on the map," Daijon said. He lay on the floor at the foot of the extra long twin bed putting himself between the girls and the door. Nothing but a sheet covered him as the girls squeezed together on the bed beneath the blanket. "The weird thing is there are actual places where the blacked-out spots are. I didn't think about it back then but it can't be a coincidence."

"There are five marked to save us," Audi said just above a whisper.

"What?" Daijon asked.

"It's something mom told me when I went back to the house."

They all lay there quietly thinking what the two things had in common.

"I think I got it," Claretta said. "Daijon, remember the lamp post at the dollar tree? The one with the symbol?"

"Yeah."

"Is there anything else you remember about it?"

Daijon thought back to the map he'd memorized years ago. It was on one of the blacked-out spots. "Those spots form a circle with one in the middle."

"A force field," Claretta said thinking back to what she did at the ranch. "I bet your mom set them up to form a force field around town in case anything happened to her."

"How are we going to get all around town? We don't have our bikes and getting someone to drive us is too dangerous for them and for us."

"I know someone who can help with that," Daijon said.

With that problem solved, they turned in for the night.

In the morning, when there were fewer people around, Daijo climbed out the window and met the girls out front. His eyes went straight to the sky and a sigh escaped his lips when he saw his mothe still there.

"Who's this person we're going to see?" Audi asked also glancing at the sky as they walked back through campus to the bus stop.

"He's a friend of mine, a junior at the high school."

"*You* know an upperclassman?"

"Let's just say I got him out of some trouble so he owes me a favor." As much as he didn't want to risk his friend's safety, they needed help.

The bus pulled up and stopped with a screech. Daijon got out first and with a quick look knew the driver was human. Trusting his powers, Audi and Claretta followed behind him.

A short bus ride later, they got off in a residential neighborhood on the corner of Tucker Avenue and 23rd Street. Two blocks later, they arrived at a tan colored one-story home. The attached garage stood open and jazz music flowed to the sidewalk from somewhere deep inside.

"That's how we're going to get around," Daijon said pointing to the go-karts sitting outside. "Hey Lee!"

A tall teen with short dark hair turned down the music and walked towards them. He had a wrench in his left hand and wore a sleeveless shirt that showed off his tan and slight muscles.

"Hey man, what brings you here?"

"Just came to collect on that favor."

"Sure thing, whatever you need man." Lee looked at the go-karts that were up on cement blocks. His dad had gotten them from a place going out of business a couple years ago. They started working on them together but when his dad's business picked up, Lee was stu working on them alone. "This got anything to do with that video of yours that went viral?"

"Maybe," Daijon said helping him lower the now fixed go-kart. Over the past couple years; he'd managed to secretly gather footage of Shadow People in shadow form and human form.

"Is it real?" Lee asked.

Instead of answering his question, Daijon walked over to Claretta and asked if she could put pure light into the metal. She shrugged her shoulders, as if to say, we'll see, then walked to the full gassed up go-kart nearest her. Claretta took a deep breath and closed her eyes letting the pure light move to her hands. She left it there letting it build until her hands glowed. When she was ready, she plac both hands on the go-karts metal frame letting it soak in the light. Stepping back, she looked over at Lee who stood there speechless.

"Does that answer your question?" Claretta asked.

Lee just nodded his head and stared at the go-kart.

While Claretta did the same thing to the other two, Lee and Daijon talked.

"Try to bring the go-karts back in one piece," Lee said.

"We'll try," was all Daijon could promise.

After making sure they were all on the same channel, Daijon took the lead as they left Lee's house with Claretta in the middle and Audi bringing up the rear. With their tanks full of gas and thanks to

100

some modifications by Lee, they rode soundlessly through the neighborhood making their way to Tripmont Amusement Park. There, they would find the first of the remaining four posts that needed to be lit.

CHAPTER 10

In the future...

It had been two days since Daijon talked to Audi on their wa[y] home from Walmart and they weren't any closer to rescuing her.

"We can't just leave her there!" Daijon shouted standing by h[is] horse's stall. He looked at the others standing around him.

Autumn sat on a wooden bench outside the stall across from him. She stared at the ground twirling a strand of dark hair around he[r] finger as she thought about Andrew. The five-inch cut on his thigh wasn't deep enough for stitches but was causing too much pain for hi[m] to come to the barn. For now, he laid upstairs waiting on their decisi[on].

"No one's saying that," Lee said from beside him.

"We need a solution with the fewest casualties," Mr. Cooper said by the entrance. "Preferably, none at all."

"Even if we get Audi out the house, we still have to make it back here," Parker said.

The others around them remained quiet.

"Anyone that wanted to train to fight the Shadow People has been," Daijon said.

"Yes, to protect themselves and anyone else if they *need* to," Mr. Cooper said. "Not to fight an army."

"You're right and I'm sorry," Daijon said. "I know this is new to you guys but if you have any ideas how we can save Audi just let [me] know."

"Don't worry, we'll save her," Mr. Cooper said as everyone filed back inside. He thought it best to have their meeting away from the others. Most of them were already panicking after Andrew came back hurt, it'd probably be worse if they knew what they were planning.

"Perfect timing," Melody said running to meet Daijon and his father, "a vehicle pulled up outside."

"Has anyone gotten out yet?" Mr. Cooper asked.

"No, but a lot of people aren't happy about it."

"We'll check it out."

Loud voices greeted them as Daijon and Mr. Cooper entered the house.

"Quiet, everyone!" Mr. Cooper yelled.

"It's been out there for three minutes now and no one has gotten out," a man with a wife and two kids said.

"We should leave them out there, what if it's a trap!" A young man just out of high school shouted from beside his younger sister.

"Then it's a good thing that's not your decision to make," Daijon said. "I'm the only one that can decide who stays."

The young man remained quiet.

"Autumn take everyone upstairs. You and one of the fighters will guard the back entrance while the other fighters guard the upstairs hallway. Dad take the foyer. Parker and Lee, you're with me."

With solar lights in hand and everyone inside was in place, Dajion opened the door and walked out followed by Lee and Parker.

Daijon turned his head left and right scanning the area just outside the solar lights. Now the darkness around them belonged to the night but for how long, he didn't know. On the other side of the street a Jeep Liberty was parked with its headlights on facing away from town. Its lights turned off as the boys approached the car blocking the driveway to prevent anyone from getting in. They stopped a few feet behind it as the passenger door opened. A woman in her 40's walked around to the driver's side where her husband of the same age got out

"Is this still the safe house?" The man asked.

Safe house, Daijon chuckled, *I guess it is.* "I have to search you individually before you can come in."

The woman looked at her husband. He glanced into the backseat of the jeep then up and down the road. "We'll do it."

"Whoever wants to go first, stand in the middle of the road," Daijon said.

The man, wanting his wife out of harm's way, sent her forward

Daijon walked to the other side of the car and stood in the small space between the solar lights and the vehicle. He looked for the familiar aura but none surrounded her. Her shadow was still as Daijon waved her closer to the solar lights.

"One last thing," Daijon said stepping forward. "I'm not going to hurt you." Normally looking for the aura was enough but not with the way things were now.

The woman looked over her shoulder at her husband as Daijon reached her. Standing a few feet away, he pressed the solar light against her collar bone. When nothing happened, he gave a sigh of relief.

With his wife safe on the other side of the solar lights, the man glanced into the back of the jeep once again then came forward.

"Whoever's in there come out now!" Daijon shouted once the man was safe inside.

A boy, the same age as his sister with black hair, walked around from the passenger side. He stopped at the back of the jeep but in view of the others. Daijon started to walk forward but stopped when he looked at the boy's shadow.

"Stay where you are," Daijon said.

"What's going on?" Parker asked coming to the edge of the driveway.

"He's not a Shadow Person but there's a shadow attached to his. We can't let him in."

"We can't just turn him away."

"If we can't get rid of it, we won't have a choice. Lee, see if you can find out who he is from the couple he came with."

Daijon turned to the boy, who looked up and down the street with large eyes. He took a small step forward but Daijon held up a hand for him to wait.

"The man said the boy's their grandson. They were watching him while his parents went out of town to celebrate their anniversary," Lee said coming to stand by Daijon.

With his back to the boy, they went over the plan.

Daijon approached by the jeep's rear attempting to keep the focus off Parker who went around the front. Lee, who held his solar staff at his hip, approached from the boy's left. Daijon kept his eyes c the boy not wanting to alert the shadow that remained on the ground. When Parker stood behind the boy, Daijon blinked once. Parker struc his solar staff straight down but the shadow was faster. It left the boy shadow and hid in the darkness. Taking the opening, Daijon grabbed the boy's arm pulling him towards the house. Before they could mak it to safety, the shadow latched itself onto the boy's leg making him and Daijon fall.

Getting to his feet, he turned and looked down at the boy. The shadow had wrapped itself around the boy's left calf. Every time, he tried to get up, the shadow tightened its grip. Parker ran forward and tried to strike the shadow again but it was ready for him. With its gri still on the boy, it stretched out, tripping him. Parker fell onto his bac with a loud grunt then rolled out the shadow's reach.

Daijon helped Parker up while Lee rushed forward to where t shadow retracted itself.

"Lee, watch out!" Daijon yelled.

Before Lee could even turn his solar light upside down, anoth shadow rose in front of him. Quick on his feet, he stepped back out o its reach and joined the others by the solar lights. "How many are there," he asked?

"Five, including the one holding the boy. The others aren't close though. They're just sort of hanging back." Daijon said. He'd hoped they could've resolved this problem before more shadows arrived. They'd just finished fighting and he didn't want them to have to fight again so soon. *If I'm quick, I might be able to help the boy, without the others having to fight.* "Lee, give me your solar light."

"Why? What are we about to do?" Lee asked.

"**We're** not doing anything," Daijon replied. "**I'm** going to try and save the boy. I don't want either of you to move unless I say so."

Taking Lee's solar light, he knew it was their last chance of saving the boy from the shadows. Using the right solar light, Daijon moved forward to hit the shadow on the ground just as the others had.

The shadow wasn't expecting what happened next.

Not knowing what would happen; Daijon raised his left arm and tapped the boy on the back. The pure light danced as though it were alive within the solar light. When the movement stopped, it flashed twice making the boy shield his eyes and the nearby shadow retreated. The shadow attached to the boy's leg was stubborn and remained in place. As though sensing its defiance, the pure light flashed again, twice as bright, forcing the shadow to back away. Daijon grabbed the boy's arm and pulled him up. Together, they ran to the driveway before the shadows could regroup.

After much complaining, Mr. Cooper helped Andrew downstairs and onto the couch. He knew he should be resting his leg but while being confined to the house was bad enough; being confined to one room was even worse.

As the day went on, Daijon continued to practice with those he

107

trained. No one had come up with a plan to save Audi but Daijon kne everyone was trying their best. Every now and then, they'd hear cars pass the house. For some reason, people thought they'd be safe if the left town. That may be true, for now but Daijon doubted it'd last long

When the beeping of a car horn was heard once again, Daijoı turned to the door. Flanked by Lee and Parker, they walked out to grε the newcomers. This time, the vehicle was smaller and parked at the edge of the driveway.

Proceeding with caution, Daijon stopped when the door open and a girl, Audi's age, stood there.

It was then; Daijon knew how he'd save his sister.

CHAPTER 11

In the past...

"Can you both hear me?" Daijon asked talking into the phone in his left hand while his other hand gripped the steering wheel.

"Yeah," Claretta said.

"Loud and clear," Audi said.

They'd all driven go-karts before. The next town over had a place the kids from school liked to go to as soon as the weather got warm. Driving on the street with cars was a different matter entirely. Though the go-karts had metal frames on the sides and on top, there were no doors just them and their seat belts.

Daijon, Audi, and Claretta stuck to the large bike lane praying they didn't get pulled over by the police. As they rode through the streets with their phones on speaker between their legs, Daijon and Audi kept an eye on the Sun. The last thing they wanted was for it to go completely dark without them knowing.

All around them, people stared at the teens from their cars.

As they got closer to the amusement park, Daijon saw the first shadow. "Two vehicles ahead under the van to our left," he said.

The girls swerved left slightly to look for themselves. Under the van, a shadow glided back and forth between the rear tires. Stretching itself out, the shadow poked its head up while still moving with the van. As the car in front of Daijon reached the shadow, it stretched it arms out of the ground and grabbed onto the darkness beneath the car. It pulled itself into the car's shadow receiving minor burns from the Sun.

Audi, Daijon, and Claretta were stuck between the flowing traffic and parked cars as the shadow got closer.

"We need to get off the main road," Daijon said. He guided t go-karts to the left to veer into traffic. Just before it crossed the edge the bike lane, a truck honked its horn and sped by. Daijon pulled bacl over forced to stay in their lane.

When the shadow reached them, it hit the front wheel of Daijon's go-kart. Hoping no one was watching, Claretta removed one hand from the wheel and shot a pure light orb at the shadow with her staff.

"Stay close and get ready for a sharp turn," Daijon said wher the shadow let go.

As the car in front of him became trapped in the thickening traffic, Daijon saw what he was looking for. The girls pulled over rig behind him and when he was right on top of it... "Now!" He yelled a: he made a sharp right turn into a neighborhood that was shaded by ta trees. While being in the shade put them at a disadvantage, they weren't too worried. Claretta dimmed the pure light that was in the g karts to avoid more attention on the road. As soon as they passed beneath the first tree, a shadow grabbed the back of Audi's go-kart. Claretta quickly connected to the pure light amplifying the brightnes: burning the shadow's hand.

Daijon slowed down to get behind the girls leaving Claretta t lead. This way he'd still be able to see any Shadow People and Claretta would have a clear shot.

Claretta glanced over her shoulder as Daijon pulled in behind Audi. Her eyes darted around the area before her and her heart quickened in pace. Past the glow of the go-kart, the trees drooped from the extra weight of the shadows. *Calm down, calm down,* she told herself realizing no good would come if she panicked. Claretta reached for the solar staff that was wedged between her thigh and the seat.

Now she was ready to shoot at the first sign of movement.

"To your left, bottom branch!" Daijon yelled.

Ashes sprinkled down onto the perfectly manicured lawn as the pure light hit the branches.

Having seen something hit her tree, a woman in her mid-20's that had been watering her plants shouted "What are you kids doing! You can't ride those here!" She continued to the side of the road. Claretta started to lift her foot off the gas pedal forcing the others to slow down.

"She's not one of them!" Daijon said looking at the woman again. "Aim for her shadow."

Claretta pulled close to the sidewalk. She waited until she was right on top of the lady, who continued shouting, then aimed at the ground. An orb of pure light struck the center of the woman's shadow expanding outward until it was completely lit. When the ground was dark again, a light breeze blew the layer of ash off her shadow sending the woman running back inside.

"How far are we from the park?" Claretta asked Daijon as trees lined the street of the next intersection they crossed.

"We're almost there."

"I've got an idea," Claretta said eyeing the road that was sprinkled with various sized potholes. "Stay close and use the potholes."

"What?" Audi asked confused but did as instructed.

Claretta, thankful for the bad roads, put pure light into every pothole she saw. Once each one was filled, she lifted the light up like beam. Shadows glided down the road as they weaved around the potholes. Unable to lose the shadow that followed close behind, Aud waited until the last possible second then steered the go-kart over the pothole and through the beam of light.

Arriving at Tripmont Amusement Park, they parked as close as possible to the entrance. Not sure if their solar lights would make it through the security check, they were forced to leave them behind an hoped they'd still be there when they returned.

"How come you haven't taken your powers back?" Claretta asked the question that had been on her mind the past few days.

"I can't." Audi said.

"Really?" Daijon asked. "Then how did you learn to transfer powers?"

"Mom taught us how years ago, in case of an emergency, which this was. We can transfer powers but once that person does; they're unable to take them back from that person. That's just a side

112

effect. The only way I can control pure light again is if someone else gives me their powers."

"I'm sorry," Claretta said.

"It's okay. It was my choice," Audi said. "To be honest I did try taking them back when you were asleep in Prima's room but it didn't work."

Claretta looked at her shocked.

"I know, I should have woken you but I didn't want to get your hopes up."

"That's okay at least you tried," Claretta said as they neared the gate. "We may have another problem."

"Huh?" Daijon asked.

"Do either of you have enough money for three tickets?"

They were in such a hurry with the new information that had come to light that they hadn't thought about it.

"We'll have to sneak in," Daijon said.

Scanning their surroundings, they searched for a way in.

"We're going to need a distraction," Audi said two minutes later as she led them over to the far-right lane.

"I can handle that," Claretta said as they stepped behind a girl with long blonde hair who wore cream-colored shorts with a lace pattern over them. She was with a large group of rowdy kids and two adults. One of them, a short woman with long brown hair, searched the backpack she'd been wearing. A first aid kit and bottles of water spilled out as she tried to find the tickets. The other slightly taller woman tried getting the kids whose tickets she had under control. Staying close to the group, Audi and Daijon shielded Claretta from view. When security started checking the other woman's bag, she sent a ball of pu light just big enough to knock the open bag over. As the security helped pick the items up, the three of them rushed through to where the other kids stood.

Once inside and away from the groups of kids, Daijon stoppe when he saw the crowd of people. There were at least twice as many here than on the college campus. He looked around trying to search everyone that passed but still missed most of them. Seeing her brothe just standing there, head darting back and forth, Audi put a hand on h arm.

"It'll be okay," she said.

Daijon looked at her and simply nodded.

They walked forward only to reach a fork in the road and be greeted by lamp posts from every direction. It was a park; after all, it had to be lit at night.

"We don't have time to check all of these lights," Claretta sai "How are we supposed to know which one it is?"

"If the lights are going to connect to form a force field, its gonna have to be tall," Audi said. "The map didn't happen to show exactly where it was, did it?"

"No, just that it's in the park somewhere," Daijon added. "Don't forget it'll be the only one with our mother's symbol on it,"

Several lamp posts later, they still hadn't found it.

114

"Maybe, we should split up," Audi suggested.

"We can't risk any of us getting caught. You just got away from them," Daijon said looking at the sky. It was cloudy out; not a good sign. He continued looking through the crowd when he spotted a teenage girl in ballet flats, capri pants, and a tank top. The smoky aura around her identified her for what she was. "Let's go in here. We're being watched." He led them into a gift shop selling tee-shirts with different pictures of the various rides on it and cups that he could never find his name on.

"Are they on to us?" Claretta asked.

"It doesn't matter; we have to find the lamp post. Mom made it so I doubt they'll be able to destroy it."

Audi walked over to the counter and picked up a map of the park. "So, we're here and this is the area we've already covered."

Daijon glanced at it, then back outside where he'd lost track of the girl. He kept watch while Claretta and Audi got help from the woman that worked at the shop. Turned out, the largest lamp post was in the next area.

Having the directions, they needed, Audi, Daijon, and Claretta left the gift shop. Daijon had a bad feeling and suggested they go into the one adjacent from them. "Pretend you're looking for something." He went to one side of the store while the girls went to the other.

The teenager Shadow Person came into the store and this time she wasn't alone. Two park security officers, who were also Shadow People, stopped behind her in the entrance. The girls turned and

115

whispered to them. Nodding, the men spoke to the cashier then went over to Claretta.

"You need to come with us," the taller of the two security guards said. They told the cashier that they'd been informed Claretta was shoplifting. What the cashier didn't know was that they were Shadow People. Without their solar lights, the Cooper siblings could do nothing but follow as they took Claretta away. The only good part was the Shadow People were going in the direction they needed to g

The Shadow People kept a firm grip on Claretta's arms as the walked through the maze of games and screaming children to take Claretta to the closest office. Audi and Daijon followed them trying t think of a way to save their friend. Audi saw the Shadow People struggle to get around the kids who were more interested with the games than watching where they were going. Getting an idea, Audi walked up to a small group of boys a couple years younger than her.

"I'll give you five dollars," Audi said pulling a wad of one-dollar bills and lent out her pocket, "if you do me a favor." The boys nodded and seconds later, they were running through the park where they bumped into the two Shadow People. They lost their grip on Claretta who ran into the crowd where Daijon and Audi found her.

Claretta, Audi, and Daijon continued to run until Claretta stopped them by a water game, the one where you shoot water at a target and something races to the top.

"Come on," Claretta said motioning to it.

The man running the game made a last call for anyone that

116

wanted to play. They quickly sat; putting down the only money they had then placed their hands on the water guns. Audi quickly looked over her shoulder and saw the men approaching. "They're coming," she said turning around before they could see her. Audi's grip loosened on the water gun and she rose slightly to get up.

"Don't move," Claretta said putting a hand on her friend's arm making her sit back down. "When he says go, turn and shoot."

Audi looked at her with a raised eyebrow.

"On your mark," the man said.

The men got closer.

"Get set."

They could hear the footsteps of the men behind them.

"Go!"

Claretta, Audi, and Daijon turned in their seats and squeezed the trigger. Golden color water shot out of every gun at the game. Surprised gasps escaped the lips of the other players who were too busy looking at the water to care where they were aiming.

The Shadow People were helpless. They stood too close to back away which resulted in them getting a full shot of pure light water. Their bodies slowly turned to ash as it traveled up and down their bodies. When the water finally stopped, Claretta, Daijon, and Audi dropped the guns and ran towards the roller coaster. Behind them, the remaining three feet of the Shadow People continued turning to ash.

"I told you that video was real!" Someone shouted.

People ran in every direction away from the ash piles. The water may have stopped them but the female Shadow Person who ha hung back wasn't far behind.

Audi, Daijon, and Claretta were nowhere in sight by the time the real park security got to the scene. Up ahead, they could see the roller coaster. It was made entirely of wood with seats that only had a buckle across your waist and a security bar you pulled down on your lap. By the time they reached it, word had spread of what had happened in the other part of the park.

CHAPTER 12

Still in the past...

A crowd of people remained in line at the wooden roller coaster that had been temporarily shut down. The operator in his early 20's tried to calm the crowd. "I'm sure the ride will be up and running in no time."

Claretta, Audi, and Daijon approached the coaster from the side away from the line. Daijon looked up but couldn't see the symbol to be sure. "Can I borrow those?" He asked a man standing nearby with binoculars hanging from his neck. With the man looking on, Daijon swept the post's length. "This is it," he told the girl's moments later handing back the binoculars.

Claretta, Daijon, and Audi were able to approach the front of the line with no problem. Most of the crowd had given up waiting and those that remained idled.

"Aren't you that kid who posted the video?" The operator asked leaning in to get a better look at Daijon.

"Yeah," Daijon said seeing no point in hiding it, "and they need to get to the top of the coaster." He pointed to Claretta and his sister.

"Why?"

"Trust me, you really don't want to know but you'll be helping us save the city."

While no one was looking, he started the ride praying he didn't get fired.

Claretta climbed in the middle row of the first car while Aud
sat behind her. She wanted to be close but give her enough space to c
what she needed. The few people that now hung around demanded
they be allowed to ride as well.

"Everybody settle down!" The operator yelled.

"Trust me; you're not going to want to get on!" Daijon shout(
at the angry crowd.

Out of the corner of his eye, he saw the Shadow Person girl
standing where they just were. He watched her for a few minutes. Th
girl appeared to be talking to herself but really, she was having a
conversation with her shadow. While it could move about alone, the
shadow was still a part of her. It was the same for all Shadow People
who hailed from the dark side of the moon. The shadow was merely :
extension of the person. They could live without their shadow but if
the Shadow Person was destroyed so was the shadow.

Understanding what it was supposed to do, her shadow went
after the girls.

"Take a deep breath in, feel the pure light flowing through
you," Audi tried to get Claretta to relax as the roller coaster made its
steady climb.

The shadow was halfway to the girls when Daijon went over
the controls. When Claretta's seat reached the top of the climb right
before the drop, Daijon had the operator stop the ride. When the safe
bar was released, Claretta pushed it up. With shaky hands, she stood.

Even though, the coaster had stopped, she feared the wrong move would tip them forward.

"This is crazy," Claretta said as Audi stood gripping the back of her seat. They both looked at how far the lamp post was from them when they heard a commotion below.

More Shadow People had arrived and were trying to restart the ride.

Daijon was doing his best to fight them off while the operator stood guard of the controls helping in any way he could.

Audi's scream returned Claretta's attention to her current task. A shadow grabbed Audi's arm trying to pull her over the coaster's side but Claretta caught her other arm just in time. With her free hand, she hit the shadow with a pure light orb sending it past the other shadow that came their way.

"We have to hurry," Claretta said having a solution.

She placed her right hand on the track's side but nothing happened. Removing her hand, she closed her eyes trying to ignore the shadows and the hundreds of feet below her. Taking a deep breath, Claretta placed her hand back on the track. The pure light flowed from her hands forming a light bridge up to the lamp post. Claretta held Audi's hand and helped her climb over the back of her seat. Together, they crossed the smooth bridge that was dense like marble.

Down below, the man Daijon had borrowed the binoculars from had alerted the crowd to what was transpiring above. They stopped as though, suddenly, frozen and watched the two girls.

"Someone get security!" A woman holding the hand of her toddler yelled.

"Go on, get out of here," Daijon said to the operator. *There's too many of them. They'll have to find another way down.*

Finally overpowering them, the Shadow People turned the ric back on.

Claretta and Audi heard the creak of the coaster then watched over their shoulders as it made the drop. Right below where the coast had been, shadows zipped back and forth between the beams that supported the start of the bridge. Small pieces of wood fell to the ground as they smashed into it. Having made it across, Claretta put both hands on the post and sent pure light up.

"Get behind me," Claretta told Audi once she finished. She p her hands on the bridge and when she stood, tendrils of light separate from the bottom. One after another, they separated from the bridge ar attacked the shadows as the girls ran back across the bridge. When they reached the track, the path behind them was clear.

"How are we going to get down?" Audi asked as they stood (the edge of the bridge.

"Remember when we use to go rock climbing," Claretta said She created thick rope and climbing gear from pure light within moments. "Just picture the roller coaster as a giant rock wall and use the wood beams to kick off on."

Audi hesitated when she saw how short the rope was but she trusted her friend. As she descended, the rope continued to extend pa its initial length.

They were halfway down when the shadows resumed their assault. Audi kicked off and descended just out of reach of a shadow whose arms clutched nothing but open air. Claretta watched from five feet above her. Her forehead crinkled in confusion as to why they didn't try again. As they got closer to Audi, she threw pure light orbs at them. It wasn't until she missed and the shadows passed them that she understood their plan. *They're going for the wood around the rope.*

"Audi stop!" Claretta yelled.

Audi stopped nestled in the climbing gear and rested her feet against a wood beam.

Claretta continued to kick off again, keeping her arches small, in order to reach Audi quicker. The shadows got higher and Claretta got lower. Pushing off one last time, she looked up again. *I'm not going to make it.*

The wood broke and the rope fell.

"Audi!" Claretta yelled. Quicker than she thought possible, she made a ball of pure light the size of an adult human head and sent it towards the ground seconds before the beam supporting her rope was destroyed. She gave a high-pitched scream as she fell towards the ground. Claretta was unable to see the ball of light she created but she didn't need to; she could feel it and knew what had to be done if they were to survive.

Below, Daijon and the crowd could only watch in horror as the two young girls fell. That's when they saw the light hit the ground in the space between the fence and roller coaster. They looked upon the golden light as it first stretched wide and long until it resembled half the size of an Olympic swimming pool. It then grew thicker and thicker until it was the height of a bounce house. Not long after the light stopped moving, Audi landed on it. No one moved or said a wor as Daijon climbed over the short fence that surrounded the ride. Audi bounced on the soft light then slid to the edge where her brother helped her down and out the way. Claretta hit it the lights moments later and slid off into Daijon's waiting arms. The crowd continued to look on silence.

"There's no way we're gonna make it out of here without having to answer any questions," Audi said as they remained by the inflated light.

"Oh yes, we will," Claretta said. "Follow me."

With the clap of her hands, the inflated light busted filling th air around them in a golden dust leaving the crowd in a mixture of fe and fascination. Through the dust and commotion, Daijon, Audi, and Claretta hid amongst the crowd and made it out the park and to their go-karts. Claretta stood by hers, gave a quick look back at the woode coaster in the distance where she could swear, she saw a shadow standing on the tracks at the big drop.

The Sun had set but the sky had yet to attain its full darkness when they entered the business district. They guided their go-karts through the streets that were void of its usual clutter of cars and park around back of a twenty-five story office building.

"We've got to break into that?" Claretta asked staring up at the black building. "Are you crazy?"

"Relax, we're not robbing it," Daijon said. "Besides, I know a way in."

"My brother, the master planner," Audi joked as they followed him to the side of the building leaving their solar staffs behind. When they reached the front, she stopped. A lone, black sedan was nestled two spots down from a handicap sign. She looked to the glass windows that covered the entire front of the building and noticed they were all dark except for the ground floor and a single office six floors up. "Someone's here!"

"Yep and right about now he'll realize he left his late-night snack in his car," Daijon said as they continued walking.

"He?" Claretta asked wondering how he knew all that.

Before Daijon got a chance to answer, an average height man in a dark navy suite came out the locked door with only a set of keys in his hands.

"Leave something in your father's office again?" The man chuckled.

"Yeah," Daijon replied with an apologetic smile. "Sorry to bother you."

"Leave it like you find it this time," the man smiled as he continued to his car.

"Sure thing."

Daijon checked the hallway for shadows as they walked

125

through the building and entered the elevator. Numbers flashed on th wall, marking their climb to the top floor. Daijon leaned against the wall by the buttons with one foot raised and eyes closed. Claretta slic to the ground her back against the wall across from the doors and Au stood in the corner to her left with her arms crossed.

The numbers continued to flash the floors by until the elevato slowed down.

"No one else is here," Daijon said pushing off the wall. "The janitor won't be here for another hour."

Claretta stood as the elevator stopped.

Ding!

Expecting the worst, no one moved as the crack in the door grew larger. Now fully open, an empty hallway greeted them. *Who pushed the button,* Claretta thought wishing she had her solar staff.

Her question was soon answered.

When only a slither of the hallway could be seen, a cloud of shadows swarmed in knocking them to the floor. The elevator doors closed and continued to climb higher.

"Close your eyes!" Claretta yelled as she managed to stand. She spread her arms wide then brought them together with a loud cla that filled the elevator with a blinding light. The shadows released their hold on Audi and Daijon as they collided with each other. Desperately, they looked for an escape from the painful glow but the was nowhere to hide. When the siblings opened their eyes, they saw Claretta standing there with a slight glow and a floor full of ash.

Thankfully, they made it to the 25th floor with no further problems. At the end of the hall to their right, they passed several vacant offices; there was also a locked staircase leading to the roof. It posed no problem for Claretta who blasted it open with an orb of pure light. As they exited onto the roof, lights shone in every direction from the city that expanded below them. Audi and Daijon stood guard by the door while Claretta lit the lamp post.

This one was unlike like the others. Instead of a regular light pole that stood on a curb or in a parking lot, this one was a flagpole.

When Claretta was done, they returned to the elevators. Claretta pushed the button but nothing happened. The light showed it remained on their floor but the doors refused to open.

"Where's the emergency exit?" Audi asked.

"It's this way," Daijon said leading them back down the hall they just left.

They made it down two flights of stairs when they heard a door below them open. Claretta looked over the rail and into the open space between the stairs. Shadows started gliding up the stairs followed by a few Shadow People.

"Go back up," Claretta said.

They ran back up the stairs but didn't go through the door. Instead, Claretta sealed it closed with a layer of pure light.

"What are you doing," Daijon said, "We'll be trapped."

"I'm more worried about them coming in behind us," Claretta said. She started making two layered orbs whose size matched that of a

127

golf ball and had the others place them on the floor.

Meanwhile, the shadows continued to climb. Some stood nex to their human counterparts taking their time to the trapped children while others continued to slither up the stairs.

Claretta looked over the railing again. "We don't have long; they're getting closer and these are about ready to explode."

Audi and Daijon looked at her with wide eyes almost droppin the orbs she handed them.

"Not those, just these," She said. Grabbing the golden orbs from the floor that vibrated, she tossed them over the railing. They whizzed from the weight and speed in which they traveled.

"Let's go," Daijon said starting down a few steps.

"Not yet," Claretta said still looking over the railing.

The shadows looked up as the golden orbs fell, unfazed when they missed them. That is until the first one exploded. The shadows watched in horror as the golden orbs sprayed pure light when they burst open. Those that weren't hit directly assumed they were safe until a second orb revealed itself to be hidden inside the first one and burst seconds after the outer orb did.

"Run!" Claretta yelled.

They made it down three flights before the shadows reached them. With their solar staffs left behind, Claretta led the way. As she rolled a few more down the stairs, a shadow sprang off the wall and grabbed her wrist, hindering her movement. Its' mouth grew wide an moved closer as if to swallow her whole but Claretta knocked it awa with a lit palm. Thinking about the man that let them in, Claretta hoped he had stayed in his office and was unable to hear what transpired in the stairwell.

The three teens threw the orbs in every direction trying to fight the dark forces that vastly outnumbered them. Audi fell as a shadow pushed her causing a domino effect. The three of them fell down a few steps and onto a landing.

"Come on, this way," Claretta said opening the door to the 15th floor. She searched the ceiling until she found a sprinkler. With no time to find a lighter, Claretta tried something she wasn't sure she could pull off.

"Whatever you're going to do, you might want to do it now!" Audi yelled as she and Daijon struggled to keep the door closed.

With her left hand out, Claretta created pure light. Placing her right hand above it, she let the light absorb some of her body heat leaving her chilled. When she had given it enough, she turned it into a golden flame. Since the light was a part of her, it spared her hand from the dangerous fire. The rest of the building, however, wouldn't be so lucky if she dropped it. Directing the flames with her fingertips, Claretta sent them to the ceiling to tickle the sprinkler.

Just as the sprinklers went off, the stairwell door burst open. Shadows rushed towards the Cooper siblings that lay sprawled near its entrance. Claretta stepped forward and just like she'd done before filled the water that showered down with pure light. The shadows and Shadow People had no choice but to go back the way they came.

129

After helping her friends up, they stepped into the now wet stairwell. With golden water now raining down on them, Audi, Daijo and Claretta made it down and out the building.

Now back in their go-karts, they rode through the darkened streets to a bell tower downtown that had been there since they were born. It used to be a tourist stop until it closed down a few months ag It was said the person that donated it was worried about vandalism which had grown to be a problem over the last year. Now that it was closed to the public, local teens had been daring each other to go to tl top and ring the bell.

Audi, Claretta, and Daijon sat on a wooden bench with their backs to the bell tower that sat across the street from them on the corner. Claretta glanced over the rose bushes behind them at the ston structure. It was circular in shape and equaled in size to the office building they'd just left. Claretta took a few deep breathes to calm herself as the surrounding trees cast shadows on the building. Daijon searched the darkness for any trace of shadows or Shadow People. H didn't see any but knew they were out there lurking in their natural element.

When they approached the bell tower, there was no one in sig so Daijon picked the lock on the wroth iron door not wanting the sound of Claretta bursting the lock open to attract any unwanted attention. When they entered, the only things at the base were an elevator and a staircase. Remembering what happened at the office building but needing to hurry, they chanced taking the elevator.

Reaching the top, there was no sign of a lamp post.

"Where is it?" Daijon asked.

Solar staff in hand, Claretta got down on her knees and looked in the only place there was. On the inside, two inches from the bottom was their mother's symbol and hanging down was a sun shaped clapper. "She used the bell," Claretta whispered.

"Look at this," Daijon said from the far-left corner. A plaque just above their heads confirmed what Claretta had found. Elegant writing told them that the bell was donated by their mother 20 years ago.

"Mom must have convinced them to close it to the public," Audi said, "so nothing would happen to it when the shadows attacked though, I doubt she told them that part."

Above them, shadows could be seen moving in the clouds. Others jumped off the tips of the tree branches and onto the roof. Claretta knelt once again and put light into the clapper inside the bell but then nothing happened. The bell, itself, was still the same copper color and when she stood you couldn't see the light at all. Seeing they had failed, the shadows attacked. Daijon fell backwards onto the bell causing a vibrant rich sound to fill the air around them. Through the bell's brief movement, the bottom started to match the color of pure light. Noticing the light vibrating away from the bell, Claretta started pushing it but it was too heavy to be done alone.

"Guys, I need your help!" Claretta yelled.

Audi and Daijon fought their way to her while Claretta held

them off with pure light orbs and her staff. When Audi and Daijon's hands touched the bell, Claretta turned and helped them push. It was well before the hour when the bell should have rung and the children cringed every time it did knowing they were drawing attention to themselves. Waves of light vibrated from the bell and into the darkne around it. Shadows scattered as the teens ran down the stairs in hope: of distancing themselves from the commotion they'd caused.

The light continued to spread into the night as they rounded tl lighthouse. Their victory was short lived, however, when a light shin in their faces.

"Stop right where you are," a male voice said.

The light was lowered and a police officer stepped forward ju as the now golden bell stopped ringing. He was in his late 40's with dirty blonde hair and a goatee. Upon seeing the teens, his expression turned from alert and tense to alert and annoyed. The bell had stoppe ringing but it was too late, they'd already been caught.

"What do you kids think you're doing?" He asked. "There's r trespassing in the bell tower."

"It was just a joke," Daijon said happy the officer wasn't a Shadow Person.

"Well, you can explain that to your parents when you call the at the station."

With no other choice, the three of them climbed into the back of the police car. Around the corner a block away, outside a closed tourist shop, their go-karts waited for them to return.

Once they reached the station and called their parents, they were left under the semi-watchful eye of a younger officer. Precious time wasted away as they sat in their chairs by his desk unable to do anything. A few officers stood around a radio a couple desks over. The radio jockey interviewed people who'd witnessed the strange events that have occurred in the last several days. Audi and Claretta looked at Daijon hoping none of them had seen the video. It wouldn't be long before the police realized their parents would not be picking them up.

"We can't stay here," Daijon said forever searching the shadows.

"I know," Claretta said. "I need to use the bathroom," she said standing up.

The young officer glanced at her then pointed to a door just past the sea of desks. On the way, Claretta noticed lamps that must've been there since the precinct opened on all the desk. While no one was paying attention, she tossed small pure light orbs into the bulb of each lamp she passed. When she rejoined Audi and Daijon, Claretta set off a chain reaction. The few officers that remained turned at the sound of the first bulb bursting then the next and the next. While they tried to figure out the cause, Audi, Daijon and Claretta ran for the door and back to the go-karts.

CHAPTER 13

Still in the past...

It was late in the night and they needed a place to stay when Audi made the decision for them to go back to her house. "It's close t where the last lamp post is," Audi said.

"But it's not safe there anymore," Claretta cautioned.

"Nowhere is safe when it's dark out," Audi replied. "At least know every part of the house dark or lit."

Solar lights in their neighbor's yards struggled to help light th way as they pulled into Audi's driveway. When they reached the threshold, Audi looked around then opened the front door. Before she could enter, Daijon stopped her.

"Turn the lights on first," Daijon instructed.

Audi reached for the second switch in and that's when they heard the screams. They moved into the living room and saw a shado go into the next dark room.

"Our mom must have put pure light in the bulbs," Audi said impressed. "I never knew that. Then again, we all had our powers an mom was home so they never came in."

Daijon closed and locked the door, then followed the girls around the house as they turned on all the lights. Claretta also made ὰ spiderweb of pure light on all the windows downstairs. With all the lights on, the sounds of their yawns followed them upstairs to the master bedroom where they planned to sleep.

That night they slept in the Sun's king size bed; unaware a shadow had already slipped into the fuse box before the lights came on. It waited there until the house went quiet then wrapped itself around the switches, and turned the lights off. While it could do nothing about the windows upstairs, it was able to open a small window in the basement corner they'd forgotten about letting his comrades in.

Hours later, Claretta rubbed her eyes and stretched her arms and legs. Turning onto her back, she opened them. "Guys, get up!" Claretta said grabbing the solar staff that leaned against the bed next to her. "The powers off."

Daijon got up and looked out the window on the other side of the bed. Though it was almost midnight, a couple of the neighbor's lights were still on and that was all the proof he needed.

When they left the bedroom and entered the hallway, Audi noticed the once closed doors of her sister's bedrooms were now open. On their left and right, Shadows stood in their entryways. Claretta threw a pure light orb at the shadows closest to the stairs on the left clearing a path. Audi led the way downstairs but before she reached the fourth step, more shadows blocked the way. At the bottom, a Shadow Person leaned its back against the front door.

Shadows continued to swarm all around but that didn't deter them. The teens continued to fight as Audi led them through the hall to the back staircase that led to the kitchen. Audi hoped to reach the back door but it too was blocked leaving them no choice but to run through the dining room.

"The windows," Claretta whispered to Audi as shadows blocked both doorways.

Claretta pulled her friends around the dining room table to the two windows. Without saying a word, they understood what she was going to do. The shadows climbed on the table in human form and advanced from both sides. When the shadows and Shadow Person were close enough, Daijon, Audi, and Claretta ducked as the spiderweb lit windows shattered inward. Claretta held them off with glowing shards of glass as they climbed through the window and ran the go-karts.

The city could no longer wait; the last post had to be lit now.

CHAPTER 14

In the future...

Audi left Kiki's room with a nature guidebook in hand. Every night, she'd slept in a different bedroom curled beneath the blankets of her sister's beds. Placing the book on the living room table, Audi went straight for the pantry. There was no point opening the fridge, everything had spoiled days ago. Her stomach growled in protest as her eyes scanned the food but she decided to wait a bit longer; it would only make her thirstier. Grabbing the water jug, she took a sip. *Even at this rate, it'll be empty by nightfall.*

Returning to the living room, Audi started to pick up the nature guide when her cell phone rang on the couch. Looking at the screen, she gave a heavy sigh. It was Mrs. Brownstone from next door, checking up on her again. Putting on a fake smile in hopes it reached her voice, Audi answered.

"Hello, Mrs. Brownstone," Audi said.

"I saw a strange man in your yard the other day," Mrs. Brownstone said getting straight to the point as usual. "Are you alright?"

"Yes, Mrs. Brownstone."

"You know I can come over if you're not ok by yourself."

"No, I'm fine," Audi said quickly. As much as she needed water and as annoying as Mrs. Brownstone could be, she didn't want to put her in danger.

"Are you sure, because..."

"Sorry, Mrs. Brownstone, I've got to go my mom's calling," Audi lied. She tossed her phone on the couch and picked up the book again. Just as she opened the cover and turned the page, her phone rang again.

I swear if that's Mrs. Brownstone calling about a car driving by, she doesn't notice, Audi thought slamming the book on the table. This time her face lit up at the caller ID. It was Daijon. *It's time.*

Daijon tried to remain focused as they prepared to turn onto t street of the home that held his earliest years.

"Whatever happens, you did the best you could," Mr. Cooper said tapping his gloved hands on the steering wheel.

"Yeah," Daijon said as he glanced at the piles of blankets and coats that littered the floor in back.

As they turned onto the dark street, Daijon went to his saved messages. Using his thumb, he clicked on the first one. On their left, the lights outside a two-car garage turned on. A few houses down, Daijon sent another saved draft. This time, the garage lights of a sma house with wind chimes turned on. Parked outside in front of the hor was a classic Chevy. Though each home on the street had plenty of room to park in their driveway, those with garages parked on the stre After days and hours of late night and early phone calls, Mr. Cooper was happy to see his efforts paying off.

"Why haven't they attacked yet?" Daijon wondered out loud they passed the third intersection.

138

Mr. Cooper wondered the same thing as another garage light turned on. *It's not like they don't know this vehicle.*

They kept driving until they reached a house across the street and two doors before Audi.

When Audi pulled back the dark curtain in Prima's room the first thing she noticed was all the light coming from her neighbor's yards. The last time she looked out the window, Shadow People glared back at her and pounded on the glass. Seeing something unusual, Audi ran downstairs for a better look. Leaning against the back of the couch, she pressed her face close to the glass. In the yard across the street, were solar lights. These weren't your cheap Dollar Tree solar lights or even the fancy type you could find in another store. No, these were something exclusive. Two feet tall, with little brass spirals that formed a cage around the glass ball that held the light. *What is my brother thinking?* Audi thought as she noticed the car, he described sitting two houses down.

Dressed in jeans, gym shoes, a short-sleeve shirt and a jacket, Audi had been waiting hours for him to finally arrive. Now that the moment was here, she wasn't a 100 percent sure she was ready. Daijon knew she didn't have her powers; how did he expect her to make it to the car. Now that she thought about it though, she didn't recall seeing any Shadow People or shadows when she just looked outside.

With only minutes before it was time to step outside, Audi got an idea. Running into the kitchen, she grabbed a small reusable shopping bag, a pair of thick work gloves from a drawer by the back

139

door and a hammer. Going through the house, she removed a few ligl bulbs from each room. Now, locked in her mother's bathroom, Audi wrapped the light bulbs in a towel then placed them on the counter. Using the hammer, she broke them into chucks about half the size of the palm of her hand. Once they were safe on the bottom, she was ready to go.

Standing at the front door, with the bag handles held in a tigh grip, Audi flipped the porch light on.

Seeing the light, Daijon sent a message to the others. Up and down the block, the sound of engines roaring to life filled the darkne: Heart racing, Audi reminded herself who she was then opened the door. Her gloved grip on the bag loosened when she didn't see any Shadow People. Stepping away from the threshold, she wished for th first time she had Daijon's powers.

The night seemed to have grown darker and the moon provid no comfort for it was blocked by dark clouds. Tree branches swayed the windless night giving away the shadow's hiding places. *It's like they're not even trying to hide. They're just sitting there.* As she neare the end of the driveway, Mr. Cooper drove towards her.

That's when the Shadow People attacked.

Before she could reach the car, a Shadow Person swept her uj over his shoulder. As it started to carry her away from her father, Auc dug into her bag and pulled out a chunk of glass. Gripping it carefull: she sliced up the Shadow Person's side. Ash spilled from between its fingertips as it tried to hold itself together. From the ground, Audi smiled.

GO! Daijon sent in the group message. Before the car could completely stop, Daijon jumped out. "Keep driving," he said to his father. Looking at the back door one last time, he closed the door and ran to Audi.

The sound of garage doors opening filled the street. Shadows started to move towards them, momentarily, forgetting their objective. At first, nothing could be seen inside the garages but darkness. Then the headlights came on. Daijon had Parker switch out all the headlights for the brightest ones he could find. Now, those very lights shined at the shadows. They knew it would only irritate the Shadow People and shadows but every bit of light helped.

From the ground, Audi saw half a dozen people run from the garages and grab a special solar light from the yard.

"Get them!" The Shadow Person in charge of the mission yelled pointing to the Cooper siblings. After what happened at Walmart, the Shadow People only expected Daijon and his father to show up. What they didn't know was that cars had been coming in shifts so as not to draw attention.

That's why they let me get this close. They want both of us, Daijon thought.

"Please tell me you have another plan," Audi said as they cut across the grass to the road.

"Nope, just the one," Daijon said. While he told Audi the basic parts of the plan, he left out the most important part knowing she wouldn't like it.

All around them teenagers fought the shadow and Shadow People. Less than a minute into battle, the cars exited the garages. They drove up and down the streets into yards shining their lights on the shadows the people were fighting.

As a car approached Audi and Daijon, she noticed a girl fighting a Shadow Person a yard away. Leaving her brother's side, Audi ran to the girl. When a Shadow Person approached the girl's blind side, Audi threw one of the shards lodging it in its leg. It screamed in pain unable to remove the golden glass. More Shadow People came when a car pulled up in the grass.

"Get in!" Daijon yelled from the passenger side.

Audi hesitated for a moment not wanting to leave the girl who fought to rescue her.

"Go on," the girl insisted pushing Audi forward.

Audi watched from the window as the girl continued to fight. Before the girl could be overwhelmed with Shadow People, a car drove by and picked her up. Audi smiled glad to see she was safe and turned towards the front. Beside her brother in the driver's seat was someone she didn't know.

"Who's this and where's dad?" Audi asked staring at the man with a black cap and dark jacket.

"This is Malcolm, he and everyone out here is staying at our house," Daijon said. "Don't worry, dad's still around."

All around them, cars picked up fighters and dropped them of in different locations.

"Time to get out," the man said.

"What's going on?" Audi asked her brother.

"Keep moving," was all Daijon said.

As the fighting continued, Audi ran out of shards and was using a solar light as her main weapon. They were several yards down from Audi's home when a car picked them up for a third time. This time instead of dropping the fighters off, they returned to the garages. When the door was closed to the three-car garage they hid in, Daijon jumped out.

"We don't have much time," Daijon said as he opened the back door and reached for Audi's hand.

As she got out, others circled their car. That's when Audi noticed a young girl climb from beneath coats and blankets in the back seat of her dad's car. Mr. Cooper hugged his daughter but their reunion was cut short when Audi took a good look at the girl. There was barely an inch difference in height between the two and if you were to add a wig, the girl could pass for Audi.

"What's going on?" Audi asked as Daijon dug around beneath the coats and blankets.

Saying nothing, he handed the girl a bag.

"I'm not doing it, it's too dangerous," Audi said as the girl put on a wig that matched Audi's hair.

"Cynthia agreed to this on her own."

"I know the risk," Cynthia said, "and I want to help."

143

"You two need to switch clothes now," Daijon said.

Once the girls were in each other's clothes and Audi had on a wig that matched Cynthia's original hair color, Daijon explained the rest of the plan. "Audi, you're going to ride with Lee while Cynthia will ride with me and dad. They'll expect us to be together. Everyone will meet back at the house."

With Audi safely buckled into the passenger seat of Lee's car, Daijon walked around to the driver's side. "Keep my sister safe," he said. Lee nodded and started the car.

When the doors opened one last time, the cars sped out into tl street. Moments later, they were joined by a dozen other cars that car from other streets. Daijon and the others blended in with the other ca going their separate ways but staying in groups of two. Not knowing who was in what car, the Shadow People scrambled to find the Coop siblings. Thanks to Audi they knew where every road led to.

Taking a right onto a street with a cul-de-sac, Audi wondered what he was doing. Lee, saying nothing, didn't slow down as he drov through a yard and onto a dirt path between a house and some trees. Branches scrapped the side of the car, digging into the paint but Lee didn't stop. Not long after, another car with Autumn in the passenger seat followed. Audi saw a Shadow Person race through the trees but per Daijon's instructions, she did nothing to stop it. She was to do nothing that gave away who she was.

On the other side of the neighborhood, Mr. Cooper raced up t street as Daijon tried to guide him past the shadows. While a few followed the other cars, the majority trailed theirs. Cynthia used the solar light Daijon gave her to try and keep them away from the windows. Shadow orbs whizzed past the car and, eventually, one struck the back tire. The car skidded, turned on its side, and flipped over twice before landing on its wheels. With the car out of commission, the Shadow People descended.

"Get out," Mr. Cooper whispered to the children holding his head. "Get out, now."

In the back, Cynthia was slumped over unconscious and in the passenger's seat Daijon's vision was slightly blurred. Struggling with his seat belt, he managed to unbuckle it and get out. Dizzy, he tried to fight the Shadow People that removed Cynthia from the car. Her wig that got tangled in the seat belt fell off when they removed her ending the deception. The car that trailed them approached, followed by another that had seen the accident.

When Daijon couldn't get to the girl, he tried to save his dad.

"Run," his father told him pointing towards the headlights.

"I can't just leave you."

"You must and you will," Mr. Cooper said finally freeing himself. He took a solar light and started to clear a path for his son. "Go!" He shouted one last time.

With tears in his eyes, Daijon ran past his father and the Shadow People and into the waiting car.

"What do we do now?" Parker asked from beside Daijon in the back.

"We have to go," he whispered through tears.

Looking back at the crash then Daijon's face, Parker didn't question him further.

"You heard him, let's go," Parker said to the driver, a woman about his mother's age.

With that, they turned down a side street and into the dark that waited.

CHAPTER 15

In the past...

It was morning and still dark when they rode to the last post. Despite the Mayor's advice to stay put until they figured out exactly what was going on, some families were out loading their vehicles to leave. The only ones who *could* help were now crossing railroad tracks.

Claretta, Audi, and Daijon pulled up to a small clearing next to a large hill. Just behind a thick cluster of trees was the last lamp post. Audi stepped forward but Daijon put his arm out stopping her.

"There's too many," he said.

They looked at the shadows dancing among the trees. The Sun looked down on Claretta and her children from where she hid in the light of the moon. Knowing her time was at an end, she made one last sacrifice for her children, the city, and the Earth. The Sun came from behind the moon letting its rays shine out before it. Seeing this, the shadows left the ground and went into the cloudy sky.

This was their chance. Claretta ran into the trees with Daijon and Audi who stood guard while she lit the last lamp post. As they backed away, something different happened. Pure light from the post shot into the air and to the sides. All around the city people watched as the other lamp posts did the same thing. Once they were all connected, pure light fell down around the city creating a force field. While the shadows that left would be unable to return, there were still several

147

that remained inside the force field. Some of those very shadows blocked their path back to the go-karts.

Above them in the sky, beams of pure light shot out of the Su as she desperately fought the shadows. Claretta, Audi, and Daijon looked towards the sky a few feet from the trees and noticed how the beams touched the Earth nearby. Using both hands, Claretta moved tl closest beams across their path gaining them entrance to the trees. Daijon and Audi stayed close while Claretta manipulated the beams (light. They circled around them at such a speed that no shadow was able to get through.

The beams vanished as they reached the road. Daijon and Au looked to the sky once again as they stood by their go-karts. The Sun glow dimmed as the shadows circled it. Weak beams of light flickere as they expanded towards the shadows but it was no use. The shadow continued to circle the Sun, the once golden beams now turning blacl until there was nothing of the Sun left.

Daijon held his sister in his arms as they cried over the loss o their mother. Claretta leaned against the furthest go-kart giving the siblings some space. Tears ran down her face as she thought over everything that has happened.

"Guys, I think I know where the shadows have been hiding," Claretta said moments later remembering something that had happen well before Audi relinquished her powers. She'd been fixing the brak on her bike near the park when she saw shadows coming out of the pond. It was evening and she just assumed the Sun was playing trick:

on her. She knew better now.

They arrived at the park and were thankful to find no other people there. Though with the Sun being gone, she couldn't imagine anyone being there in the dark. Due to construction on the lower parking lot, they were forced to the parking lot on the hill. Down below past the concession stand and the tennis courts lay the man-made pond where the shadows lived. Claretta had no intentions of letting Daijon or Audi go into the pond with her, they just didn't know it yet. Seeing how full most of the trees were, Claretta touched their trunks as they passed. The trees soaked in the pure light, all the way to the tips of the leaves. This was the first time she put light into something living but she knew it would work.

Standing side by side among the trees, Claretta, Daijon, and Audi let the shadows come to them. The more they could defeat outside the lake, the better. They fought the Shadow People and the shadows with their staffs and pure light orbs but it wasn't enough. Seeing the shadows were becoming too much, Claretta told Audi and Daijon to run for the stage that stood before rows of wooden bleachers. Claretta waited until they were behind where the curtain would fall then threw down a large pure light orb at both ends. A thick sheet of golden light met in the middle then rose upward.

The second Audi and Daijon were safe, Claretta turned and made the leaves fall from the trees like golden confetti giving her enough time to make it to the pond.

Claretta walked down the cement steps empty handed and into

the water until it was up to her chin. Before she could talk herself out of it, Claretta closed her eyes, took a deep breath and immersed herself. Opening her eyes, she started swimming through the darkness that lay ahead, not sure of where to go and what she'd find. Just when Claretta could hold her breath no longer, she swam through a dark shadow resembling a door. She fell onto a damp stone floor, filling her lungs with much needed air. Soaked, she pushed herself off the floor and stood in a darkness she hadn't experienced before. *It's like an underwater tunnel,* Claretta thought as she reached to her right and felt a stone wall. With her back to it, she counted it to be about six feet across and who knew how long.

"Claretta," a familiar voice whispered.

Claretta stopped inching down the hallway and turned around. A hummed tune that used to haunt her at night as a child filled the corridor. *It can't be,* she thought dropping the small orb of pure light she'd been carrying to try and lighten her way.

"You do remember me," the voice said before it reached out and pushed her down.

She remained on the floor as memories of the shadow that tormented her most nights started to fill her mind causing her orb to distinguish.

"I thought you..." she whispered.

"Weren't real," the voice finished for her. "I'm very real and have just begun to play. Though it appears I'm playing alone again."

The shadow rushed toward Claretta and picked her up by the

arm.

"Not this time," Claretta shoved him away remembering she was no longer that scared little girl. She closed her eyes and took a deep breath to clear her mind and remembered all that she'd done in the past several days.

"Then let's play," his voice threatened a few feet away.

Claretta created identical two-foot staffs made of nothing but pure light and advanced on the shadow. Though she couldn't see, Claretta remembered the shadows were slightly darker than the darkness they hid in. It was like seeing a wave of heat while driving down the street on a hot day. It wasn't much but at least she had a chance.

As Claretta got closer, more shadows came through the entrance.

"You all have your orders," the shadow said to the others. "I haven't finished playing yet."

The shadows moved around them leaving Claretta untouched. The shadow man, as she called him when she was little, created a shadow staff equal in length to one of hers. Wasting no time, he brought the staff straight down at Claretta. Holding tight to her staffs, she raised them high crossing them to block his blow. With his height and the strength of the blow, Claretta was forced to take a step backwards with her right foot. Pieces of ash fell from his sizzling staff but he was quick to repair it.

Claretta pushed him back and stepping forward swung the right staff at his side. The solar staff scraped the wall as it missed its target sending off sparks as Claretta spun around attempting to knock the shadow man off his feet. He jumped, barely missing the staff and kicked Claretta who was still crouched. Landing on her butt, she leaned back on her forearms and sent a pure light power kick to the shadow man's chin.

Claretta turned and as she tried to run down the dark hallway, sent a blast of pure light in front of her hoping to light the way a little It hit a wall a few feet ahead showing left as the only available option

"You're not playing nice, Claretta," the shadow man said not far behind.

She sent another pure light blast forward and, in its impact, sl saw a door with bars near the top in the middle.

"Audi, is that you?" A girl asked.

Approaching the door, Claretta sent light through it towards t ceiling and was happy to see all four of the Sun's daughters sitting or the ground.

"Claretta," Prima said shocked. "Where's Audi?"

"She's safe."

"But you're not." The shadow man grabbed Claretta by the back of her neck and threw her against the side wall making her drop her staffs. He kicked her in the side but before he could do it again, she put up a shield.

"I could use some help," Claretta gasped.

"We can't use our powers," Kamyra said. "They injected us

with something that stops them from working."

Claretta stood and held her side as the shield cracked from the force of the shadow orbs. She stepped forward and to the right hoping it led to another hallway. Instead, Claretta found herself stumbling down the stairs with a shadow orb following her.

Having missed his target and tired of playing, the shadow man descended from the ceiling above but Claretta was ready for him. She opened her balled up fist and blew particles of pure light at the shadow man. He fell to the floor but didn't stay there for long. Wrapping a whip around Claretta's arm, he pulled her down the hallway. Claretta grabbed the whip and sent pure light up the rope coating the shadow man in layer upon layer of pure light until he was nothing more than a golden statue. Inside the golden layers, his entire body turned to ash. Claretta waited a few moments, in case, the shadow man was able to break through. When nothing happened, she created another pure light staff and smashed the statue.

"Looks like *I* win this time," Claretta said as pure light and ash fell to the stone floor.

With her childhood tormentor gone, Claretta returned to the cell holding the Sun's daughters. "Stand back," Claretta said melting the lock with pure light. "This hall will lead you to water then keep going straight to get out the pond." She brought up the rear ready to fight any shadow that might try to stop them. When everyone was out the pond, Claretta remained at the edge. She put her hands in the water and when she was finished a layer of pure light that now sealed the shadows in could be seen glowing across the surface.

Claretta expected shadows to be waiting for them when they had emerged from the pond but was shocked to see none. With their leader gone and unable to leave because of the force field, they went into hiding in hopes to regroup. She then returned to the stage where she left Audi and Daijon. To keep them there, she'd made the pure lig glass was too hot to be touched by anyone but her. It was the only wa to ensure they wouldn't follow her. Once the pure light was removed, Audi and Daijon ran off the stage and into their waiting arms.

After a long bus ride, Claretta and the Cooper siblings finally reached Daijon's house. Claretta's parents waited right inside the doo happy to see their daughter safe while Mr. Cooper stood at the edge o the force field ready to welcome his other daughters to their new home. As they walked up the steps, Claretta stopped in the doorway when she saw someone out the corner of her eye looking in their direction. The person continued to grin and stare and at first, she thought it was a Shadow Person until the person got smaller and win; sprouted from her back. Not sure of what to make of it at first, Claret closed the door and joined the others. For now, she just wanted to sleep but even sleep wouldn't make her forget about the little fairy or its wicked grin.

CHAPTER 16

Still in the past...

Grief overcame the silence that dominated the Cooper home earlier that day. Work was called off and little to nothing was done as the day progressed. When the time had come for sleep, the sofas and training mats welcomed the warm bodies that covered them for no one wanted to be alone and though silence took back its control some hours later, a sniffle or sob could still be heard.

The next morning, if you could even call it that anymore, darkness filled the world outside. After everyone changed and had a quick breakfast, Mr. Cooper had the children gather in the training area. "We should hold a ceremony for your mother. Something simple."

"How would *you* know what she'd want?" Prima cried staring at their father who leaned against the kitchen counter. "You haven't been around since after Audi was born."

Mr. Cooper looked at his eldest child who sat with her back against the mirrored wall. Prima had all of her mother's features from her long legs to a rounded nose but it was her almond shaped eyes that belonged to him.

"Knowing what your mother wanted is what has kept you all safe until recently." Mr. Cooper said. "I'm sure you all know by now, Daijon has the power to distinguish Shadow People from normal humans and can easily spot their shadows."

"I knew, the others didn't," Audi said looking around the room at Claretta and her siblings on the training mats then the adults in the kitchen. "I told him I was giving Claretta my powers and that's when he told me."

"I'm sorry," Daijon apologized to his father for breaking his promise and to his other sisters for keeping them in the dark. "I made her promise not to tell anyone."

Prima, Kiki, Klarissa, and Kamyra all looked at their little brother. From an early age, their mother told them it wasn't safe to vi Daijon and their father. They knew that Daijon was normal like him but didn't really understand why their family was separated. They dic see their brother at school and in the city, every now and then, but the weren't allowed at each other's home. The girls weren't even allowed to know their father's address.

"So, we got the power to fight the Shadow People and Daijon got the power to see them," Kamyra said, sitting near the outside doc beside Klarissa. "Wow."

"When Audi was born, the entire family was there," Mr. Cooper started to explain. "Daijon and Kiki were playing on the floo of the waiting room when he saw his first shadow. I looked away for second and when I turned back Daijon was chasing it across the floo and Kiki had run after him. Thankfully, I got to him in time. I picked him up and ignored the shadow in hopes that it looked like they were just playing. Months passed and the Shadow People never attacked b your mother and I knew we couldn't stay. By the time, Audi turned one, Daijon's powers grew stronger so I took him and left. At the time it was better that no one, especially the Shadow People, learned what he could do."

Though his absence from their lives had been explained, his daughters remained silent. It was a lot to take in after years of getting no answers from either parent.

"Hopefully, one day you'll forgive me," Mr. Cooper said. Moments passed before he spoke again. "I think you girls should go back to the house. I know it'll be hard but grab whatever you need to bring back here."

"It's time we get going as well," Mr. Arbogast said coming from the kitchen as the others went outside.

"What!" Claretta said turning from the doorway towards her parents.

"We should leave them to grieve," her mom said.

"I may not be the Sun's daughter but we knew her for years," Claretta said. "I want to be here for them. Besides, I'm also not sure it's safe to go home."

Mrs. Arbogast looked at her daughter's pleading eyes. "*We should be taking care of you not the other way around,*" she whispered hugging her only child.

"But I'm the only one with the powers to stop the Shadow People. You just have to trust me."

"We do trust you," Mrs. Arbogast said. "We're just going to need to time to get use to all of this."

Claretta understood how they felt. I mean, they did just learn about Shadow People and pure light a few hours ago.

"Don't worry," Mr. Cooper said putting a hand on Mr. Arbogast shoulder. "My son and I have trained her to fight with and without the pure light. She's come a long way."

Mr. Arbogast still didn't fully understand everything but he nodded as Claretta hugged him. Releasing her, she then joined the others outside where Prima sat behind the wheel of a minivan that hadn't been there before.

"What's with the van?" Claretta asked sliding the blue side door open and climbing in next to Audi in the middle row.

"It's been in the garage for years. Dad got it in hopes we'd be together again one day." Daijon explained as Prima backed out the driveway.

"And do what? Take a family vacation in *this?*" Kiki said.

"We'd be ready to kill each other by the time we made it there," Kamyra said.

"More like ready to kill Kiki," Klarissa laughed pinching Kil who sat between them in the back.

"And I have my own car," Prima said.

"Yeah, he didn't know we'd be apart this long," Daijon said.

They drove the rest of the way in silence back to the girl's home that would never feel whole again. A few days ago, it would've been like any other summer day filled with work, fun, and morning traffic while trying to keep cool from the summer heat. Now, it was

158

colder than usual for a June morning and there *was* traffic on the roads but not from people going to work. Everyone was rushing to the stores to buy extra light bulbs; whatever portable lights they could find and batteries. Parents were afraid to let their children play outside without supervision for they heard rumors there was now more to fear than strangers lurking in the dark.

When Prima pulled into the driveway, the first thing everyone noticed was the police tape.

"What did you guys do?" Klarissa asked climbing out the back.

Police tape roped off the overgrown grass a few inches from the dining room windows that were now covered with plywood.

"We didn't have a choice, the shadows were in the house," Audi protested following her.

"How are we going to fix this!" Prima yelled.

"It's not like we're going to be staying here anytime soon," Audi said.

"We have to come back," Kiki insisted, "it's our home."

"For now, we're staying with dad end of discussion," Prima said using her, *I'm the oldest so what I say goes voice*, they'd come to recognize over the years. "Now, go get your stuff." She knew Kiki was right though. It was *their* home and they couldn't stay away forever, even though, they'd be living with their father now.

While the others were focused on the police tape, Daijon looked at the cream-colored house. He hadn't paid much attention to it

159

when he, Audi, and Claretta spent the night here but now that he saw behind the yellow light of a street lamp, a memory he'd forgotten can back. He was only one at the time but Daijon remembered the house used to be yellow. His dad complained all the time how it looked like school bus so his mom agreed to change it to cream as long as he did the work himself.

"Aren't you coming?" Audi asked from in front of the van.

"What?" Daijon asked leaving his thoughts to address his sister. "Yeah, I'm coming."

Taking no chances, Daijon went straight for the basement and checked for shadows. Though most had been defeated or trapped in t lake, no one knew for sure if any still lurked around. With the house now lit, everyone went their separate ways to pack. Claretta sat on Audi's bed and listened to the silence that now filled a home that was once filled with so much noise the neighbors constantly complained. For right now, all she could do was stay by her friend's side while Daijon explored the house as he waited for the others.

"What's going to happen to the house?" Audi asked once everyone returned to the living room.

"Well, mom and dad own the house and I'm the only one that can legally live on their own," Prima said as she looked across the entryway to the dining room. "I'm not sure what to do. For now, it'll stay like it is." *I guess I can stay here while I finish college so my sisters could stay but then what about dad? He seemed happy to have us all at the ranch house and I don't know if he could pay to keep bot*

160

houses. I guess we'll figure that all out later. "I think we should each take something to remember mom until everything gets sorted out."

For the girl's, the choice wasn't that hard, they'd lived with her their entire lives but for Daijon it was much harder. He walked from room to room searching for the perfect thing to help remind him of the mother he'd known for two short years. While the others returned to their rooms to pick something their mother had given them at one point in time, Daijon opened the door to their mother's room and sat on the bed he, Claretta, and Audi had slept in not too long ago. Looking around, there was plenty to choose from: a silver bracelet, a worn copy of *Nineteen Minutes* by Jodi Picoult, and a picture of the family on the dresser. He had plenty of pictures though, his father made sure of it. That's when he saw it, a blue and sea foam green patchwork blanket, sitting on a rocking chair in the corner. Daijon held it up to his face and inhaled until he could draw in no more air. It still smelled of strawberries just like it had when his mother wrapped him in it when he was little. *This is perfect,* he thought.

By the time they left, there were fewer people out. *I wonder if I'll ever get used to this,* Claretta thought looking at the golden glow of the force field. Thin lines of pure light snaked across it from one side to another as though helping to keep watch over the city. Though its glow was bright, it had little to no effect lighting the darkness inside. Beyond the force field, the dark was in control while the stars watched from afar.

CHAPTER 17

In the future...

"Where's my brother?" Audi asked the moment they reached her father's house knowing he and their father were together. "Where Daijon!" All around her, cars parked in the driveway or along the street.

Grabbing the solar light off the back seat, Lee got out the car do the job that was asked of him.

"**Where** is Daijon?" Audi slammed the door closed and walked around the car until she stood in front of Lee.

"I don't know!" Lee yelled. "I don't know," he said this time a softer tone as he looked into her tear-filled eyes. "Let's get you inside."

It was then Audi noticed the solar lights in the yard. She'd bee too busy searching the streets and passing cars for Daijon to notice them before. *We don't have anything like this at home,* Audi thought, as she walked to the closest one with Lee right behind her. Taking on out the ground, Audi turned it over in her hands. *All this time, she'd been protecting them to. That explains where the ones in the neighbor's yards came from.* Her entire life they were never allowed visit or know where their father and brother lived. Daijon was too young at the time to remember his first home. While they weren't forbidden to see each other outside of school, contact was too be kep at a minimal.

"You should really get inside," Lee said, "I have to help check the others for shadows."

"What do you mean...check for shadows?"

"Someone will explain everything to you later," Lee said, guiding her to the door.

Once inside, Audi was met with a mixture of smiles and frowns.

"*This* is who they risked their necks for some child," a man in his 30's said as they entered the living room. "We've all got family still out there. What makes her so important?"

"Look, when Daijon and his father get back they'll explain. If you don't like it here, feel free to leave," Lee said. Though he'd been wondering the same thing, he believed there was a good reason they braved going out into the dark again for one girl, even if she was Daijon's sister. "Make yourself at home," he said returning his attention to Audi, "I mean, it technically is more your home than ours."

Audi wiped her eyes staring at him. "Are you sure it's safe here?"

"Safest place in town. Don't worry no one would dare mess with you."

As the minutes passed, people kept entering the house but none of them were Daijon. When the last person entered, followed by Lee, Audi rose from the steps where she'd been waiting. "Where is he?" She asked once again.

"I don't know," Lee said. "Parker, his driver and two other ca
aren't back either."

Gasps escaped the mouths of those closest to them.

"Has anyone seen the cars Daijon and Parker were in?" Lee
asked the crowd of people in the living room.

A moment passed before a woman in her 20's stepped forwar
Turns out, she was one of the drivers that arrived for their getaway.
"One of the cars got in an accident and the shadows swarmed it. A fe
of the cars, behind me turned around to help but there was too many
them to see anything else."

As much as Audi wanted to be furious at the woman for not
helping them, she understood. The woman was scared. They'd gotten
dragged into a battle that had nothing to do with them. Tears welled ι
in her eyes once again but before they could fall, the door burst open

Two men everyone but Audi recognized walked in followed t
a woman and finally, her brother who was followed by a teenage boy

"Don't scare me like that. I thought they'd taken you," Audi
said flinging herself into her brother's arms.

"Not me," Daijon whispered, "but they did take dad and
Cynthia."

"What?" Audi asked thinking she'd heard him wrong.

"The Shadow People took them Audi. I'm so sorry."

For the first time that night, Daijon allowed himself to cry.
Tears escaped Audi's eyes once again as she and Daijon held each
other.

Those around them wanted answers but Daijon ignored them for now. He led Audi to her room across from his and sat her on the bed. Though still sad, Daijon had stopped crying while Audi still had tears to shed. He continued to hold her until the last one fell. Once it had, he tucked her into bed and went back downstairs where an argument was taking place.

"You send an entire team to look for a little girl but won't help any of us bring our families here!" The same man from earlier yelled.

"Keep your voice down," Lee said looking towards the stairs where his eyes locked with Daijon's.

"What's going on down here?" Daijon asked coming into the living room. "Is there a problem?"

"Yeah, I got a problem. What makes that *girl* so important?" The man twice Daijon's age asked.

"That *girl* is the only one of us that used to be able to create pure light and fight the Shadow People. Anyone who has helped fight did it willingly."

Gasps and confused looks spread throughout the room.

"Right," the man scoffed, "she 'used to', how convenient. The only reason some of us even listened to you was because of your father."

"I can't believe he said that," one of the women in the back whispered shaking her head.

Daijon scanned the room as everyone started talking at once. Shaking his head, he walked to the front door and opened it. Looking the man dead in the eyes, he spoke loud enough for everyone to hear. "This is *my* house, regardless if my father is here or not, and you *will* respect me while in it. If anyone here doesn't like the way things are being ran, you're free to leave at any time." He gestured outside where the darkness awaited. When no one moved, he closed the door and walked right past the man.

Shocked whispers followed the teen as he walked past the training mats and out the back door. Daijon took a deep breath having shocked himself as well. He'd never spoken to anyone like that before especially, not an adult. With his father gone, he knew he'd have to step up and take control if they were going to survive there. Ignoring the darkness around him, Daijon pulled opened the barn door filling the night with neighs. Grabbing a brush from the tack room, he went Jax; loudest of them all. Brushing his brown coat brought back the memory of when his father gave him Jax. Moving to the front of the stall, Daijon leaned against the door and slid to the ground as the tear came again. When the tears left him, he finished brushing Jax, and went back inside.

As the night went on, no one said a word to Daijon about the way he acted. Audi still hadn't come out her room and when Daijon went to check on her she was asleep. Not wanting to bother her, he closed the door and went to check on Andrew. He was finally able to walk on his leg and ready to help out. Having learned first aid from h father, Daijon looked at Andrew's leg and gave him the go ahead.

"How are you guys doing?" Andrew asked as Daijon started

166

pace the room.

"We're fine," Daijon said still pacing.

"Daijon," Andrew said in a strict tone that got him to stop.

"What do you want me to say," Daijon yelled frustrated. "That my sister hasn't done anything but sit in her room and cry since she arrived. That I practically handed my father and Cynthia to the Shadow People because I insisted we help Audi. I've no idea what to do next. That....that I'm scared." He whispered the last part.

"You good?"

Daijon nodded yes.

"First, your dad and Cynthia knew what could happen if they went. They all did. It's not your fault. Second, you'll figure out what's next. For now, we'll just keep going as we have been."

They talked for a bit more then both went to bed as did the rest of the house.

Hours later, in what would normally be the dead of night; Audi sat up in bed forgetting where she was. Still in the clothes that she arrived in, Audi slipped on her shoes on and tiptoed to the door. Listening for any noise and hearing none, she opened the door and stepped into the hallway. She couldn't just sit there while her father and Cynthia were at the Shadow People's mercy.

Making sure the hallway was clear; Audi stepped into the hallway and down the stairs. Reaching the last step, she leaned over the banister and looked into the living room. Everyone appeared to be asleep, even the young man on the couch she hadn't seen before. *This is my chance,* Audi thought reaching for the doorknob. Opening it, sh stopped noticing a set of keys on the dining room table. With one eye on the young man, Audi inched her way to the table. Gathering the keys all at once, she managed to keep them from jangling.

Once outside, Audi looked at the vehicles then the keys in her hand. There was no name or anything on the keys that told her which car was its owner. As she took a step, something in the darkness howled. Realizing she was wasting time; Audi chose to ignore it and ran to the driveway. Two cars later, she successfully located the right one. It was Parker's, one of the last to come in. Sitting in the driver's seat, it dawned on her she didn't know how to drive.

Before she could stick the key in the ignition, the door was pulled open. On the other side, stood the young man that Audi though was asleep on the couch.

"Get out of the car," Andrew said trying to stay calm.

Audi slid back towards the other side instead.

"Get out!" He yelled but not loud enough for anyone inside t hear. He pulled the key from the ignition then grabbed her firmly by the arm.

"Let go," Audi said hitting Andrew's hand as he dragged her out.

When he let go, she tried to run for it but he just grabbed her arm again and pushed her against the closed door. His body blocked any escape.

"Are you crazy?" Andrew said staring down at her. "You kno

what's waiting out there better than anyone else."

Audi cast her gaze to the side.

"Daijon was afraid you'd try something like this."

"So, what, he asked you to look out for me?"

"Yeah, he asked for help. Your brother has a lot to deal with," Andrew said looking back at the house. "You know, you could have hurt yourself or someone else. Or worse, the shadows could've taken you."

As though to emphasize his point, shadows rose from the ground and approached them. Well, as close as they dared with the solar light in place.

"How about we go back inside," Andrew said shielding Audi from them.

"Ok. Do we have to tell my brother about this?"

Andrew looked down to see Audi glancing over her shoulder every few feet at the shadows. "I guess we can keep this between us."

"Thank you," Audi said once they were back inside. Her tone implied she was thanking him for more than just keeping what happened between them a secret. After seeing the shadows again, waiting there for her, Audi knew he'd stopped her from making a terrible mistake.

CHAPTER 18

In the past...

When they arrived back at Daijon's house, everyone was waiting for them by the driveway. For now, their belongings stayed in the van as they followed the others past the side of the house and into the backyard. Mr. Cooper led them several feet from the house to a cluster of trees that formed a half circle to the right of the barn. The smell of hay and manure greeted them as Mr. Cooper pulled Claretta inside the barn away from the others. Daijon's quarter horse, Jax, stuck his head over the stall door as they entered hoping to receive a treat.

"I hate to ask this," Mr. Cooper said rubbing the back of his neck, "but can you make a headstone?"

Claretta's eyes grew in size at his request. She had never been to a funeral before and the only headstones she'd seen were in movies. On top of that, Claretta never imagined the man she'd known for a few short days would ask her to do something so personal.

"I'm sorry," Mr. Cooper apologized, "it's just, even if I could get a headstone this soon a normal one doesn't seem right and the others don't have their powers."

Claretta remained silent for a few moments. She watched as he scratched Jax's head and looked everywhere but at her. As hard as it was for him to ask such a thing, it was even harder for Claretta to answer. It didn't feel right to make that kind of decision not being a member of the family but she *did* want to help.

"Okay," was all Claretta whispered.

Mr. Cooper stood between the trees facing the others when he and Claretta rejoined them.

"A loving mother, wife, and friend was lost to us the other day. She was a true gift to the world and will be missed," Mr. Cooper said with tears in his eyes. "Powers or not, her legacy will forever live on in our 6 beautiful children."

The eulogy was short but by the time he finished everyone, including Claretta's parents, were in tears. Claretta waited to see if someone else was going to move forward to speak. When no one did, she stepped into the circle and faced the trees. She stood there for a moment with her arms loose by her side. She shifted her weight from one foot to another knowing all eyes were on her. Claretta closed her eyes and took several deep breaths trying her best to block out the crying that wove through the night towards her back. Her body tingled like when your leg falls asleep as pure light flowed weightlessly through her. Knowing what she wanted to do; Claretta raised her hands and walked until she was beneath the trees.

Pure light fell from Claretta's palms and fingertips and onto the ground. Her hands moved this way and that as though she were performing a dance and the light was her ribbon. Waiting for the light to form the desired shape, Claretta stood beneath the trees for a few moments more.

Eyes now open; she smiled looking at the head stone. When she stepped aside, a collective gasp filled the air. Before the trees stood a three-foot golden headstone unlike anything anyone would ever see again. It was shaped like a golden sun with rays sticking out in all directions but flat where it sat on the ground. The ray's edges were just a hint darker and seemed to sparkle. In the middle, their mother's name, Priscilla, was engraved. The other thing that caught everyone's eyes were the trees. Claretta had let the same color pure light that was at the tip of the sun's rays seep into every leaf on them so it looked as though the headstone lit them itself. She didn't know how long they would stay that way but knew the light would do no harm.

The Coopers thanked her and after seeing how happy she'd made them, Claretta was glad she accepted Mr. Cooper's request. As the minutes of the hour ticked by, everyone left the memorial when they were ready and made their way back inside.

An hour later, as Claretta left Audi's room to get a drink; she heard whispers of a conversation coming from one of the other rooms near the stairs.

"Do you think we'll ever get our powers back?" Kamyra asked from the full-sized bed that sat across from her sister's.

"I'm not..." Klarissa started to say but stopped when she heard someone coming. They both looked toward the slightly opened door and saw Claretta step into view.

"I didn't mean to eavesdrop, I was going to get something to drink," Claretta said looking from the window that stood as a divider for each girl's side to the twins.

"Its okay," Klarissa assured waving Claretta in." I thought you were Prima. I'm sure the last thing she wants is for our powers to return."

"What did the Shadow People give you?" Claretta asked as she joined them. They both had long hair the same color as Audi's and even though, they were seventeen, they never mind sharing a room, even after a big fight.

"That's what we're trying to figure out," Klarissa said from beside Claretta. "Our mother warned us about the shadows but we've never had a problem like this before so we weren't as cautious. Well, except Audi."

"When they attacked, we weren't ready," Kamyra continued. "As soon as we were injected, our powers stopped working. I could still feel the pure light inside me but it wouldn't come out."

As she listened to them talk, Claretta looked around their room. In front of her, between the door and Kamyra's bed, was the keyboard she'd brought from home to practice on. Piled beside her were several piano books so old, some of the pages were starting to fall out. On the floor at the foot of the bed beside Claretta, was an overstuffed dance bag. *That's right, they want to audition for Julliard's college program,* Claretta remembered.

Audi, who wondered why Claretta hadn't returned, ventured out into the hallway towards the stairs. "Here you are," she said coming into the twin's room.

Kamyra gave a small squeak of a yell.

"What?" Audi asked looking at each of them.

"They thought you were Prima," Claretta replied.

"Oh," Audi said shrugging her shoulders not seeing what the big deal was.

"Daijon, girls, come down here please!" Mr. Cooper yelled just as Audi sat down.

Everyone gathered in the living room where the flat screen above the fireplace was turned on for the first time since the other girl arrived. The news was showing a reporter in a black suit with a navy tie standing next to the force field that Claretta and the others had created.

"I'm Eric Dunham reporting to you live from what people are calling the Quincy Force Field. Residents have been calling in for hours with tips on how they think it appeared. While no solid evidence has appeared as of yet, what we *do* know is residents are terrified to get to close or leave the city."

It then switched to the videos people had sent in of the strange things that have been happening all around town. One showed cars stopping in the streets as their owners got out to look at the sky growing darker in the middle of the afternoon. The footage got stranger as it zoomed into the intersection that was even darker than the surrounding area. Shadows moved in and out of focus and a pure light orb soared by. It continued on like that until Prima got up and turned the TV off a minute later.

"You guys were caught on tape!" Prima yelled.

"We were being attacked! What did you expect us to do?"

174

Audi shouted back. "Besides, it was too dark for anyone to really see us!"

"You were always so reckless with your powers!"

"At least, I used mine! Maybe if you did, *you* wouldn't have gotten caught by the shadows!"

"Last time, I checked baby sis; I wasn't the only one who got caught!"

"Well, you don't have to worry about her being reckless anymore since she gave her powers away," Kiki interrupted.

"Kiki," Audi said shooting her a you're not helping look.

"Both of you stop it," Mr. Cooper said from the big couch where he and Claretta's parents sat. "What's done is done. You need to work together and decide how to proceed."

"So, are the shadows gone?" Kamyra asked.

"I don't know," Claretta said. "I mean, I defeated their leader and sealed the pond but there's no telling how many were out there to begin with."

"We need to tell people and find a way to protect them," Mr. Cooper said.

"What about necklaces made of pure light," Klarissa suggested. "It'll burn a Shadow Person's skin no matter what they have on."

"It can be our mother's symbol," Daijon said. "There's nothing like it in any store so a Shadow Person can't just go buy one."

"I don't mean to change the subject but I saw the strangest thing last night," Claretta interrupted feeling now was a good time to

175

mention the fairy. "There was a person outside watching us. She turned into a fairy."

"You're kidding right," Kiki laughed. "People don't turn into fairies."

"They don't have the power of pure light either but you all do."

"Good point. Our mother never said anything about fairies."

"For now, let's focus on the current problem," Mr. Cooper sa having heard nothing of them either. "The mayor is holding a town meeting and I think Claretta and Daijon should go."

"Our daughter isn't going to get up in front of the whole tow and tell them that she can create light," Mr. Arbogast said. "They'll think she's crazy."

"Dad," Claretta protested. "You and mom are safe because I protected you. I don't want to tell them what I can do either but what about the rest of the city."

"Claretta is the only one that can use her powers and Daijon the only one who can warn us if a shadow or Shadow Person is there Mr. Cooper said.

"How are we going to get them to listen to us?" Claretta aske

"I'm hoping the shadows will help with that."

CHAPTER 19

In the future...

"What is that sound?" Autumn asked standing barefoot on the mats. It was sometime in the afternoon the next day when things went from bad to worse. They'd just finished cooling down from training when a sound the Cooper siblings knew well filled the darkness.

Daijon and Audi looked at each other. Doors upstairs could be heard opening as people came to investigate while the children playing nearby covered their ears. Soon, everyone had their ears covered as the sound grew louder. Taking her brother's lead, Audi and a few others followed him onto the front porch.

Outside, the sound equaled that of a fire truck's siren in volume. Beyond the solar lights were more Shadow People than either Daijon or Audi had ever seen in one location. They filled the streets and spilled into the grass. Shadows darted around among their feet and in the tall grass. They stood there in true form wanting to be seen. After a few seconds, the Shadow People were silent having accomplished their goal in drawing them outside.

"What are they doing?" Autumn asked from beside Audi who stood on Daijon's left side.

"Looks like they're sending a message," Andrew said from behind them.

"What's that?" Parker asked from beside Autumn.

"They're angry," Daijon said. "They hate we beat them even if only for a moment. Also, we have Audi."

"Now that I think about it, we haven't had any new visitors," Lee said from behind Daijon.

"And we won't be getting any more," Daijon said looking around. "I doubt they'll let us leave again or let anyone get too close.

"What are we going to do?" Audi asked.

"Ration what supplies we have," Daijon said. "Besides that, I'm not sure."

The teens glanced at one another then back at the army of Shadow People. None of them imagined their summer vacation woul start like this. That an evil few knew about would take over their city

"Let's go," Daijon said turning to the door and without question, they followed. Once inside he explained where the noise came from. For now, he gave no other instructions but to ration out what they had.

With that said he motioned for the others to follow him upstairs. He led them down the hall to the only room that faced them It had been off limits to everyone besides Daijon and upon entering i they understood why; it was his father's room. While they opened the home to others, Daijon and his father still wanted their privacy. It wa the only room they needed permission to enter besides Daijon's. Inside, a king-sized bed with a maroon comforter faced the door. To their left were two windows draped with black curtains. On that same side by the bed was a wooden door that led to a closet. To their right, long dresser held an 18-inch flat screen TV.

Daijon grabbed the remote from the dresser then sat in the middle of the mattress. While flipping through the channels, the others climbed on the bed around him.

"What are you looking for?" Lee asked as Daijon continued his search.

"This," Daijon said using the remote to point at the screen.

"Eric Dunham reporting to you live outside Quincy High School. In just a few hours, a town meeting will be held to discuss the current problem Quincy has been faced with."

Daijon then switched to another channel. Behind two news reporters sitting at a desk, photos were shown of Shadow People and shadows that citizens sent in. It then switched to footage of someone breaking into a jewelry store. As they continued to watch, they learned the police would be continuously patrolling the city to cut down the new outbreak of crime. They also advised people not to confront the '*intruders*' as the police called them.

They watched for a few more minutes then Daijon turned it off.

"They have no idea what they're up against," Audi said.

"I've read reports online that scientists are trying to figure out what happened to the Sun," Autumn said.

"It's a long story but I doubt they'll even get close to the truth."

"I hate to repeat what Audi already asked," Parker said, "but what do we do now?"

They all looked to Daijon.

"We need to collect all the batteries that aren't being used for something important, just in case, the Shadow People try and knock out the power. The water line is within the solar lights so it should be fine," Daijon said.

"What about the army outside?" Lee asked.

"They can't get past the solar lights without turning to ash. I'ı more worried about people trying to take the solar lights. People are bound to realize the solar lights aren't normal and can be used agains them if they didn't know already. That's why I suggest we patrol the area in at least groups of three."

"Ok, but the solar lights cover the entire property," Lee said. "That's a lot of area to cover."

"That brings me to the second part of the plan. We're going to have to shorten our perimeter. Not too short but where we can get to anyone fast in case of an emergency."

"How are we going to do that without the Shadow People getting in?" Andrew asked.

"We'll have to leave a few in place so they can't get through.'

"I'm coming with you," Audi said.

"It's too dangerous," Daijon said.

"Giving up my powers was dangerous. All of this is dangerous," Audi said. "Besides, I wasn't asking. Powers or not, I've had experience fighting them."

"Fine. Let's go see if we can recruit more help."

With a plan of what they should do and the others supporting him, Daijon led the way back downstairs. When he finished explainiı their plan, the teens were surprised to find others were still willing to help. After what happened rescuing Audi, they weren't sure if anyone would.

"Are you sure, you can drive?" Daijon asked pulling Andrew to the side.

"It's not a problem."

"Okay," Daijon said nodding.

"Try not to worry so much, it'll be fine," Andrew said. He pat Daijon on the shoulder then led the others out front.

Daijon went out the back door to the barn to saddle Jax. The horses hadn't been out in a while and Jax wasn't easily spooked so he figured he'd start with him. Once the barn door was closed again, Daijon mounted Jax. Just then, Andrew's pickup rounded the house followed by Parker's car. Audi and Lee sat in the bed of the pickup while Autumn and two others rode with Parker. Looking down at his sister, he frowned.

"What?" Audi asked rolling her eyes

"What are doing?" Daijon asked.

"I told you I was going to help. If the Shadow People attack, I can fight them off with a solar light. Probably even better than you," Audi teased.

Lee couldn't help but laugh. Daijon shot him a look that made him cover his mouth but didn't stop him from chuckling. Shaking his head at both of them, he turned and walked Jax to Parker's car. Surprisingly, the man who Daijon argued with sat in the passenger

181

seat.

"You good?" Daijon asked.

Parker looked at the others in his car. "Yeah, we're good," he said.

"Alright everyone, we know what we need to do, so let's go!' He shouted only loud enough for them to hear. Turning Jax around, h saw a crowd standing at the glass doors. He gave them a firm nod the they were off.

Reaching the edge of the Cooper property, the others saw jus how bright and unnatural the pure light was. Out here with unclaimec land on the other side of the solar lights and a darkness they hadn't been in before, everyone was on edge. Andrew turned the truck arour and backed it up to the last row of solar lights. The solar lights themselves had been set in a pyramid fashion. Imagine three people standing in a row and behind them a person standing between the gaj This ensured no shadows could slip through.

"They're out there, aren't they?" Audi asked after Lee helped her down.

"Yeah, they're there," Daijon said.

"How many are there?" Lee asked.

"You don't want to know." Daijon said.

If it weren't for the solar lights, they wouldn't be able to see each other. Daijon, on the other hand, had no trouble seeing the 20 Shadow People and countless shadows that watched them. As the others got out, no one said anything for a moment as they stared at th

182

solar lights. A golden glow against a near black backdrop.

"It reminds me of a bumble bee," Autumn said.

Audi couldn't help but laugh. It filled the dark and wrapped around them. For someone, who'd been through so much, it was pleasant to the ears.

"What?" Autumn asked realizing everyone was staring at her.

Audi took a deep breath, and then said "it's nothing. I just remember that's what I thought the first time I made pure light in the dark." She stared longingly at the pure light then down at her hands.

"Come on, let's get started," Daijon said putting an arm around his sister.

The man, Daijon argued with, whose name he learned was Reggie and Lenora, the woman who drove Parker's car during the rescue, stood guard. They walked back and forth crossing paths when they went in opposite directions, solar lights in hand. Daijon stood guard and helped the others.

The Shadow People moved closer with every layer of solar lights they removed. Daijon could see in their hollow eyes, a slight hope that they would remove the wrong one and leave a gap for them to slip through. The teens were careful though. Andrew drove the truck while the others went row by row loading them into the bed. They cleared three of the six rows in one section then moved onto the next one. It took a couple trips but they finished the length of the back of the property. They used the large empty barn stalls to store them all.

CHAPTER 20

In the past...

Though the town meeting started at two, Mr. Cooper, Claretta and Daijon arrived at the high school a little afterward hoping to slip unnoticed. Mr. Cooper tried to reassure them everything would be okay on the drive over but Claretta and Daijon remained silent knowing he couldn't promise that. Claretta's parents, who wanted to make sure their daughter would be okay, drove in a separate car behind them. She insisted on riding with Daijon claiming it would be safer, but really, she knew her parent's worried expressions would make her even more nervous.

When they entered the gym, Claretta had expected it to be filled but found only the center section of one side filled with people and a podium center court facing them. Daijon and Claretta's parent's stayed close to the doors while Claretta and Mr. Cooper sat on the bottom bleacher with their backs to the crowd. With the arguing and shouting that had been going on, they slipped in relatively unnoticed.

"Where did the force field come from?" A young mother with a baby in her arms yelled.

"Look, I've got deliveries to make!" A truck driver in his 30's yelled from the back. "Is this thing safe to go through or not?"

The mayor, whose hair had begun to turn gray, stood with his mouth partially open, but was unable to get a word in as he was bombarded with questions. The police chief, who stood off to the right

184

stepped forward and everyone grew quiet. He was a tall, muscular man in his early 40's, with broad shoulders and dark hair. With a few years in the position under his belt, and with all the good he'd done, he earned the respect of the community and fellow officers.

"At the time, we're still not sure how the force field appeared and why," the police chief said in his deep voice. "Every officer in my department is making this their top priority. We encourage anyone with information to what's going on to step forward."

With a nod from Mr. Cooper, Claretta finally stood up. "I put up the force field," she said but no one heard her as the shouting had begun again. "I put up the force field!"

Everyone stopped talking and the room grew quiet but only long enough for them to laugh at her. *I don't have time for childish jokes,* the police chief thought. He made eye contact with one of the officers around the gym and nodded towards Claretta. *She needs to be escorted out before she makes things worse.*

"This isn't a joke, Red," Mr. Cooper said. "Let her speak."

"Claretta, sixth row center!" Daijon, who'd been searching the crowd since their arrival, interrupted stepping away from the door and into view.

Without hesitation, Claretta turned facing the bleachers. The crowd watched as a shadow separated from the young Shadow Person that stood among them. Those around her moved aside as the shadowy legs took two steps at a time towards Claretta who turned it to ash with ease. Zigzagging through the people running down the bleachers, she

185

created a pure light orb as she tried to reach the Shadow Person.

Seeing the child approach, the Shadow Person grabbed a you[n]

man close by and used him as a shield. This was no problem for

Claretta though. She threw the pure light orb straight ahead knowing

wouldn't hurt the young man unless he too was a Shadow Person.

When the Shadow Person ducked, she threw another one over the

young man's head and with a flick of her wrist sent it straight down

turning the Shadow Person to ash.

"Do you believe me now?" Claretta shouted.

The people that remained behind started to crowd around

Claretta as she descended the bleachers but between her parents, the

police, and the Cooper's, no one was able to get close.

"You have a lot of explaining to do," Red told her.

"I know and we've got a plan," Claretta replied.

With a police escort, she was able to make it out the gym

where the rest of the crowd and reporters waited for them.

"People are saying you're responsible for the force field goin[g]

up." One of the reporters said. "Is that true?" He tried shoving past th[e]

police with his pen and paper but was unable to get through.

The crowd grew in size as the police continued to escort the[m]

to Mr. Cooper's car. Claretta looked over her shoulder scanning the

crowd for her parents. Off to her right, she found them being led to

their car by another officer who whispered in her father's ear.

"Oh no," Daijon groaned as they drove pass the bell tower

minutes later.

186

"What's wrong?" Mr. Cooper asked.

Claretta looked out her window and groaned as well.

Mr. Cooper looked in the review mirror at Claretta who wouldn't meet his eyes. "What's going on?"

"We've been here before," was all Daijon would say. He never planned on telling his dad about the night the police picked them up but it looked like he was going to find out anyway.

"The trespassers have returned," the same officer who had caught them at the bell tower said as Red led them in.

"What's he talking about trespassing?" Mr. Cooper asked his son.

"We broke into the bell tower. Sorry about that," Daijon apologized to both his father and the officer.

"And I'm sorry about the lamps," Claretta said pointing to the two desks near the bathrooms. Only the black base of the once beautiful lamps remained. She'd only meant to break the light bulbs but instead shattered the mosaic style lamp shades as well. The officer looked at the desks then back at her confused.

"I'll explain later," Red told him.

The officers that had been taking care of the crowd outside the gym returned and began talking to those that had remained behind.

"We need to check the other officers," Claretta said as she glanced at them.

"Anyone could be a Shadow Person," Daijon added.

While Daijon talked to Red, Claretta walked over to her

parents and explained they'd be there for a couple of hours and that she'd be okay.

After her parents left, Claretta joined Red inside his office while the others waited outside. If his precinct was going to help, he needed to know what's going on and what they had planned.

"Well," Red said to the young girl in the metal chair across from him.

Don't tell him more than you have to, Mr. Cooper had whispered to her beforehand.

"What happened in the gym and most of what you've seen on the news is because of me," Claretta said.

They spent the next 20 minutes alone in the office. Claretta took extra care not to mention the Sun being an actual person and when Red asked about Daijon, she told him about his power and nothing else. Red could tell the girl was withholding information but as long as she could help that was the least of his worries.

"We're ready," Claretta said when they emerged from Red's office.

He led them down a hall to an interrogation room that they could use. Mr. Cooper, Claretta, and Daijon stepped into the gray roo that held a small black table, two metal chairs, and a two-way mirror that claimed one wall. Daijon could've just as easily looked at everyone as they waited in the hall but they didn't want a repeat of th chaos in the gym. Since they knew Red wasn't a Shadow Person, he stood guard of the officers lined up by the wall making sure no one l before Daijon could determine if they were human.

Daijon and his father moved the table and chairs aside wanting nothing in the way, in case, they had to fight then had the officers enter one by one. Each officer stood in the room's center while Daijon stood a safe distance away looking for a dark aura. As he checked them, his father remained by the door while Claretta stood in the corner diagonal from it bouncing a pure light orb in her hands.

Once the searches were complete, they asked for the police chief again.

"We're going to need lots of boxes," Claretta said as she worked the golden light between her hands. "Make sure everyone in Quincy gets one." She held up a long golden chain with the Sun's symbol dangling from the bottom. "I'm also going to make pure light orbs for every police officer. Pure light's, the only thing that'll destroy them."

"Anything, you need," Red said. "I'll contact the news and radio stations and have a broadcast sent out every 15 minutes."

With Daijon's help, Claretta moved the table back to the room's center and got to work while Mr. Cooper and Red went for boxes. *This is going to take forever,* Claretta thought as the pure light between her hands twisted, bended, and expanded. That's when an idea came to her.

"Stand back," Claretta said.

When Daijon was by the opposite wall, Claretta placed a small pure light orb on the table then proceeded to make it larger and larger. Once it was the size of a large pumpkin, she broke off tangerine sized balls until the pumpkin sized one was a thing of the past. Claretta the stood before the table and waved her hands over them; shaping sever necklaces at one time.

At five o'clock, Claretta closed the door to the interrogation room while Daijon went to find his father. The room behind her was filled five to six boxes high and the trash can overflowed from drink bottles and empty take-out bags. Eyes closed, she leaned her back against the door taking a quick break until footsteps approached.

"Can we make a stop on the way back?" Claretta asked, opening her eyes to see Mr. Cooper not far from her. "I need to check something."

"Sure," Mr. Cooper said leading them out the police station.

From their parked car on the side of the road of the lower parking lot, Claretta could see the glow from the pond. As she got ou her eyes were drawn to the only lamp post there but she wasn't sure why.

"You want me to come with you?" Daijon asked unbuckling his seat belt.

"No, I'll be fine," Claretta said. "This won't take long."

After making her way through the construction, Claretta arrived at the stairs to the pond. Shadows could be seen gliding belov the surface hoping for a way out but it was of no use. The seal she created was the only thing keeping the shadows and Shadow People the pond and could only be removed by her. However, it wouldn't ke anyone else from entering it.

When Claretta reached the last step before they disappeared into the water, she added another layer of pure light to the pond just to be on the safe side. The Shadows, sensing movement on the water, sped towards the slight vibrations. They gave a hollowing growl when they saw another layer of light stretch across the lake realizing it had caused the vibrations. Claretta didn't pay them any attention. She'd finished what she came to do.

"You guys have to see this," Kiki said when they walked through the door later.

The show that had been playing was interrupted by a special broadcast. In light of recent events, for the safety of Quincy and its residents, that evening, everyone inside the force field would be required to go to one of the designated locations and receive a pure light necklace that the police chief held up. Anyone seen not wearing one would be considered a threat and will be taken into custody until it's confirmed that they're human. *He actually came through,* Claretta thought. It also helped that someone had recorded the incident at the meeting and had given it to that very news station.

"I'm going to need everyone's help to make this work," Claretta said. "I need two people at each distribution center, one at the least. No one knows the rest of you had powers. If someone asks why you're helping, just tell them I showed you how to use the pure light orbs. A police officer will be at each one and others will be monitoring the border of the force field to make sure no one leaves." She continued to explain what they had to do then assigned everyone a

191

location.

I wish the police chief would've talked to me when he set up t₁ *distribution centers,* Claretta thought that night as she walked throug the park for the second time that day. It was the least ideal place for distribution and to make matters worse, it was at the concession stanⅽ right by the pond. In the distance, despite numerous protests, Claretta parents stood away from the crowd near a police officer who was armed with pure light orbs. They, along with Claretta, the Coopers, a every other officer already had their sun necklaces on.

Claretta leaned on the outside of the concession stand wall, where a long line of citizens stretched out before her holding flashlights. In just a few minutes at eight o'clock, distribution would begin. Extra lights were brought to brighten the area but it still wasn' enough and never would be for the darkness. Every now and then, Claretta looked over her shoulder at the water. When she looked bacƙ at the line, she noticed no one was standing closer than necessary to anyone else. Mothers held their children close and eyes of every colⅽ shifted to the shadows around them.

"I'll be right back," Claretta said as she walked to where the line weaved through the trees. Like she'd done before, Claretta put both hands on one of the tree trunks but this time she waited. When most of those around her looked in her direction, she winked at the little girl nearby then lit not just the one she was touching but *every* tree on the hill.

"We're going to make this clear!" An officer yelled at 8.

"Everyone is to take a sun necklace, put it on, and sign your name on the paper afterwards. Failure to do so by *anyone* will result in a ride to the police station until you can be cleared shadow free. We *will* use a bus to transport people if needed."

Claretta went back down the hill but this time she stood with her left side facing the pond. People came through the line and put on their necklaces just as they were told. What she wasn't counting on was people hanging around afterwards. To her left was a group of four teenagers around the same age as Kiki. The girls were admiring their necklaces while the boys played too close to the water.

"Why is the pond glowing?" A girl with long blonde hair asked.

"Dare you to jump in," a dark-skinned boy said to his friend, who stood beside the girl on the steps.

"I'm not afraid of a little light," the brown-haired boy replied.

"Get away from the pond," Claretta warned walking away from the concession stand.

The teenagers turned and seeing it was just a kid they didn't know, laughed and continued what they were doing.

"I'm serious, it's not safe," Claretta said coming up to the group.

"I can swim kid. In fact, I think I'll take a dip right now," the guy who'd been dared said.

He stuck one foot in the water and before he could get his shirt off, a shadow started dragging him under. The other guy grabbed onto his arm careful to stay out the water all the while shouting for the gir

to get back. Claretta rolled her eyes while working pure light into a

bottle sized dagger. Scanning the water near the boy's legs, she saw h

target and threw the dagger. It sliced through the light barrier with ea

and struck the shadow. Letting go of his leg, it sunk back into the

depths of the pond.

"Still want to go swimming?" Claretta asked the boy as he sa

on the top step, his friends surrounding him.

Just then, a high-pitched scream came from the concession

stand. A young man, a few years older than the teens, stood in front c

it. He'd thought the necklaces were just a ruse to get the Shadow

People out of hiding. Unfortunately, his actions lead to the necklace

falling from his hands as he turned to ash. *It's going to be a long day,*

Claretta thought as the officers ushered everyone away from him.

At a distribution center across town in a neighborhood park,

Kamyra and Klarissa watched the crowd's movements. They grew ur

accustomed to not knowing if those around them were human. Still,

they were nervous the shadows and Shadow People would make an

appearance.

"You sure you girls are up to this?" A police officer asked

standing next to Klarissa near the front of the line. He knew the

Coopers would be helping but he still had his doubts they'd be of any

actual help.

"It's not us you should be worried about," Klarissa said,

holding a pure light orb against her hip. Her brown eyes searched the other side of the crowd for her twin. She found Kamyra on a swing close by pumping her legs slow and playing with a pure light orb. *I wish she were taking this seriously,* Klarissa thought, though she couldn't help but smile at her playful nature. As if sensing her twin's worry, Kamyra found Klarissa in an instant and smiled.

Kamyra got off the swing and proceeded to climb the slide stairs. Little kids who already had their necklaces, played below with their parents watching close by. Careful to not drop her orb, Kamyra scanned the playground then looked over the top of the crowd. The line that started by the water fountain at the other end of the playground was diminished by half before an incident occurred. A woman about their father's age put a sun necklace on and began to scratch her neck. She tried to sign her name quick and step out of line but the burning was too much for her.

"Mommy, why is she falling apart?" A little girl asked pointing to the woman in front of her.

"She's one of them!" The girl's mother shouted scooping her daughter up and backing away.

Klarissa ran a few steps forward, orb raised but stopped when she saw the woman turning into ash. Out the corner of her left eye, she saw someone leaving the line near the back.

"Stop, where you are!" The officer she'd been standing next to yelled at a man in a green shirt.

Klarissa ran after him.

She threw her orb but it missed landing where his foot had

195

been moments before. Kamyra, having seen everything, ran down the slide and threw her orb as she jumped off the end. It soared through the air hitting him right on the shoulder before he could make it past the end of the line.

"Nice shot," Klarissa said running up to her.

As the distribution continued, Klarissa and Kamyra each took opposite sides and ends of the line. They passed each other as they walked up and down until the line was gone. Once the extra pure light orbs and necklaces were packed into the back of a police car, they made their way to the fairground to meet up with the others who had finished.

Inside the fairgrounds, there were no games, rides, or laughter as the citizens waited in line. Through the darkness, the fairground lights shined covering the pathways, arenas, and main entrance. At the end of the arena, where the equestrians entered with their horses, Prima stood next to a police cruiser whose trunk was open. Inside, boxes of sun necklaces and pure light orbs filled every inch of the cloth interior.

Underestimating the number of people that would arrive, Red had extra police officers put in place around the arena's fenced perimeter with flashlights and pure light orbs. Prima, who never used her powers, tapped the pure light orb in her hands while she surveyed the area.

"Chief, I think we've got a problem," one of the officers said over the small radio. "There's a dark cloud coming up behind you."

Prima and Red both turned around. High above the police cruiser, a dark cloud glided in front of the moon moving towards the arena. There were several out but none of the others moved as the wind had been still all day. When they passed before the moon, Prima saw the shadows moving inside bringing it closer and closer.

Everyone watched as the clouds stopped over them. The moment it did, screams filled the air as shadows dropped from the clouds. Everyone scattered as the shadows fell and joined the Shadow People that went after the officers. Unable to contain the crowd any longer, they grabbed more orbs from the trunk and focused all their attention on the shadows and Shadow People.

With less than half the people wearing necklaces, Prima threw an orb at anyone that got close. *There are too many,* she thought as the shadows glided towards her. She may have been able to fool everyone else about her true identity but the shadows could never mistake a daughter of the Sun.

Ash fell around her as more shadows kept coming. *They planned this,* Prima thought reaching for another orb only to find the box empty. Without them, she had nothing to fight with and only her necklace for protection. For the first time in her life, Prima wished she had her powers back.

Off to her left, Prima saw two teenagers fighting. Neither wore a sun necklace but a shadow leaving the bigger girl was all the proof she needed. Taking off her necklace, Prima wrapped the long chain around her hand once and held it tight. When she was close, she swung

197

hard hitting the Shadow Person in the back.

"Run!" Prima yelled at the girl. The Shadow Person turned and growled at her as ashes fell to the ground behind it. Prima swung at it again this time making contact with its face. Outraged, it shoved Prima to the ground but was stopped by two orbs before it could attac again.

"So, I take it everything's not going well," Audi said stepping over the ash to help her sister up.

Prima couldn't help but smile happy to see her. Nearby, Clare and Daijon helped drive back the Shadow People and shadows while Kiki and the twins could be seen helping the police wrangle the rest c the crowd.

When everything had settled down, Prima was surprised that the majority of the people had stuck around. When everyone there ha a necklace, Claretta decided to take a walk along the border.

"I'll go with you," Daijon said as they prepared to leave.

"Me too," Audi added as her sisters went their separate ways

CHAPTER 21

Still in the past...

Nestled on the hill near a strip mall, Claretta, Audi, and Daijon walked along train tracks that weren't used much. It became their favorite spot a year ago when they discovered part of the town could be seen through an opening in the trees. They were afraid the darkness would ruin the view, even though, they needed flashlights, it was still amazing. Above them, the moon glowed on the city below adding to the town lights that danced around like fireflies.

"I wonder if there are shadows outside Quincy?" Claretta asked stopping on the track. Just beyond the force field, they could see one of the many parts of Quincy that remained in the dark.

"Probably," Audi replied stretching her leg out so her foot landed on the next wooden railroad tie.

"I wouldn't be surprised if the rest of the world thought it was a joke," Daijon said skimming his hand along the force field like he was sitting in a boat on a lake. "I mean, Claretta had to get attacked at the meeting for anyone to take her seriously."

"I'm still worried about the fairy," Claretta blurted as they continued walking.

Daijon groaned rolling his eyes. Audi slapped him in the chest with the back of her hand.

"Don't be a jerk," Audi said. "If she says, she saw a fairy then I believe her."

Claretta turned around to look at her friends. "I haven't seen i
since that night. I've got a bad feeling about it."

They walked a while longer until Audi got a call from her da
saying someone was at the house that needed to talk to them.

Overhead, past the force field in the night sky, hand sized
fairies flew around. For now, they did nothing as they watched the
three children climb down the hill.

"These are the ones that defeated the Shadow People," the
fairy Claretta had seen said.

"Mere children," a male fairy beside her sneered.

"That *child* defeated their leader," she said pointing to
Claretta.

"Humph. We will make her fear us as she once feared the
shadows."

When they arrived back at the Cooper house, Claretta, Audi,
and Daijon stood outside and looked around. The house still had its
force field around it and all was quiet. With Claretta in the lead,
powers ready, they entered the house to find everyone sitting in the
living room. To their right, a peculiar guest sat on a stool in front of t
fireplace. A man in his 30's leaned forward on a stool with his head
down and arms resting on jean clad legs. He appeared to look just lik
anyone else until you saw his face. Claretta, Audi, and Daijon couldn
help but stare as the man stood. His long brown hair came down
around his ears that resembled those of a Siberian Husky while hone
colored eyes stared back at them. His nose, while not the length of a

husky, was still the same shape and black color. Even his bare feet were covered in hair.

"I am Finian of the Et Lunam," the man said. Apart from his identity and the request to speak to the children, he had remained silent until now.

"You said there was something you needed to tell them," Mr. Cooper said.

"I'm sorry to hear about the Sun's death," Finian said before anyone else could speak. "There is another way to save everyone but we must hurry. She *will* send others, if they're not already here."

"What in the world are the Et Lunam?" Kiki blurted out.

"Don't be rude," Mr. Cooper said.

"Well, he's clearly not human," Kiki replied waving her hand at Finian, "and we've never heard of the Et Lunam."

"He's definitely not a Shadow Person," Daijon added.

"Wait," Kamyra said, "did you say something about there being another way to save everyone."

"Yes," Finian replied.

"What others are you talking about?" Audi asked.

"The fairy," Claretta whispered.

"The stars can explain," Finian said. Before more questions could be asked, he walked out the sliding door and into the backyard.

The others followed, wondering what stars that couldn't speak could possibly tell them.

With a glance behind him to make sure everyone was there,

Finian pulled a black stone with white stars on it from his pocket. "Show them what they're up against," he said looking at the sky. Wh᷈ he opened the stone, all the colors of the northern lights shot from its center into the sky. Stars moved the lights until they formed shapes, showing them clips of what they assumed to be a longer story.

"That is our queen," Finian narrated as they watched the sky. "Because the light burns her skin, she was forced to live on the dark side of the moon and became very bitter." The light showed a woman with a crown standing in darkness looking out at the light in the distance that was once her home. "The Shadow People were the first of her followers. They too wanted the world full of darkness away from any light."

The Stars then shaped the light into a small fairy that grew larger until it was of human form.

"That's what I saw that night," Claretta exclaimed.

"That's a Crater Fairy," Finian explained, "they dwell in the craters on the dark side of the moon and that's who she'll send next." He closed the rock and the sky returned to normal.

"That doesn't explain how we can save the world now," Claretta said.

"We should go back inside," Finian said his eyes searching tl sky for any lights that shouldn't be there. Once they were out of eyesight, Finian faced the others that waited impatiently on the training mats. "When the Sun is on its last days, another is chosen. It a secret held by the stars since their creation. They do have a human

202

form, though I haven't had the pleasure to see one leave the sky."

"What do you mean another?" Claretta asked.

"When the Sun is on its last days," Finian repeated, "the stars will choose someone to be the new Sun. She'll start getting her powers if the Sun is attacked directly. There's a ceremony that must be completed by the end of the second day after the Sun's death. If it's not, the Earth will be in darkness forever."

"So, who is she," Claretta asked, "and how are we supposed to find her?"

"The new Sun's name is Paige," Finian said. "The stars will guide you to her."

"That doesn't give us much time," Claretta said. It was nearly the end of the first night.

"I'm coming with you," Daijon said.

"You're the only one that can see the shadows and tell who's a Shadow Person," Claretta said, "You need to stay here."

"If you end up going into the countryside then you'll need me," Kiki said. "Let's just say I know my way around."

"You need someone that can drive," Klarissa said.

"She also needs someone that's good with pure light," Prima said, "that's more important."

"She's right," Claretta said, "and from what I saw at the fairground that would be Kiki and Audi."

As they started to prepare what they'd need for the trip, Finan wished them well and left to return to his temporary home on Earth.

Claretta, Audi, and Daijon retrieved their go-karts from the park then Audi and Kiki went to the go-kart track to get one with two seats so Paige would be able to ride back with them. While they were doing that, Claretta made pure light necklaces, orbs, and staffs for Klarissa and Kamyra. They'd be going to warn the rest of Quincy that sat outside the force field distributing necklaces and bringing anyone inside the force field that wanted the protection. Daijon, after helping the twins, was to work with the police if anyone was caught without a necklace *and* to help Prima prepare everything for the ceremony.

With the final preparations done, Claretta had the others scatter along the border looking for a sign from the stars. Claretta, Audi, and Kiki waited patiently in the drive-way, go-karts started and ready to go.

It was hour before midnight when a sign presented itself.

"I see something," Klarissa said into her phone. "It's a bright red star."

"Where are you?" Claretta asked.

"Down by the old movie theater."

"We're on our way!"

Claretta called Audi and Kiki connecting them for a three-way call. "It's by the old movie theater!" She shouted over the engine. "Stay close to me and remember we don't know what's out there waiting for us." She hung up the phone, hit the gas and sped out the drive-way followed by Kiki in the two-seater then Audi.

When Claretta passed the movie theater 20 minutes later, she saw the red star right away. She also saw the tunnel of darkness that swallowed the country road. Every few feet, another red star showed them where to go. The stars offered no extra light and even though the go-karts glowed, it still wasn't enough. With no headlights to light the road ahead, Claretta sent pure light into the lines on their side. The once white and yellow lines now shined a golden color twelve feet ahead of her and three feet behind Audi disappearing on the road as they sped along.

As they continued on their way, Kiki realized the surroundings looked familiar. When they passed a tractor with a for sale sign and a stop sign that had been run into one too many times, she was positive she'd been that way before.

About an hour later, another red star shined above a one lane road that appeared to lead nowhere. *Seriously,* Claretta thought but drove up to the black gate anyway. She got out and searched the darkness around her as she opened both sides of the gate wide.

Tall American Beech trees lined the sides of the road as the girls continued to follow the stars deeper into the forest. As the trees became less dense, Claretta saw two wooden cabins up ahead. The last star shined above the cabin to their left, its glow so bright part of the lake could be seen behind the cabins. Once they turned off their go-kart, Audi and Kiki grabbed their staffs that were wedged beside them then followed Claretta up the worn grass path to the door. Before she could knock, the door was opened by a female Et Lunam.

"We started to think no one would come," the woman said

standing in the doorway.

"But then we saw the red stars and heard vehicles," a male E
Lunam said.

"Please come in," the woman gestured for them to enter as
they moved aside. "I'm Emilan and this is my husband, Bastille."

"Where's Paige?" Claretta asked after she introduced herself
and the others.

"She's in the other cabin," Bastille said as they entered the
kitchen.

"Then why did the stars lead us here?" Kiki asked.

"Paige doesn't know she's to be the Sun," Emilan said. "We
saw her create a small orb of pure light late one night when she
thought no one was looking. The shadows didn't see her and they dor
know who she is or they'd have taken her by now."

"We've been keeping watch over her ever since she was
chosen by the stars," Bastille said.

"I'm sorry but didn't they notice you're not human?" Kiki
asked.

"You don't always have to say the first thing you're thinking,"
Audi said glaring at her older sister.

"I don't," Kiki replied, "just most of the time."

"The stars placed us here years ago and gave us amulets to
blend in when among the humans," Bastille said.

"We've been friends with our neighbors ever since," Emilan
said. "We do have another home. It was the stars that suggested we

stay here every summer when we came to Earth. One could assume they'd made a choice long before recent events."

"What do you mean the stars placed you here?" Claretta asked.

"That's how our kind get to Earth," Emilan said as her husband went to keep watch, "the stars bring us."

Having explained everything, Emilan left to gather Paige's family. Knowing they'd be safer over here, especially, now that the others had arrived.

"I'll come with you," Claretta said in case Emilan needed help getting them to leave.

Necklace now secure around her neck, she knocked on the door while Claretta had her back to it choosing to face the dark instead.

"Hello Lauren," Emilan said when someone finally answered the door. "You must gather your family and come to our cabin quickly. It's an emergency, I'll explain everything then."

Lauren looked at her old friend through the crack in the door then at the child standing next to her. She'd never seen the girl before and knew Emilan had no children but she nodded okay anyway. She assumed something must be wrong if her friend was waking her at this late hour.

Less than 15 minutes later, Paige's family, which thankfully consisted of just her and her parents, now sat fully dressed across from Claretta and the others while the Et Lunam stood between them at the side of the table. Not wishing to reveal their true identities, Emilan and Bastille continued to wear their amulets underneath their shirts.

Though they were able to blend in, Claretta thought it strange to see them without their dog-like features.

"What's so important you had to drag me and my family out our vacation home in the middle of the night?" Paige's father asked irritated.

"Reginald," Her mother said patting his arm to get him to relax.

"Your daughter has incredible powers," Emilan said, "and because of it there are...people after her."

"Powers! You dragged us over here for this nonsense!" Reginald shouted. "We're leaving!"

"We saw the ball of light," Bastille said.

"I don't know what you're talking about," Paige lied.

They got up and headed to the door but before they could mal it there, Claretta stood and created a ball of pure light. She sent it pas them on the left whipped it around the front and brought it back on their right to her. They turned around and that's when Claretta did the unexpected. She sent the orb right at Paige's mother. Paige sidesteppe in front of her caught the light with her hand then threw it to the floo just as Claretta thought she would.

"You were saying," Claretta said.

Paige looked at her parents with worried eyes and told them everything. The girl, near tears when she finished, was shocked when her parents hugged her tight.

"I don't understand any of this but nothing will ever keep us from loving you," her father said bending down to look her in her eyes; her face between both his hands.

Emilan and Bastille suggested Claretta and the others take Paige into the guestroom where they'd be sleeping while they talked to her parents some more.

Not long after, everyone was asleep and the cabin grew quiet. The Et Lunam stood guard making sure every entryway was secure but it was already too late. A Crater Fairy had found Finian and tortured him into telling her where the others went. They had almost missed their chance but the faint glow of the red stars could still be seen well enough to follow.

CHAPTER 22

In the future...

"Where have you been?" Emilan asked as Paige closed the front doc

Paige rolled her eyes. She let out a sigh then turned to face he "Just out," she said pushing the black hood of the zip up hoodie off h head.

"You shouldn't be out there."

"I can't just sit around here all day."

"You should be practicing using your powers," Bastille said entering the room.

"That's all I've been doing so I gave myself a break."

"You know what's at stake if you get caught."

"Yeah, I know," Paige said walking through the living room the hall on the right. It was a small house with only two bedrooms an stairs at the end of the hall that led to a loft. That was her favorite spc and was where she headed now.

Reaching the wall, she took off her sneakers and climbed the carpeted stairs on her right. Her small feet sank into the plush navy carpet as she made her way to the large window that took up the entii wall. Pulling the thick black curtains aside Paige stared into the dark where the beautiful garden was. She'd gotten a chance to play in it bu only for one day before the world went dark.

Walking to the railing that overlooked the hallway, Paige sat i the egg-shaped seat that hung from the ceiling in the corner. Leaning back with her legs folded beneath, she thought about everything that happened while she waited for him. It was the start of summer vacation and her family was getting ready to go to the cabin for a week. She and her parents did it every year, one week of family time, no work, and no summer activities. She had decided to stay behind while her parents went to the grocery store then drop off their load. Their home was less than two hours from the cabin so she'd be fine.

That's when Emilan and Bastille showed up. They were in human form then their matching amulets hidden beneath their shirts. Paige knew them; they had the cabin next to theirs so she let them in. At the end of that first day, she wished she never opened the door. Finian had been with her parents and through speaker phone; they'd learned everything about the Sun and her destiny. In truth, Paige knew something weird was happening, she just never told her parents. Thankfully, it never happened outside the house but sometimes late at night her hands would glow. She just thought it was her imagination that she was half asleep and her mind was playing tricks on her. That was until pure light came from her hands.

She'd been having a weird dream about shadows that moved on their own and people that turned into these black silhouettes. When she woke from the nightmare, a ball of light shot from her hand and hit the wall across from her bed. She'd never been afraid of the dark and still wasn't but ever since then she never looked at the dark in the same way. When her parents learned about their daughter, they didn't take it well. Even when Paige told them what Emilan and Bastille said was true about her powers, they believed it but didn't want to accept it. They didn't come home and tell their 13-year-old daughter that everything would be okay. No, they stayed at the cabin claiming they needed time to deal with everything they just learned.

Emilan and Bastille took her to their odd shaped home with tl loft that hung over the outside patio. When the world went dark, they assured her and her parents she'd be safe. When the stars first started bringing the Et Lunam to Earth, they wanted to ensure they'd be safe So, they made their first promise. As long as a star remained in the sk no Shadow Person, shadow, or other dark force would be able to ente an Et Lunam home.

Paige hadn't understood how she was supposed to practice using her powers until one of the stars arrived. When a certain constellation appeared above the house, a star would be able to come from the sky undetected by the Shadow People. With him or her ther no dark force would be able to see the pure light from outside.

Just then, a white light descended from the ceiling and filled the room bringing Paige back to the present. Her favorite star, a youn man three years older than her with white wings and black armor sto where the light once was. A star in human form for that is what they were.

"Are you ready?" Mathis asked.

"Yes," Paige said trying to hide her smile. She still couldn't believe her first crush was with an actual star. She moved to the cent

212

of the room and started with her usual warm up. Pure light lit her hands in seconds. It was always present and at the forefront, ready for use the second she needed it.

Approaching the window, Paige created a pencil of pure light and drew on the glass like it was a sheet of paper. Her left hand moved with ease filling the center and all four corners with a golden target. Height wasn't a problem. She mearly let the pencil go and lifted the pure light into the air using her finger to direct it. Paige stepped back and smiled at her work.

Warmed up, she prepared for the real work. When she was younger, Jacks was her favorite game. Her mother had taught it to her and though no one really played it anymore, she still liked it. So, that is what she created now, a handful of small golden Jacks that resembled the real thing. With a nod to Mathis, he turned back into his original form. A bright ball of white light now floated next to her. He dimmed his glow enough so Paige didn't have to shield her eyes then shot toward the window. As soon as he hit the glass, Paige was quick to act. She threw a Jack at the top left corner and hit him with ease. Mathis moved as fast as a blink and Paige struck him again. Though the Jacks were pointy and she used her powers to travel faster than normal, they didn't break the glass. Upon hitting the glass, the Jack absorbed into the glass and became a golden dot.

When they finished, Paige got rid of the Jacks and Mathis returned to human form. "It's time, we took your training to the next level," Mathis said.

"I'm tired, can't we do it tomorrow?"

Mathis smiled at the girl he'd grown close to in the last couple days. The North Star thought it would be better to have someone young help her train. That she would connect and be more open to someone closer to her age. "Now's the perfect time. You need to be ready, no matter how you feel or where you are."

Once again, the room filled with light. This time when the light dimmed, two more stars floated near Mathis.

"This time all three of us are your target."

"Ok," Paige said still looking at the new stars.

"And we'll be using the entire room to move in. See if you can hit us."

"How am I supposed to know if I hit you?"

"If we're hit by pure light in our true form, our natural light will turn gold for a second then return to normal. I'll let you know how many times you hit each of us when we're finished. Instead of Jacks use orbs."

Paige took a moment to survey the loft. On the wall to the left of the stairs was an entertainment center with a flat screen nestled in. In the center was a dark brown cloth couch that fit three people. She'd been up their countless times, but never thought about it like she did now.

Mathis said nothing as he watched her. This is what he hoped she'd do: plan, calculate, and see everything as an opportunity to beat her opponent. "Ready?"

Paige nodded, and so they began.

Turning, she backed up to the railing and waited for their first move. One of the stars flew towards her and Paige ducked. This time one came straight for her but instead of ducking, she faced it. That wasn't the one she was after but the one behind it. Sending a pure light orb up towards the ceiling, Paige ducked under the other one, stepped forward and sent it down on the other. The Star turned golden, her first hit for the night.

Out the corner of her eye, Paige saw a Star trail down the wall on her left aiming for her feet. She waited for it to get closer then ran to the couch. Jumping onto it, she quickly created four orbs, one after the other. Still on the couch, she sent one under it from each side hitting her target. With her focus on the four orbs, Paige didn't see the Star coming at her from behind. Thankfully, the couch wasn't that high up and should leave nothing but a bruise on her left shoulder.

Getting back up, Paige stood in the corner created by the wall and entertainment center. Shaking off the fall, she readied herself for the two Stars that now came towards her. Creating an orb, she threw it at the floor before them where she then sent it upward splitting it in two along the way.

They continued like this for another ten minutes when Paige finally had enough. She moved to the center of the room and created so many orbs they fell from her hands unable to hold them all. All at once, she sent them into the air. It was like looking at half a room of floating lights. Some floated around her creating a moving barrier while Paige sent the others around the room. They had one job to see out the Stars. Using her hands, Paige sent them flying in every direction. By the time the last one vanished, Mathis had returned to human form holding his hand up for her to stop.

Paige stood there in silence as Mathis whispered to the other Stars. When they left, back through the ceiling, he finally spoke.

"The North Star chose well," was all Mathis said then he left ending their session.

The next day, Bastille and Emilan warned Paige again about going out and she took their advice until lunch time rolled around. Even with the Shadow People taking over, downtown would be booming with those required to still work. The more people, the more chances she got to hear what's really going on; not the downplayed version the news likes to give. So, when the doorbell rang that afternoon bringing the arrival of Et Lunam who Paige hadn't met, she slipped out while they talked in the kitchen.

Running to the bus stop, Paige made the short trip downtown getting off at an intersection. With her hood up, she ignored those that told her it was dangerous to be out alone and kept walking. Up ahead on her right was the twenty-five-foot office building she was looking for. She could always count on a crowd hanging by the food truck just a few feet away. Having skipped lunch, Paige brought a sandwich, chips, and juice then stood off to the side. With her hood still up and eyes down, Paige ate her lunch as she eavesdropped on her first of many conversations.

"I can't believe there's still all this traffic with those things running around," a woman drinking yet another cup of coffee said.

"The town can't exactly shut down," a man in a business suit laughed, "but I get what you mean. Shadows moving on their own and the dark figures. Did you know the little corner store a block over closed down? The owner said shadows chased them out. Thought he was crazy so I went to take a look and the old man was right. Dark shadow figures were standing around and shadows darted in and out beneath the door."

"I don't have enough caffeine in me for this," the woman said taking another sip.

Paige continued to eat as she made a mental note to avoid that area. Looking up, she noticed a man in jeans, a white button down shirt and a dark tie approach.

"I couldn't help but overhear you mention the shadows," white button down said.

Yeah right. More like you were eavesdropping too, Paige thought.

"Have you heard about the safe house?" White button down asked.

The other two looked at him confused.

"Well, somewhere near the edge of the city they say there's this house surrounded by lights. People having been fleeing to it to escape the shadows. I haven't seen it myself and most people say it's a bunch of crap."

Leaving them to their conversation, Paige dumped her trash and headed back to the bus stop. All the times, she had sneaked out, this was the first she'd heard of a safe house. *I wonder if Emilan and Bastille know about it,* she thought taking the same route she came. This time things were different. The tap of heels and expensive shoes were absent from the sidewalks. The air was free of cheap perfume a the missing warmth of rushing bodies left a chill in the air. Hearing tl scuff of shoes, Paige turned around. A teenage boy and a girl walked few feet behind her holding hands. Giving them back their privacy, Paige turned back around.

When a shadow glided past her, Paige stopped where she was Glancing over her shoulder this time, she really looked at them. They were Shadow People in human form and now, there were more of them. *I didn't know they still took human form,* she thought. Realizin; Paige was staring, the girl nudged the boy whose hand she held. He looked up and winked at Paige with a cocky grin. With his eyes lock(on Paige's, the boy sent his shadow towards her. Pretending not to notice, Paige turned back around only to find the boy's shadow standing two feet in front of her. Unable to keep it in, a high-pitched scream escaped her lips.

Paige ran around the shadow towards the bus stop. She'd hop(the teens would leave her alone once they realized they scared her bu the thud of several feet behind her told her they weren't done yet. *Please let the bus be on time,* Paige thought. She wiggled her fingers then clinched her fist knowing that using her powers would put her ii

218

more danger. Paige looked to the stars as she continued to run pleading for their help. Taking a left at the corner ahead, she almost set her powers free when someone grabbed her hand.

Jumping at the sudden contact, Paige tried to pull her hand away but the person wouldn't let her go. She looked at the boy holding her hand.

"Who are you?" Paige asked. He didn't answer but she didn't need him too. One look into his yellow green eye and she knew it was Mathis.

With the sound of footsteps drawing closer, they continued to run. When they were two blocks from the bus, Mathis pulled Paige into an empty apartment alcove.

"What are you doing?" Paige asked looking around the corner.

"Trust me," Mathis said. He knew he shouldn't do it and was bound to get into to trouble but he had no other choice. Checking the dark for shadows, he wrapped his arms around Paige and drew her close. Her checks turned pink as she looked at him with wide eyes and he couldn't help but smile.

Paige didn't know what was going on but wrapped her arms around him anyway. She gasped as thousands of dot sized gold and white lights circled them. A weightlessness filled her as the pure light in her felt alive moving through her body. Looking down, Paige saw their legs matched the light dots. Mathis' were white and hers' golden. She continued to look down as their bodies changed. When it reached her waist, she looked at Mathis who was still smiling.

Once the light reached Paige's neck, Mathis focused on guidii their light into the dead bulb above. Just as their combined light fille(the bulb, the young Shadow People passed not giving them a second glance.

Mathis released them from the light bulb with enough time to run the last two blocks and hop on the bus. The hum of the engine an the voices of other passengers was all that could be heard as the two sat in the back-left corner of the bus. When they reached their stop, Mathis stayed with her the short distance home.

"There you are. You had us so worried," Emilan said rushing over to give Paige a hug before she could even close the door. Lookii over Paige's shoulder she noticed Mathis standing there. "Okay, what happened?" She asked taking in the young man's jeans and sweater.

"She was almost caught by the Shadow People," a man Paig(hadn't seen before came down the hallway that led to the loft. He wa: tall man that wore armor just like Mathis. He had a deep commandin voice and dark long hair he kept in a low ponytail.

Emilan ushered them into the living room where Bastille sat they could all talk.

"Hello, Master Linen," Mathis greeted that man that taught a the stars how to fight with a bow.

"You know the rules," was all Master Linen said ignoring everyone but the young man before him.

"What's he talking about?" Paige asked moving to Mathis' si(as Emilan and Bastille remained silent. They knew the stars were stri

220

when it came to their rules. One of their main rules for the Et Lunam was that they were to always wear their amulets when around humans. If a human were to see an Et Lunam's true form, they would be banned from living on Earth.

"When I put us in the light bulb, I not only mixed our two lights sources but I also changed your form."

Seeing that the girl was confused, Master Linen elaborated. "Changing the form of a human the way Mathis did is forbidden. It gives the human power over the star."

"She's not a normal human," Mathis said realizing he hadn't actually broken a rule.

Well thanks, Paige thought rolling her eyes.

"I know what she is boy," Master Linen said loud enough to make everyone cover their ears. "She's still half human."

"What does he mean half human?" Paige asked.

"Even though, you were chosen to be the new Sun, you're still human. Because of that it also makes you half light," Mathis explained. "As you've seen, our true form is a white light because we, the stars are the only other source of pure light."

"I thought stars were made of gas."

"That's what we want humans to think. They don't need to know the stars can take human form."

"Wow."

"Since she's half human, the rules don't apply to her," Mathis said challenging Master Linen.

Silence filled the room, as Master Linen looked at them all in turn. Then surprisingly he sighed. "I was... wrong and for that I apologize," he said not use to being wrong, "but don't forget who makes the rules."

Mathis knew what he meant. The North Star was the ruler of the night skies. He was a kind man in his late 30's that never seemed age. He knew more about humans than even the Sun. To break one o: his rules, without being granted his permission, meant death. He wou take their light and banish the star to Earth. There was no greater dea for a star than to lose one's light. To live as human and be reminded every night you look up of what you once were.

"Was there another reason you're paying us a visit?" Bastille asked. "Surely that matter could have been handled when Mathis returned."

"The Et Lunam queen is becoming impatient and wants the Shadow People to start clearing the city of humans." Master Linen said.

"But they can't get in here because Emilan and Bastille are E Lunam," Paige said, "so we'll be fine...right?"

"You're correct," Master Linen said looking at the young girl "the house *is* protected because of who they are. The problem is we could no longer come to the house..."

"Which means I can't train or use my powers at all," Paige said. Master Linen nodded.

"If you stay here, it wouldn't be long before the Shadow

People take over the entire area," Mathis said. "You'd be surrounded."

"Where are we supposed to go?" Emilan asked.

"That is not for us to figure out," Master Linen said and it was true. When it came to Earth and the humans, the Stars only had two things they were required to do; secure Et Lunam homes, and their journey to and from Earth, and protect the person who was chosen to be the next Sun. It was the Sun and her daughter's jobs to protect the humans of Earth. All the Stars knew the Sun's daughters had been captured but they also knew one remained out of their captivity and so did her son. The Stars would not intervene until there was no other option.

Having delivered the North Star's message, Master Linen turned to leave.

"What about the safe house," Paige said remembering what she'd heard earlier.

"That place is surrounded by Shadow People," Bastille said. Emilan looked at him confused. She knew nothing of it and Bastille hadn't mentioned it to her.

"You know about it?" Paige asked.

"Yes. It's a house on the edge of the city that's surrounded by solar lights created by the Sun herself."

"You knew about it. Then why aren't we there?"

"Until the Sun's daughters are freed, there's no way for you to become the new Sun. Protecting you is our first priority. The longer we can keep your identity a secret, the safer you'll be," Emilan said.

223

"If Master Linen's right, I'll be in danger if we stay here," Paige said. "Can't you help us?" This time her question was directed Mathis who had stayed behind.

"I can't do anything without the North Star's permission," Mathis said.

"You have already," Paige argued.

"Yes, and look how bad that could've turned out."

"It doesn't matter because we're not leaving," Bastille interrupted.

"What!" Paige yelled.

"He's right," Emilan said. "The safest place for now is right here."

Realizing, they weren't going to budge on their decision, Paig stormed off to her room. Mathis stood outside her door trying to reason with her but even he wasn't allowed to enter. When he finally left, Paige kicked off her shoes. Draped across the width of the full-size bed, she stared at the ceiling pouting like the child she was. *Wha could be better than a safe house,* Paige thought swinging her feet back and forth. *I wondered if my parents are there.* Pulling her phone from her back pocket, Paige unlocked her screen then pushed mom. The generic ring tone broke the silence as she waited for her to answ When the voice mail picked up, Paige tried again. This time, her mor answered.

"Hi mom," Paige said.

"Hi sweetie, how are you?" Her mom asked.

"You would know if you called. Where's dad?"

"He's out getting more firewood."

"You're still at the cabin?"

"Well yes, that's where we planned on going remember?"

"Yeah, I remember we were going as a *family*," Paige said, pacing her room. Silence filled the conversation as neither of them said anything. "When are you coming home?" She asked though what she really wanted to know was when they were going to be together again.

"With everything that's going on in the city right now, this is the best place for us."

Tears filled Paige's eyes as she stopped by the window. They fell as she watched the family across the street pack their van with bags and boxes. "The *best place* for you right now should be with me," she said then hung up before her mother could justify not being there. Throwing her phone on the bed, a bang followed Paige into the hall as the doorknob hit the wall. Going to the loft, she grabbed a book from the entertainment center along with her iPod and curled up on the couch.

A few hours later, a loud continuous knock reached Paige. Removing her earbuds, she left the comfort of the couch to stand by the banister. *No one ever comes by*. Straining her ears, she tried to hear what was being said.

"If you're going to eavesdrop, you might as well come down and meet our guest," Bastille said a smile on his face as his true form came into view. The first time Paige had seen it, she couldn't help but stare and not the stare for a few seconds then look away kind of stare It was more like two minutes of taking in the Et Lunam's every feature. Her eyes had stayed on their ears the longest which is how Bastille had heard her move to the banister. Even in human form, the had great hearing.

Paige couldn't help but smile at being caught. "I'll pass," she said returning to the couch.

The faint sound of conversation swept down the hall like a continuous rhythm. Then silence. No more laughter or the clinking o a spoon being stirred in a tea cup. The thud of bare footsteps padded towards the loft. Assuming whoever it was going either out back to tl garden or to the kitchen, Paige didn't bother to move. When the pers(did neither and she heard the light creak of the fourth step from the bottom, she turned around.

"Paige run!" She heard Bastille yell from somewhere below but it was too late, her exit had been blocked

"Who are you?" Paige asked using the couch as a barrier between her and the Et Lunam that now stood at the top of the stairs. She too wore an amulet that signaled what she was.

The woman removed the amulet and her features changed faster than a leaf falling from a tree. Her russet colored hair was pull(in a low ponytail and she wore one earring with a chain that led up tc cuff around her ear. "By the lack of shock on your face, you already know what I am," the woman said as she moved closer. "As for who am, it's not important. *You* on the other hand seem to be of some

226

importance for Bastille and Emilan to fight for you."

"What did you do to them?" Paige asked out of both fear and anger.

"They're tied up at the moment. Though, I'm sure they'll free themselves soon enough. So," the woman said clapping her hands together, "let's get going."

"I'm not going anywhere with you."

"I promised the Queen a pet. I don't plan on disappointing her."

She doesn't know who I really am, Paige thought as the woman advanced. Backing up, she stopped inches from the glass. Thinking back to when she played tag with her friends, Paige waited. When the woman got closer, Paige ran to the left in an arch around her. With the stairs in sight, Paige started to reach her right hand for the railing but she didn't make it. Paige grimaced as her arm was pulled backward and she was forced to her knees. Removing the thick twine, she used to tie up her hair, the woman pulled Paige's other arm behind her back and tied both her wrists together.

Paige was being lifted to her feet with rough hands but then they were gone before she could get her footing causing her to stumble. Lifting her head up, Paige saw Master Linen standing at the top of the stairs with a weapon that made her think of an apostrophe. Turning around, the woman held her bleeding arm and a weapon like Master Linen held was stuck in the wall by the window. Paige ran to him. He caught the girl with his free arm and cut the twine with the other half of his Chakram.

"Mathis waits for you downstairs," Master Linen said steppi in front of her as the woman prepared to attack again. "Go to him!"

Paige took off without a word. Just as he said Mathis was waiting for her in armor and a hand stretched in her direction. Giving her hand to him, Mathis led her down the hall and out the front door. Parked outside in their small four door car, Bastille and Emilan waite for her with the car running.

"Go, it'll be okay," Mathis said letting go of her hand and giving her a light push.

Paige gave him a quick hug then ran to the car ignoring everything else around her. As the car pulled away, she turned in her seat to see Mathis go back inside. *I hope they'll be okay.* "Are you gu okay?" She asked turning to Emilan and Bastille.

Bastille, who was driving, had blood coming down his ear an Emilan had a bruise under her left eye. "We'll be fine," he said as Emilan held a cloth to his ear.

"Where are we going?" Paige asked.

Emilan looked at Paige then Bastille.

"To the safe house," Bastille said changing lanes.

CHAPTER 23

In the past...

The Crater Fairies hovered above the cabin until everyone was in position. They removed the glowing red whips that hung curled up on their hips and brought them down on the roof. The Et Lunam, who'd fallen asleep, after a long night as well, jumped to their feet from where they slept on the couches.

"Everyone get up, now!" Emilan yelled as she rushed into the guest room then the master bedroom where Paige's parents slept.

"What's going on?" Claretta yelled.

"Crater fairies! You must leave!"

All around them pieces of wood fell from the ceiling as the roof caved in from the Crater Fairies powerful whips.

"Where's Paige?" Audi asked.

Her parents hadn't seen her and she was nowhere in the cabin. Their worst fears were confirmed when they made it outside and saw one of the go-karts was gone and the others destroyed. That was the least of their problems at the moment. 10 Crater Fairies circled high above. At first glance, Claretta thought their entire bodies glowed orange but now realized it was their wings behind them that made it seem that way. The men all wore silver pants and black shirts that hugged their bodies while the women wore silver dresses of various styles.

Trees were sliced in half as the Crater Fairies cut through them with their whips. They fell onto the cabin and in the grass nearby shaking the ground and filling the air with a thud sound. They huddled togeth as the Crater Fairies continued their assault from the sky.

We're gonna need something better than staffs, Claretta thought. "I just need a minute, cover me," she said. Claretta worked the pure light between her hands remembering the weakness Finian told them about.

"I was hoping Finian exaggerated their wings," Kiki said as ؛ gust of wind knocked them over.

No sooner than they got up, another gust of wind from the Crater Fairies' wings knocked them down for a second time.

"Okay, I've had enough of this," Claretta said.

Finally finished with their new weapons, Claretta handed Auc a pure light bow and quiver that held 20 thin golden arrows that coulؤ pierce the fairies' wings. For Kiki, she gave her a mini crossbow that would shoot small pure light orbs at a rapid speed. She also handed h a container that she could clip onto her jeans like a phone case that held extra orbs. For herself, Claretta created small golden daggers. Since they were made of pure light, she could move them wherever she needed.

Fighting the shadows was *nothing* compared to fighting Crate Fairies. Audi, who was no stranger with a bow, had a hard time aiming. The Crater Fairies movements were quick and their wings were almost as fast as a humming birds. Kiki held the mini crossbow in both hands to try and steady her aim. She ran to the remains of the go-karts and used them as a makeshift shield. Crouched down on one knee, she looked for a target. Seeing her little sister in trouble, Kiki steadied her hand and aimed at the Crater Fairy that had backed Audi into a tree. The orb was a blur as it flew through the air only slowing down when it hit the corner of the Crater Fairies wing. It screamed and turned towards her.

On the other side of the yard, Claretta stood protecting the Et Lunam and Paige's parents.

"Do you know where Paige would've gone?" Claretta asked.

"There's a skating rink we take her too," Reginald said barely dodging the Crater Fairies whip, "but it's closed."

Claretta threw a dagger. When it missed, she turned it back around with her left hand and threw another one with her right. The fairy dodged the first dagger and blocked the other with its whip.

"We'll try to draw them away while you get them to safety," Claretta said to the Et Lunam. "Don't worry, we'll find her," she said to Paige's parents as the Et Lunam guided them past the cabins to the lake behind.

Claretta ran over to Audi then Kiki whispering to both of them exactly what to do. When they reached the road, Audi and Kiki hesitated for a moment then ran into the dark. When they were a good distance ahead, Claretta threw two daggers then ran for one of the trees. She filled it with pure light and when it reached the top sent it in an arch to the one across from it. Now standing back in the road,

231

Claretta thrust her hands out from her like she was pushing someone away. The golden arch of pure light followed the movement of her hands lighting up one tree to the next until the road of darkness was now a tunnel of light.

Audi and Kiki were amazed at what Claretta had done and thankful to be running in the dark no longer. They passed the black gate and kept running until they reached the woods on the other side the road. They covered the glow of their weapons with twigs and leaves then laid on their stomachs near the forests edge and waited fc Claretta.

Even though, the Crater Fairies didn't dare come into the tunnel, they still followed overhead but Claretta planned on changing that. When she was close to the gate, Claretta turned to face the tunne Keeping its shape, she diminished the tunnel until its width matched that of the road. She then clapped her hands and pushed her palms to the sky. The tunnel collapsed into pure light particles then rose up int the air towards the Crater Fairies. Claretta ran through the particles a across the road only slowing down enough to motion for the others tc follow her deeper into the woods.

"I can't believe Paige ran away," Claretta said as they walkec through the forest and back onto the road a few minutes later. "Now we have to chase after her."

"How long will it take to get back?" Audi asked.

"About 12 hours," Kiki said not needing to look at her phone

"How do you know that?" Claretta asked.

"I used to come to parties out this way," Kiki replied. "Come on, the skating rink isn't far from here."

"Why would she even go there, it's not like its open," Audi said.

"Oh, it's open," Kiki said as they hurried along the roads shoulder. "The owner's son is a senior and has a key and likes to throw parties there. With it being out so far, we've never had a problem with police."

Claretta looked to the sky as they continued on their way. From what she could tell, there were no Crater Fairies following them.

Chaos awaited them at the skating rink that sat off from the road. Teenagers ran in all directions trying to get away from the Crater Fairies. Seeing only fields of wheat and corn nearby, Claretta and Audi understood what Kiki meant about the noise not being a problem. Unfortunately, it did attract the Crater Fairies. Kiki and Audi tried to divert the fairy's attention away from the party goers while Claretta looked for Paige.

Claretta ran across the parking lot and through the doors. Techno music bounced off the walls of the empty building as the last of the stragglers put on their shoes to leave. Claretta moved to the middle of the rink for a better view. Not seeing Paige anywhere, she went to check the bathrooms.

In the last stall by the wall, Paige squatted down on the lid of the seat with her left hand braced against the cement wall. A Crater Fairy that had entered above Claretta's head flew down into the stall

233

Paige was in. She screamed, jumped off the toilet, and ran out the sta banging the door against the tile wall.

"Paige, this way!" Claretta yelled waving the girl to come towards her.

The Crater Fairy, having made the mistake of reverting to human size, emerged from the stall, its wings folded behind it. Claret pushed Paige behind her then sprang forward and turned on the close faucet. With a single touch, pure light was put into the water then aimed at the Crater Fairy. It hit the wall hard not only burning it but leaving its wings soaking wet.

Taking Paige's hand, they ran outside to join the others.

"This way!" Claretta yelled leading them to a field of corn th stood above their heads.

She led them further into the field then stopped ceasing the movement of the corn. They huddled together as the Crater Fairies started to descend from above, the orange glow of their wings signaling their every move. As they got closer and closer. Paige start to move but was stopped when Claretta placed a hand on her arm.

"Not yet," Claretta whispered.

When the fairies descended deeper, Claretta could see the cor sway in the glow of fairy wings nearby. She waited a second longer then put both hands out beside her touching the corn closest to her.

"Run!" Claretta yelled when the pure light reached the tops c the corn. Every move, they made sent the corn swaying back and for which made the pure light corn hit the fairies.

"How do we get out of here?" Audi asked as they kept running.

"This way," Kiki said turning left.

Crater Fairies wings fluttered as they tried getting away from the burning corn. As they continued running, a Crater Fairy that was in human form reached out between the stalks and grabbed Paige.

"Ahhh!" Paige screamed. Without even thinking, she sent a blast of pure light at it with her right hand.

"Keep going!" Audi yelled from behind Paige who stood there stunned.

They made it out the field and continued running through the dark streets putting as much distance between them and the Crater Fairies as possible.

When they finally slowed down, Claretta sent an orb of pure light out in front of them to light the way. They zipped their jackets as the day turned cold, while crickets chirped and the occasional deer ran across the road. They were still not sure what lurked in the darkness but were slightly comforted with their new weapons and knowing they'd see the Crater Fairies coming.

"Why'd you run away?" Claretta asked Paige.

"I heard what they said," Paige said. "I didn't go to the bathroom; I listened to the rest of the conversation. Why didn't you tell me I'm the new Sun?"

"You lied about even having powers like you would believe you're the new Sun," Kiki said shaking her head.

That's true, Paige thought remembering what she'd just done *If I didn't have these powers, I wouldn't have believed them.* "I'm onl 13, I don't want to be the Sun," Paige said. "I haven't even been on m first date yet. The last thing I want to do is spend my days in the sky. This is crazy."

"I was scared when Audi gave me her powers and I had to fight the Shadow People," Claretta told her, "but I knew I was the on one left that could defeat them."

Paige just stared at her not expecting to hear that.

"Your powers are different from Claretta's though," Audi sai "You have the Sun's direct powers. Our powers came from our moth but yours are more powerful. What you did in the field is nothing to what you *can* do."

"They won't stop coming for you. The force field won't turn the Crater Fairies to ash. They're more powerful than the Shadow People. The only way to beat them is to catch them or completely destroy their wings," Claretta explained. "The only way to keep everyone safe is for the Sun to return to the sky."

With the cabins far behind them, they neared a subdivision or their left. Two black lamp post stood on both sides of a bridge that le up to it. A brick wall at the bridge's edge surrounded the perimeter an a cement sign that said Ridgedale in large black letters could be seen the lamp post glow. Needing water and a few other supplies, since everything got destroyed with the go-karts, they left the road and ventured over the bridge.

236

CHAPTER 24

In the future...

Bastille cursed under his breath at the number of cars on the road. Paige noticed this too. The neighborhood they drove through was busy with people loading their families and belongings into vehicles. As much as she wanted to go to the safe house, Paige had hoped Master Linen was wrong.

"We have to do something," Paige said watching the Shadow People terrorize the citizens.

"I can't see them but I know the Shadow People are out there," Emilan said turning to look at Paige. "If you reveal yourself now, none of us will make it to the safe house."

"Fine," Paige said crossing her arms.

Halfway there, Bastille took the left at the fork in the road. Paige, who shut the world out, opened her eyes and took off her seat belt. With her knees on the seat, she looked out the back window. Paige's heart raced and her breath came out in pants.

"We have a problem," Paige managed to say moments later.

"Did you say something, sweetie," Emilan said not realizing the girl had spoken after being silent for so long.

"Shadows are following us," Paige said watching the shadows that followed them at the fork in the road. Her eyes moved to the scenery around them but she couldn't help to keep looking down.

They rode in the center lane of the main road with cars all around them. Their car swerved into the right lane as if it was struck by a shadow. Paige slid sideways falling on her butt as her shoulder h the car door. Quickly turning, she put her seat belt back on. The car beside them slammed on its breaks as the back end of Bastille's car grazed the driver's side door. Holding the wheel tight, he continued o through the intersection. Paige hoped the passengers were okay but s knew they couldn't stop.

"Why are they following us?" Emilan asked. Paige hadn't us her powers...unless.

"Thalese," Bastille said referring to the Et Lunam that attack them at their home. "When the Stars came to our aid, she must have realized that Paige is no ordinary girl."

"But Finian is the only other Et Lunam that knows about the ceremony," Emilan said.

"Even so, the Stars helping us would be enough for Thalese t go to the Shadow People." Bastille weaved through the traffic trying shake the shadows.

"Honey, don't!" Emilan shouted as Bastille hit the gas and ra a red light.

Paige's hands covered her eyes as the intersection filled with squealing tires, honking horns, and shouts. Removing her hands, she gave a sigh as they made it to the other side in one piece. "I have to c something," Paige said.

"You can't," Bastille said. "Right now, all they know is you'r

238

someone important but they don't know about *that*."

"If I don't, we won't make it," Paige said.

Emilan lightly touched Bastille's arm and gave a slight nod.

"Okay, but be careful," Bastille said.

Looking around, Paige noticed the car had a sunroof. Removing her seat belt once again, she leaned forward and pushed the button. The tinted glass slid towards Paige into the roof. Standing on the middle armrest between the two-front seats, she lifted herself out until she was able to seat on the roof. "Hold onto me!" She shouted to Emilan.

The woman grabbed a leg in each hand as Bastille slowed down to the speed limit. The wind pushed at her back as the scenery rushed past her. *Okay, now what*, Paige thought as she looked around. Cars honked and people stared but she tried to ignore them and focus on what she was really looking for. It was dark but the cars and street lamps provided enough light for her to see. Blocking everything else out, Paige found the shadows weaving through the traffic behind them. Her hands rested on either side of the sunroof and her heart started racing once again.

"Are you ok?" Emilan asked peeking through the sunroof.

"Ummm... yeah," Paige said but it was far from the truth. Before, she had no real reason to fear the Shadow People. They had no idea who she was. But now that she was about to show them, she feared what would happen next.

There's no other way, Paige thought. Remembering her last

training session with Mathis, she created a pure light orb and threw it on the ground behind them. The car behind them slammed on its breaks, almost making the vehicle that followed collide with it. The shadow gave a short-hollowed scream before it turned to ash. *So that what happens to them,* Paige thought having destroyed her first shadow. Having the element of surprise, she threw another one at the ground but this time they dodged it. In fact, they backed off keeping what they hoped was a safe distance. Paige couldn't help but smirk. I was quickly wiped from her face when the car was struck with such force that Bastille slammed into the car next to them.

Paige screamed as she was jerked sideways then slid back into the car.

"Are you ok?" Emilan asked again.

"I think so, though, I'm sure I'll be covered in bruises in the morning," Paige said through tears.

"Will it start?" Emilan asked as the man they hit shouted all sorts of profanities at them.

"I'm not sure," Bastille said turning the key for a third time a he glanced at the rain cloud above. *This isn't good,* he thought.

"We need to go, now," Paige said as Shadow People in true form quickly approached.

Just as they were about to reach them, the car roared to life. Climbing back through the sunroof, Paige noticed the Shadow People didn't chase after them. Looking down, she realized they didn't need too, they sent their shadows instead.

Sirens could be heard in the distance as they sped away from the accident. Wiping away her tears and ignoring the ache in her side, Paige focused on the five shadows that followed them. Wanting to get rid of them all at once, she filled both hands full of pure light Jacks and threw one hand full at the ground. The shadows dodged them as they laughed at the child and her sad attempts to stop them. Watching the shadows moments, Paige noticed some of them moved in short sharp movements while others stretched out their full length before moving forward. This time, instead of just throwing them, Paige tossed them in specific locations based on the shadow's movements. As soon as they hit the ground, she made certain points of the Jacks spread out until they touched each other. The Jacks that landed a distance behind them hit the shadows that trailed behind.

Paige grinned as they turned the corner leaving piles of ash behind. Thinking she was done, Paige gripped both sides of the sunroof. Glancing back up before lowering herself, she saw a large shadow slide around the building in their direction. *I can't tell how many there are,* Paige thought. They somehow managed to blend their shadows together masking their numbers. *Jacks aren't going to cut it for this.*

As a few separated themselves from the group, Paige thought back to the one training session she hadn't liked. "How long until we get there?" Paige asked.

"10, 15 minutes," Bastille said, "depending on traffic."

Paige took a look at her surroundings and noticed there were no more tall buildings and the houses were farther apart from each other. *Ugghh,* Paige internally groaned. Closing her eyes, she created handle that was easy to grip and control. Using her right thumb and index finger, Paige made a thick rope of pure light come from the handle. Laying it before her, she twirled the rope in a circle until she had a nice size pile. Taking the handle in her right hand, Paige cracke the whip. Sparks of pure light came off it as it snapped in the air. She flinched at the sound but tried to remember she controls where it wer

The shadows came and Paige was ready for them. The crack (the whip filled the air as she struck any shadow that got near. Those that made it pass the whip's tip thought they were safe, and perished for underestimating her. Paige simply separated part of the whip to g after it.

Seeing their comrades turned to ash, the large shadow broke apart and it was then Paige learned their true numbers. *I'm not sure i; can keep a barrier up with us moving in the car. If I keep weaving the whip around I'm bound to miss some shadows.* Not giving it another thought, Paige stilled the whip just long enough to create several pur light orbs. She sent her army of orbs to float around the entire car.

Just a little longer, Paige thought as she grew tired. There we; fewer houses now as they neared the edge of Quincy.

"We have a problem," Bastille said stopping the car just as th rain escaped the clouds.

"What is it?" Paige asked. Turning around, she saw an army Shadow People and Shadows surrounding a farm house that had

242

hundreds of solar lights in the yard. There were so many of them, Paige knew she couldn't beat them all using her whip. "Help me," Paige whispered looking up to the sky.

Using both hands, Paige created an orb of pure light the size of a small suitcase and tossed it in the air. Arms outstretched, she guided it even higher. When it was about 10 feet up, two stars shot across the sky and caught it in their arms. Mixing the two lights, they helped the young girl guide it to the rain cloud she was aiming for. Once it reached the cloud, the Stars vanished once again leaving them to fend for themselves.

"Split," Paige whispered. She ignored everything around her knowing it would take her full concentration in order to work.

Above, the large orb split multiple times until there was one in the six clouds that surrounded them. Once they were in place, Paige made them expand and what happened next was something the Stars hadn't seen in many years. Not liking what they saw, some of the Shadow People and shadows fled the area but many stayed behind.

"Start the car," Paige said getting back into the car and closing the sunroof.

Bastille looked over his shoulder at her but did as she said.

"You'll know when to go," Paige said and that he did.

When the first drops of pure light rain fell from the sky, Bastille hit the gas.

"No matter what, don't stop until we're behind the solar lights!" Paige yelled as he drove through the shadow and Shadow

243

People.

All around them, ash fell to the ground along with the pure light rain. When they reached the driveway, there was no room to pai and they were forced to get out. Paige shielded them with her orbs as they stumbled behind the barrier.

"Daijon!" Audi had screamed from upstairs when she saw th pure light rain. *How's that even possible,* she thought. Running down the stairs, she noticed the curtains on all the windows were still draw closed. "You need to see this," she said dragging her brother from the couch and over to the back door. A gasp left his lips as he saw the golden clouds.

Then there was a knock at the door.

Daijon told the others to stay there as he and Audi went to answer it. Opening it, they saw a man and a woman who had the features of a dog and a young girl they didn't know holding a whip ot pure light. "Who are you?" Daijon asked. Though he was concerned, he knew no shadows or Shadow Person could pass the solar lights.

"The new Sun," Paige said voicing it for the first time.

"How do you have the same powers as me and my sisters?" Audi asked as Paige turned the whip to fine glitter.

"I just told you," Paige said.

"This doesn't make any sense," Audi whispered more to herself than anyone else.

"If we could come in, I'd rather not discuss it outside," Bastil said.

Daijon looked behind them. The rain had stopped and the clouds, now their normal color, were moving past them. For the first time in a while, the darkness around their home was just that, normal darkness. They didn't know how many were turned to ash but Daijon knew they would be back. Waving them inside, Daijon and Audi led them to the living room. Those that had been downstairs were still by the glass doors. Paige moved closer to Emilan's side as the others approached.

"What's going on?" Lee asked standing by Daijon wondering how they made it past the Shadow People outside.

"That's what we're about to find out," Daijon said. "I need you to gather everyone on the training mats."

Lee glanced at the newcomers once again then headed upstairs.

"Stop starring," Daijon said nudging Audi in the side.

Whispers filled the room, as Paige, Bastille, and Emilan stood by the counter that separated the kitchen. Though, she knew none of them were Shadow People and there were no shadows in sight, Paige couldn't help feel a little nervous as she stood between the Et Lunam. Looking around, she noticed there were children and adults, yet the children seemed to be in charge.

Daijon and Audi stood at the front of the group. Lee, Andrew, Parker, and Autumn were spread out in front of the group behind them, just in case.

"Who are you?" Daijon asked again.

"I'm more concerned with who **she** is," Audi mumbled.

"I already told you **I'm** the new Sun," Paige said.

"How's that even possible," Audi said. Her mother had never told her that if something happened to her a new Sun would take her place.

"We'll explain everything," Bastille said. "We should warn y that it's going to be a bit of a shock."

And that is was.

When Bastille and Emilan removed their amulets, parents dre their children closer and whispers grew into loud voices. Their eyes remained the same but their hair came down around their ears that resembled those of a Siberian husky. While not the length of a Siberi Husky, their noses were still the same shape and black color. Even their hair, covered their now bare feet. By the time they finished changing, the voices were even louder.

"Quiet down everyone," Daijon said.

"What are they?"

"Where did they come from?"

"If everyone could quiet down, we'll find out," Daijon loudei this time.

"How could you let them in here not knowing that they're no even human? What if they're with the shadows?"

"Everybody shut up!" Daijon shouted having lost his patienc He turned to scan the crowd and not one person uttered a single worc The only sound that could be heard was a soft chuckle coming from Andrew who stood with his arms crossed.

I swear if we get one more interruption, Daijon thought as he turned back to face their new guest.

"We are called the Et Lunam and we come from the light side of the moon," Bastille explained.

"The Stars brought us here and gave us these amulets because we wanted to live among the humans. We've been watching over Paige here ever since then," Emilan said.

"You expect us to believe the **stars** brought you here," Lee said stepping forward.

"You will," Paige laughed. "I didn't believe them at first either."

"Guys, you're gonna want to see this," Andrew said having spotted the light first.

Right outside the glass windows, two Stars fell from the sky. They dimmed their light so they could be seen but made no move towards the house. Ignoring Daijon's protest for her to stop, Paige opened the glass door and ran to Mathis.

"You're okay," Paige said as he wrapped his arms around her. Letting go, she looked at Master Linen who surveyed the area. "Thank you for saving me, both of you."

"I'm glad you made it here in one piece," Mathis said.

"So am I but we have important matters to attend to," Master Linen said. All business as usual.

With their wings spread out and battle armor on, Paige led the Stars to the waiting crowd inside.

"I am Master Linen, fighting master of the Stars," Master Linen said stopping just inside the door. "And this is Mathis, Paige's protector. We have been sent by the North Star to explain the situation."

"The North Star sent you," Audi said.

"That is correct, Audi, daughter of the Sun," Master Linen said.

"How do you know who she is," Daijon said.

"It's the star's job to know the names of all the Stars children Daijon."

"Our mother never told us any of this," Audi said.

"I think we should clear the room first," Mathis said looking around the room at the fear and confusion on the others faces.

Daijon followed his gaze and realized Mathis was right. Thes people had already dealt with the Shadow People; they didn't need to deal with this as well. Going over to Lee and Andrew, he asked them both to take everyone upstairs then to come right back. Parker and Autumn were the only others he allowed to stay.

When the two young men returned, Daijon turned to the Stars "What's going on? What do you, the Et Lunam, and the girl have to c with the Shadow People?" Daijon demanded.

Master Linen stared at the boy. He noticed that how despite h age, the others listened to him. He also noticed the dark circles under his eyes. For those reasons, he didn't reprimand the boy's rudeness bt got straight to the point. "When the Shadow People grew stronger an the Sun looked to be in danger, the North Star chose a human to replace the Sun if she should die. Paige is that person. It's the job of the Stars, Bastille, and Emilan to protect her."

"What about our sisters," Audi said. "You just let the Shadow People take them."

"*We* did no such thing," Master Linen said. "Your sisters knew about the Shadow People and have been told their entire lives to be careful by your mother. They chose not to practice using their powers and to not be aware of what has been going on."

"We're just kids," Audi said. "We just wanted normal lives."

"You are the Sun's children. You weren't meant to be normal but to fight the Shadow People," Master Linen said. "You, yourself have lived a normal life and had no problem fighting off the shadows even when you gave your powers away."

Audi lowered her eyes and remained silent.

"We made a promise to the late Sun and we will keep it," Master Linen continued.

"Why do the Shadow People even want the Earth?" Daijon asked still not fully understanding.

"The Et Lunam queen lives on the dark side of the moon and has ordered them to take over Earth so she can claim it as her own."

"How do we stop them?" Daijon asked.

"First, we have to save your sisters." Master Linen said.

CHAPTER 25

In the past...

Though it could barely be seen, water from a large fountain o
each side of the bridge rose into the air in wet arches splashing back
down into the water below.

Finally entering the neighborhood, they welcomed the light
that greeted them every few feet from lamp posts identical to the one
by the bridge. Solar lights in their last hours of stored light glowed
from just about every yard. A few homes even had lights still on
inside.

"I'm hoping, we'll find a house where no one's home," Claret
said. Without Daijon, there would be no way to distinguish a Shadow
Person from a human but as much as they didn't want to stop, they
needed the supplies. *Hopefully, we can make it out without running
into anyone.*

When they reached the second block from the main road, the
found a house whose garage door was still open.

"Do you think someone's home?" Audi asked.

Kiki looked around then proceeded into the empty garage.
When she reached the door leading inside, she found it slightly ajar.
"Is anyone here?" She yelled stepping in further. Hearing no reply, sh
waved the others forward.

Audi, Claretta, and Paige entered the kitchen and stood next t
Kiki. Cabinets were left open and dirty dishes littered the sink. Toys,

phone charger, and other random items that were left behind remained on the counter as though hoping someone would return for them.

"Look for any bags that will hold supplies, preferably, backpacks," Claretta instructed. "Also look for: first aid supplies, food, water and glass jars with lids that screw on."

Having everything they needed, they left the house but were greeted by the residents across the street.

"Mind telling me what you're doing in my neighbor's house," a man about the same age as Claretta's father said as he stood at the end of the driveway. "You all aren't from around here."

Claretta mentally rolled her eyes as they kept their distance, wishing to avoid the entire situation. The man glanced at the bags they hadn't entered with waiting for a reply. "We're on our way to Quincy and came to see if a friend of ours wanted to tag along," Claretta lied.

"A bit young to be walking that far," the man said not believing her story.

"What's this about going to Quincy?" A woman interrupted in a loud voice as she came over from next door. "I heard on the news they got this strange light surrounding part of the town."

To their misfortune, her loud voice started to attract more people. Audi, Claretta, Kiki, and Paige tried to leave but kept getting bombarded with questions, even though, they never *said* they were from Quincy. Paige, unable to answer any questions, stood there in silence.

"What?" Claretta asked after Paige pulled on her shirt for the fifth time.

Paige pointed in the direction she'd been looking in. Between two of the houses, outside the crowd, was a human sized Crater Fairy. To the left of it was another one. Realizing, they'd been spotted; the Crater Fairies became small again and flew towards them.

"Everyone back inside!" Claretta yelled backing away from the crowd as the tip of a whip hit the cement in the middle of the crowd.

Audi removed the bow she'd slung over her left shoulder and reached for her quiver Claretta had replenished. Kiki took the mini crossbow from the bag she now carried and pulled Paige, who had th other bag behind them. Still two blocks from the main road, Kiki looked for a shortcut. *If we cut through the yards, we should make it,* she thought.

Kiki led the way as they ran through the resident's backyards. Dogs barked behind a fenced in yard up ahead. They didn't know wh had them so bothered until they rounded the fence and saw a Crater Fairy. The children almost collided from the sudden stop they made but they managed to stay standing and went around the house next door. Claretta turned throwing a pure light dagger at the charging female fairy. It side stepped it then expanded its left wing to knock Claretta over but the girl ducked underneath it. Claretta spun around and ripped through the fairies' wing with a dagger she'd made at the last second. The Crater Fairy yelled and lashed out with its whip hitting Claretta on the arm. The Crater Fairy returned to its normal si

252

struggling to stay in the air but before it could try and get away, Paige unscrewed the lid of a jar Claretta infused with pure light and captured it.

Audi helped Claretta, who held her bleeding forearm, off the ground. She took a quick look at it while Kiki held off the other fairy. "It doesn't look too bad," Audi said. "Can you keep going?"

Claretta nodded as silent tears left her eyes. She held her arm as they continued to run. Even more people were out now, leaving their cozy beds to see what was going on. Audi yelled at them to go back inside as she let an arrow fly loose, while Claretta prayed they'd make it to the bridge before more fairies arrived.

When they finally reached the bridge, Claretta told the others to go across first.

"Are you sure?" Kiki asked looking at Claretta's arm.

"Yes, now go!" Claretta shouted.

Claretta let go of her arm that wasn't bleeding as much anymore and let it hang by her side. She turned to walk backwards but with good reason. Though her left arm was useless at the moment, she was determined to pull off her plan. Trying to ignore her throbbing arm, Claretta focused on the fountains nearby. The sky may be the Crater Fairies advantage but the water was hers. She let pure light sit at the bottom of the pond until the fairies were closer.

"Wait!" The Crater Fairy she'd soaked in the bathroom yelled but it was too late, his comrades had already flown over the bridge.

That's when the pure light left the bottom of the pond and into the ropes of water that shot out the fountain. With one hand, she used those ropes and directed them at the fairies. Ignoring her order, Audi and Kiki rejoined Claretta on the bridge shooting at any fairy that escaped the water's grasps. As the Crater Fairies kept up their assault the girls grew tired. Seeing no way across, the fairies were forced to retreat.

"Where's Paige?" Claretta asked letting the water return to th fountain.

"We left her by the road," Audi said.

When Claretta got to the road, she noticed Paige up ahead wi her thumb stuck out trying to hitchhike. A car sped by them and stopped by Paige. The others weren't far behind but not close enough Without even asking her where she needed to go, two men jumped o and tried forcing Paige in the car. She kicked and punched trying to g away.

Audi was the first to reach Paige and grabbed onto one of the men that held the girl. Audi noticed the man flinch at the sight of her necklace. "Shadow People!" She yelled. The Shadow People let Paig go and hopped back into the car. Before they could get away, Claretta sliced the tires with pure light daggers then tossed an orb through the open window. It exploded seconds after she let go turning the Shadov People and their shadows to ash.

"First, you run away and now you want to hitchhike!" Claret yelled. "In case, you forgot, Crater Fairies and Shadow People are trying to kill us."

"I told you I don't want to do this!" Paige yelled back.

"You think we do!" Claretta continued to yell. "My *entire* life had been turned upside down and *they* lost their mother."

"I'm sorry but I can't change any of that!"

"But *you* can make it better!"

Both girls stood there in silence done yelling at each other. Audi looked at Paige and fully realized what she'd done to Claretta.

"Do you hate me?" Audi whispered feeling sorry for Claretta and Paige.

"What are you talking about?" Claretta asked looking at her best friend.

"I'm sorry I ruined your life by giving you my powers. I should have just faced the Shadow People that day."

Claretta sighed. "You didn't ruin my life; it's just a bit more colorful."

Both girls laughed.

"Things would be a lot worse if you hadn't. We're best friends. I'd do anything to help you."

Audi and Claretta hugged for a few moments then everything was okay between them again.

"Are we still going to make it?" Claretta asked no one in particular.

"We should if we take a shortcut," Kiki said.

"What shortcut?" Audi asked seeing nothing but trees and a cement road.

"There should be a river that comes out this way," Kiki said. She looked around, even though it was impossible to see anything in the dark. "We just came out the subdivision," she said more to herself than anyone else, "so if we go this way." She led them across the stre and into the woods. No more than 15 minutes in, they were greeted with a river no wider than the country two lane road they left behind them.

"That's great, you found a river," Paige said sarcastically. "To bad, we don't have a boat or a raft in our bags."

"I'm pretty sure I can make one," Claretta said standing by th river's edge.

"What are you going to do, chop down a tree? I didn't realize you were carrying a chainsaw. Is it invisible?"

"Why don't you try shutting up and not causing any more problems for once," Kiki said from beside Paige.

"I've got something better than a chainsaw," Claretta said. Bending down, she put both hands in the water then created pure ligh It flowed from her hands and wrapped around the water making a lor log shape that floated to the top.

Paige moved towards the log that floated to the riverbank. Sh reached out with her hand and was surprised to find the log was solid *Wow, that is better* Paige thought but refused to say aloud.

Claretta continued making logs until it was big enough to hol them all. Then, without even touching it, tied them together with rop of pure light.

"Is that really going to hold us?" Paige asked still a bit apprehensive.

"Yes," Claretta said stepping onto the raft without hesitating.

"This river should take us most of the way," Kiki said as she got in the back. "There will be a fork in the river. We have to go right and get off there. Then it's just a straight shot."

"Do I even want to know what you've been doing out here?" Audi asked from the middle of the raft beside Claretta.

"Just a couple of parties," Kiki explained, "but mostly, I was practicing my powers. I loved having them and figured no one would see me out here. Remember, when we learned how to send letters through light?"

Audi and Claretta laughed.

"What's so funny?"

"That's how Claretta got dragged into this." Audi said. "Her future self sent a letter to her past self through the light. No doubt she learned from one of us."

"Yeah and it said I had the power to create pure light," Claretta added.

"And who else would she have gotten them from but me," Audi said.

"I'm glad you didn't ignore it and showed the letter to Audi," Kiki said.

The girls sat in silence as the current pulled them in the direction they needed to go. Before they got too far, Claretta made a lantern of pure light and attached it on the front of the raft. It shone back and forth across the river allowing them some view of what lay ahead. Every now and then, Claretta steered it around fallen trees and back into safe water. As they continued to drift, Paige took the fairy she'd caught out her bag. He flapped his wings furious as he pushed on the lid that had three small holes for air. They watched as he attempted to revert back to human size hoping the glass would break in the process. It refused to budge and he was forced to stay fairy size. Knowing the pure light burned them, Claretta only infused light on the outside of the glass. They would still be unable to break it but wouldn't get hurt at the same time.

"What are we going to do with him?" Paige asked putting it back in the backpack.

"I'm not sure," Claretta said. "Maybe Finian can ask the stars to take him back to the dark side of the moon."

They returned to silence after that for awhile enjoying the rushing sound of the river that accompanied the sweet melody of crickets. The wind that had grown still picked back up again making the branches sway as though they were alive and dancing to the music the crickets and river provided. Claretta caught one of the leaves that fell then placed it in the water. Seeing more leaves fall like a dropped handkerchief, she sent tiny orbs through the air. The leaves soaked them up as they continued to fall all around them. Once they hit the water, the light left them and they were normal leaves once again.

They had almost made it to their turn, when the Crater Fairies

258

appeared from behind them.

"If we get out the river now, we won't make it on time," Kiki told them.

Claretta moved Paige to the middle of the raft and took her spot at the helm. There was no way she'd be able to steer and make pure light ropes. They would have to rely on their weapons. The Crater Fairies advanced their whips uncurled and ready. The raft shifted as the girls stood in a triangle form around Paige but trying to fight while sitting wasn't an option. Having a sense of how the fairies moved, their aim had improved but they were still outnumbered and had nowhere to run.

A Crater Fairies' whip struck Audi on the side of her ear causing the arrow she just notched to fall into the river. She grabbed her ear and felt blood dripping down her neck. The Crater Fairy cracked its whip again but this time Audi held up her bow diagonally.

"Claretta, the whip!" Audi yelled once it had wrapped around her bow. She pulled on the bow bringing the Crater Fairy closer. Claretta turned to her left and cut the whip with her dagger making the fairy fly backwards into a tree branch.

Kiki twisted and turned firing at the Crater Fairies that surrounded them. "Claretta, I'm out!" She yelled. She passed the empty container to her. Claretta took it and held her hand over the container until it was full then passed it back to her. Kiki continued to shoot when she noticed some branches overhanging the river. "Branches up ahead!"

Claretta looked up and saw them. Right as they were going under them, she lit the leaves with light and Kiki hit the branches making them fall. It slowed the Crater Fairies down but only for a moment.

"We're almost there!" Claretta shouted as the Crater Fairies continued their attack.

Their whips beat at the raft breaking it apart. Soon, water started to leak from the broken logs. Daggers flew through the air turning to dust whenever they hit the shoreline or tree. Paige jumped out the way of the fairy's whip nearly falling out the raft. Claretta caught her arm steadying her. This was not the time to try and teach her how to use her powers so Claretta made the girl a shield. She did know how long it would hold up against the Crater Fairies powerful whips but she could always make another.

The raft slowed down as it continued to lose water now from three different spots.

"We're going to have to jump!" Claretta said.

"What!" Kiki yelled.

"Can you swim?" Claretta asked Paige.

"Yes," she answered.

"Then everyone follow me!" Claretta yelled. "One, two, three!"

Claretta jumped into the river that was deeper than she though The sound of more splashing let her know the others had followed. Thinking fast as the current pushed them towards the fork in the rive

260

Claretta sent four orbs to the left. Her arm still hurt a little but she kept swimming as the Crater Fairies took the bait. When the fairies were out of sight, the girls broke through the rivers surface gasping for air. Somewhere behind them, the raft collided with a fallen tree along the shoreline sprinkling the ground and water with pure light particles.

The current had slowed down and the girls swam to shore with no problem. Remembering the fairy in her bag, Paige opened it and found the Crater Fairy standing in a few inches of water. She tipped the jar over letting the water out then put it back in the bag.

They ran a short distance to the road and soaking wet, they continued on their journey home. Exhausted from running and fighting and with only a few hours sleep, they decided to find a place to take a break while they could. The ride on the river gained them 20 minutes thanks to the current. It wasn't much but they were thankful for the time allotted them.

CHAPTER 26

Still in the past...

They didn't have to go far before they came to an intersection Claretta sent some orbs ahead and noticed a cement culvert beneath the road. "Let's check it out," she said.

They carefully made their way down the sloping hill to the culvert. Grass and weeds grew tall near the cement that stretched out from it and hugged the grass. Standing at the edge of the culvert, Claretta sent a few orbs into it to check things out. It was 15 feet wid and littered with leaves and dirt. When the light had reached the end, and no shadows or animals were found, Claretta led the others inside

"What about the shadows?" Kiki asked when they stopped a few feet in.

"Right now, I'm more worried about the Crater Fairies," Claretta said as she and Paige sat across from Kiki and Audi.

"How's the arm?"

"It's not too bad."

"We should change it though. Who knows what was in the water?"

Audi went to sit next to Paige as her sister tended to Claretta's arm. While the others were preoccupied, she whispered to Paige who sat there as though uninterested in anything she had to say.

"You do know you can dry our clothes," Audi said no longer whispering.

262

"Really," Claretta said surprised leaning against the wall with her eyes closed.

"Of course. We used to do it all the time when we got caught out in the rain."

Claretta opened her eyes ready to learn something new.

"All you have to do is let the pure light flow through your body. Move it to your hands but don't create any light. Your hands will glow and heat up from the unused light. Then all you have to do is move your hands over what you want to dry."

Now dry, they were able to relax a lot better but not for as long as they'd like because they were careless and forgot to hide the glow of pure light coming off their weapons. The Crater Fairies had realized to late the light they followed was a decoy. Back tracking, they went the other direction, but were not sure where to go until they saw the light off the road.

Claretta opened her eyes having fallen asleep by accident and spotted a small group of Crater Fairies up ahead. She woke the others and urged them to hide their weapons not realizing it was too late. The Crater Fairies whips hammered the road causing cement to fall from above. The fairies attacked from both sides leaving them no way out. Claretta looked up and could've sworn the culvert was getting smaller but assumed she was imagining things. Audi and Kiki cleared the way and they hurried to the next culvert. Claretta looked behind her as they ran and noticed what looked like red glitter falling onto the road above the culvert. She slowed a little to get a better look and realized the culvert they'd hid in *was* getting smaller. *Its fairy dust,* Claretta thoug as the road above the culvert crumbled.

"Guys, don't let the fairy dust touch you!" Claretta yelled as she sped up.

They ran through the next culvert trying to stay ahead of the Crater Fairies but as they made it to a culvert further down, the other side crumbled to the ground just as they were about to enter it. Not fa ahead was a forest and on the other side of that was an open field rigl outside Quincy.

"Audi, cover us!" Claretta yelled.

Audi nodded turning her back to the forest. She dodged whip: and shot arrows doing everything she could to keep the four fairies from the forest. When her quiver was empty, she ran in after the others. Unable to find them, Audi started to panic and was about to shout but didn't want to for fear of attracting the Crater Fairies to her location. She went a bit further when a small pebble hit her in the head. She looked up and saw Claretta and Kiki each hiding in a tree. Paige peaked out from the large bush she hid behind then ducked bac down.

Claretta and Kiki stayed quiet, weapons ready. Audi hid behir a tree and Paige had a jar opened and ready.

The Crater Fairies flew into the forest where they were met b: other fairies. There was nearly no time left and they had to get the gii

Claretta and Kiki stayed hidden behind the cluster of leaves i the trees waiting for the perfect moment. When the fairies got close,

Kiki shot at them with her crossbow and Claretta threw her daggers targeting the fairy's wings. Paige took out another jar and handed it to Audi. Together, they caught three fairies that fell from the sky.

Their hiding spots discovered; a Crater Fairy used its whip to cut down the tree Claretta was in. She stood on the branch struggling to hold on as the tree fell forward. When it was a safe distance from the ground, Claretta covered her face and jumped. She rolled along the grass inches from where a branch smacked the ground. Another fairy sprinkled fairy dust on the tree Kiki was in. She nearly fell out trying to get away from it but her attempts failed as her hair was covered in fairy dust. Kiki and the tree both shrank away from the Crater Fairies grasps. The fairies weren't worried though the damage had already been done. Having seen what happened, Audi ran over to the tree as it finally stopped shrinking. With the tree now standing three feet tall, she was able to catch Kiki as she jumped into her hands.

"Where are they going?" Paige asked confused as to why they'd flee when they had the upper hand.

"Where's Kiki?" Claretta asked joining them.

Audi held out her hands for the others to see. Kiki, now the same size as the Crater Fairies stood in her sister's palm looking up at the others. "She got hit by fairy dust."

"Why is she smaller than the tree?" Paige asked. "They both got hit by fairy dust."

"I'm not sure," Claretta said. "It probably works differently on people."

"Can you change her back?" Audi asked.

Claretta remained silent thinking it over. *If fairy dust can mak* things smaller, then maybe pure light particles can reverse the effects Audi placed Kiki on the ground and Claretta knelt over her with her hands over Kiki's head. A shower of pure light particles fell from Claretta's hands. After a few seconds she stopped, then stood and backed away with the others. Slowly, Kiki got bigger and bigger unti she was back to normal size.

"Thanks," Kiki said.

"No problem," Claretta said. "How much time do we have left?"

Audi pulled out her cell phone. "An hour."

"Call the others and have them meet us at the edge of the for field. See if one of them can pick us up as well."

"Okay, but where?" Audi asked.

"I got a good view when I was in the tree," Kiki said. "We're between the dairy farm and the Garraway's house."

"Tell them to bring their staffs and any orbs that are left. They're going to need them," Claretta said. "Don't forget to warn the about the fairy dust."

Even though, the Crater Fairies retreated, there was no way they would make it to the force field without a fight.

The glow from the force field could be seen with ease as Claretta and the others reached the forest's edge. *So, this is what the force field looks like from this side,* Claretta thought. Tired and sore, they looked for a vehicle but there was no one there. In the distance, she could just make out the Sun's other daughters, Daijon and the Et Lunam that had protected Paige's parents standing at the edge of the force field. *Why are they just standing there,* Claretta thought until more Crater Fairies than they'd seen before came into view.

The open dark field was sprinkled with the orange glow of Crater Fairies that flew and stood human size.

"Take off your bags," Claretta said working light with her hands.

Kiki and Paige placed their bags on the ground by a tree.

"What about the fairies in the jars?" Paige asked.

"Leave them," Claretta said still working with the light while keeping an eye on the Crater Fairies who waited for them.

"There's so many of them," Audi said worried, "we'll never make it across."

"Yes, we will," Claretta said handing her more arrows for her quiver. "We have too." She handed her a shield with straps on the back she could slide her arm into. It was small but it would allow her to block the fairy's whips and still use her bow. She also gave a shield and more orbs to Kiki who was on the phone telling the others what they planned to do.

"We should turn back," Paige said lowering the shield Claretta handed her.

"There *is* no turning back. We either make it across or we don't make it at all," Claretta said. "Keep your shield up and stay with us.

When we get close to the force field you run, no matter what. Do you understand?"

Paige nodded gripping the shield in front of her tightly.

We can do this. We can do this, Claretta thought a pure light dagger in one hand and a staff in the other.

CHAPTER 27

In the future...

Seven stars fell from the sky that day. It would be the first time an event like that took place on Earth. Four of those Stars fell on the outskirts of the park forming a crude square. These particular Stars were old, the oldest of all those in the sky, with light that was so dim it was hard to see. They each carried one of Daijon's friends. Lee, Parker, Andrew, and Autumn stabbed the point of the solar lights they took from Daijon's house into the ground just like they were instructed.

Paige, Daijon, and Audi landed at the edge of the trees that separated them from the upper parking lot with Master Linen, Mathis, and another old Star. Daijon looked in each direction his friends landed not knowing if he'd see them again. He'd ordered them to leave once the solar lights were on the ground. After all they'd done to help him so far; there was no way he was going to allow them to join this fight when it could be their last.

"Don't worry, the Stars will make sure they make it back safe," Paige said following Daijon's gaze. After taking a quick glance around, Paige created a pure light orb and sent it into the air. Using her powers, she stretched the light and connected it with that of the solar lights. Paige used her hands to pull and shape the light until it formed a force field around the park. Now, they only had to deal with the shadows and Shadow People that were currently at the park.

"Where are the Shadow People?" Audi asked. She was the

only one among them that couldn't distinguish them from the regular darkness around them.

"Oh, they're here," Daijon said moving closer to her as he looked around. Shadows moved among the trees behind them, stood by the concession stand, and even played tennis with a shadow orb.

"You two didn't have to come. I mean, you can't even see them," Paige said looking at Audi.

"I've beat them before and I'll do just fine now," Audi said. "We're not leaving here without our sisters."

"If you two would stop arguing, we need to get moving," Mathis said removing the chakram from his side. Though the distance they had to cross was not great, he knew they'd have to fight to get anywhere near the pond.

The shadow continued to move through the darkness as Paige led the way to the lake with Mathis by her side. Master Linen, who followed from behind, didn't like what he was seeing. The Shadow People knew they were there and yet were too calm for his liking.

They didn't make it far.

"The Sun's last two children have finally come to surrender," tall Shadow Person in true form said coming from the direction of the pond. "They even brought the new Sun with them."

"How do you know about the child," Master Linen said moving in front of the group.

The shadows all around them stopped moving and they knew then that this was their leader.

"One of the Et Lunam named Finian was kind enough to tell me," the leader said, "after a little persuasion."

Master Linen's wings unfolded and lifted him into the air as he went after the leader. He smirked as the other Shadow People shielded him.

"Stay with Paige," Master Linen ordered Mathis as he sliced a Shadow Person with his chakram.

"Destroy them all!" The leader shouted as he stayed on the outskirts of the fight.

Thus, the fight began.

Audi and Daijon moved closer and gave each other a glance that said everything; they would save their sisters and their father or die trying. With solar lights in hand, they swung at any shadow or Shadow Person that neared them. Paige created pure light orbs and threw them at anything that moved while Mathis stayed by her side. For now, he kept his wings folded behind his armor and used the chakram.

As the fight continued, they grew tired. It seemed that for every shadow and Shadow Person turned to ash, two more took its place. Still, they continued to fight. Audi smacked a Shadow Person in the face then flipped the solar light into the ground turning a shadow to ash. Daijon fought with two solar lights just like his father taught him. All his skills were put to the test as he wielded the lights like swords. Mathis had freed his wings and jumped into the air. With a chakram in each hand, he flew forward taking out several Shadow People at once.

Paige swung her staff at a Shadow Person's legs then finished it off with a solar orb.

As more Shadow People swarmed them, Paige abandoned her staff. "Mathis, Audi, Daijon, I need you to shield me for a few seconds!" She shouted.

The others moved closer to her forming a triangle. Kneeling down, Paige created a medium sized bowl made of pure light. Turning it upside down, she sealed it to the concrete. Placing both hands on top, Paige closed her eyes. Once she was done, she stood up with a smile and backed away. Pure light orbs emerged from the upturned bowl just as she commanded them to. The moment they hit the air, they flew at any shadow or Shadow Person. Seeing the pure light orb Audi turned around. She nodded her head with a smile of approval as the pure light orbs continued to leave the bowl on their own.

Master Linen stole a glance away from the leader who fought him with shadow orbs as a pure light orb came over his shoulder. The leader noticed this to but he also noticed a flaw as he ducked the orb. There were too many pure light orbs for the girl to be able to control the movements of them all. Even still, too many of his kind were being turned to ash.

"Forget the others!" The leader shouted. "Go after the girl!"

It was in that moment that a white light covered the sky for miles around Quincy. When the light vanished, to any human that looked up, they would think it was a Star shower. Paige knew differe though as they shielded their eyes from the white light that circled

272

them. The light dimmed to reveal Stars that had been trained by Master Linen. Dressed in armor, they were ready to keep their promise to the late Sun. Past their protective circle even more Stars fell among the Shadow People.

Looking past the Stars that stood before her, Paige saw the leader slip away as Master Linen was once again surrounded. Seeing that Paige was safe, Mathis flew to help him. Daijon and Audi stayed by each other's side as they watched the Stars fight. Paige had something else in mind. The moment the Stars were distracted by the fight, Paige ran through an opening between them after the leader. *I can't let him escape,* Paige thought. Fighting her way through the Shadow People and shadows, she caught up to the leader as he slipped into the pond. Not wanting any Shadow Person or shadow following her, Paige descended the steps. Reaching the last step, Paige kneeled down and placed both hands above the water. It rippled as pure light spread across its surface in a thin layer. Once she was finished, she took a deep breath and dove in.

Moving quickly, Paige shot a beam of pure light into the water's depths. Keeping her eyes on the light, she saw a glimpse of a door before the light vanished. Returning to the surface, Paige took another deep breath then swam for the door. She reached out for the handle and realized, it wasn't a real door but a shadow made to look like one.

With her feet now on surprisingly solid ground, Paige searched the darkness for any hint of movement. Just as she was bout the create pure light to light her path she was knocked to the ground. Paige free her leg from the unexpected weight and scrambled to get up. She swiftly created an orb of pure light and threw it towards the door.

"You know those won't hurt me, right?" Audi gasped from th floor.

Paige rolled her eyes. "That was really stupid, you could have drowned. What are you doing here anyway?"

"I... came..." Audi gasped.

"You know what, never mind," Paige said helping her up, "ju follow me and don't get in the way."

Audi rolled her eyes and remained silent.

Paige led them down the dark hallway without the aid of pure light fearing it would give them away. As shadows glided past, leavir them untouched, she realized the leader was aware of their presence.

"Such foolish children," the leader whispered from somewhe in the dark just loud enough for them to hear, "thinking you could hic from me."

"We're not the ones hiding," Paige said reaching out with her right hand. It glowed as pure light flowed into the wall revealing the brick that hid in the dark. Halfway down, a shadow's ashes fell from the wall. The leader gave a hollow scream of anger.

Paige continued this process as they made a left down the onl available turn. This time she lit the floor revealing a door with bars near the top in the middle. As they neared them, Audi and Paige hear another scream. This one was feminine and not coming from the doo they approached.

"We have to do something," a female voice said from behind the door. "This is all your fault, Kamyra."

"We had to try something," Kamyra said, "and she's the only one whose powers still work."

"Audi should've never given them to her," Prima said.

"I didn't have much of a choice," Audi said going right up to the door. "At least, I used mine."

Just as they were going to continue to argue, they heard the feminine scream again.

"That's Claretta," Kiki said from somewhere inside the room.

"Who's Claretta?" Paige said coming to where the others could see her.

"The one I gave my powers to," Audi said.

"Who is she?" Kiki asked Audi like the other girl wasn't standing right there.

"I'm the new Sun but I'll explain later," Paige said then looked at Audi. "We need to go. We'll come back for them."

"Wait, where's dad?" Audi asked quickly. "The shadows took him and another girl."

"We haven't seen him," Prima said, "and trust me the Shadow People like to gloat when they've captured one of us."

"If they're here, we'll find them," Kiki said closer this time. "For now, just go save Claretta, our powers don't work so we'd just be in the way."

275

Audi nods and turns to go but Prima grabbed her sleeve making her stop.

"Go on, I'll be right there," Audi said to Paige.

Paige took a quick glance at the sisters then ran down the stai to her right in the direction the screams came from. Leaving a trail of pure light for Audi to follow, Paige turned left. At the end of the shor hall, movement could be heard coming from an open door. Not knowing what to expect, Paige created an orb of pure light took a dee breath and entered the room.

"All alone *little* Sun," the leaders voice taunted from the darkness.

"So, what if I am," Paige said searching him.

"Then you'll have made a grave mistake," the leader said closing the door.

Not long after the door was closed, Audi ran into the short ha having reached the end of the pure light trail. The door at the end opened but no one came out. *Please let this work,* Audi prayed havin a feeling she was walking into a trap. Nonetheless, she walked into tl room where she found Paige standing off to her right with a pure ligl orb in her hand.

"Where's Claretta?" Audi asked.

"She's over there," Paige said pointing to the wall across fror the door.

"Now that we're all here, let's get started shall we," the leade said slamming the door close.

Claretta whimpered from the ground.

The leader rolled his eyes. "I told you to be silent," he said walking towards the girl. Paige created another orb of pure light and moved to block his path. "I suggest you put those away," the leader turned towards her, "or you'll all die." Paige looked at the others then closed the palms snuffing out the light.

"Now, let's play a game," the leader said walking around the room with ease. "I'll call it...left behind. There are three of you in this room but only two of you will be allowed to leave. The one chosen to be left behind will never see another day."

The leader continued to circle the room as the girls took in what he said. After a minute had passed, he clued them in to the other part of the game. "As thrilling as it would be for me to watch you all struggle in choosing who will stay, I'll leave that choice up to the little Sun. I'm sure she'll make an unbiased decision."

Paige's eyes grew wide as she looked at the two girls. The leader was right, she didn't know either girl enough to favor one over the other but it still didn't make her choice any easier. "I won't do it," Paige said refusing to choose whose life would end here.

"You will do as I say," the leader said from behind Audi. He wrapped one arm around the girl and held a shadow orb in the other. "Now choose," he ordered Paige.

"Paige take Claretta and get out of here," Audi said as Paige still struggled to choose. "Trust me, everything will be okay."

Paige stared at her then looked at the leader behind her. "I

277

choose Audi to stay," Paige whispered. She looked at Audi who nodded then walked over to Claretta whose eyes were on the leader. Paige moved to her left trying to block her view of the shadow perso "It's okay, we can go."

"Claretta, go with Paige," Audi said, "She'll keep you safe."

The leader chuckled from behind her shaking his head.

"Now, it's just you and me," the leader told Audi as Paige walked out the door with Claretta.

Paige led them back down the hall and up the stairs to where the Sun's daughters were being held. "Stand away from the door!" Paige shouted through the bars. She placed both her palms on the doc then began to put pure light into the thick wood. Once she was finished, Paige told the others to shield their eyes. Connecting to the pure light, she reached out with her index finger and tapped the glowing door. It burst into a cloud of golden glitter that got into Paig hair making it sparkle.

"Where's Audi?" Prima, the first one out the door asked.

"He made me choose," Paige said. "She told me to leave her."

"But...she should still be here," Prima said coming into the hall and moving to the edge of the stairs. Behind her, her younger sister's left their cell and stood by Claretta.

"We have to go," Paige said.

"No," Prima said. "She'll be here."

"But he said..."

"I don't care what he said. She'll be here."

They waited in the hall for what felt like a long time but really only a minute had passed when they heard a door slam open. Prima walked down the steps then ran when she saw Audi turn the corner glowing in pure light. "I knew you could do it," Prima whispered into Audi ears as the two girls hugged.

Staying together, they searched every room but still couldn't find their father.

"Are you sure, the Shadow People took him?" Prima asked.

"There were so many shadows, if not them then who." Audi said.

CHAPTER 28

In the past...

Ready for battle, the girls emerged from the forest to face the Crater Fairies. Claretta dodged a whip aimed for her head and threw dagger at the flying fairy. Another one charged towards her wings spread wide. Instead of ducking, Claretta charged forward. Using the staff, she knocked the fairy off its feet then sliced its wing so it couldn't fly. Audi and Kiki were right behind her fighting off fairies with Paige between them.

Daijon, his sister's and the Et Lunam left the force field and joined the fight. They spread out a few feet along the force field.

Daijon held the staff Claretta had left them in his right hand, his knuckles turning white from his strong grip. Unlike the staff Claretta used when he first met her, these were made of nothing but pure light. He advanced forward but was stopped short when a Crater Fairies whip wrapped around his ankle. Daijon fell forward landing on his stomach. The pure light staff lay inches from his hands that had broken his fall. He turned onto his back and saw a female fairy with long dark hair, flying inches from his feet. She changed to human size and brought her whip down again.

Dirt rose from the ground as Daijon rolled out the way then kicked her in the leg. As the fairy used her wings to keep from falling Daijon crawled backwards reaching for his staff. Just as his fingers were about to wrap around it once again, another orange whip pulled away. Looking up, he saw another Crater Fairy standing by his staff. The Crater Fairy with the long hair wrapped its whip around both of Daijon's legs holding him in place as the second fairy reached into a pouch on her side and pulled out a handful of fairy dust. He struggled against the whip then closed his eyes waiting to feel the fairy dust fall but he never did.

"Don't mess with our brother," Kamyra said.

Daijon opened his eyes just as she knocked the fairy down with her staff. He turned as the whip around his ankles loosened and saw Klarissa run her staff down the other fairies wings burning the small threads that lay in the middle.

Not far from them, Prima fought side by side with one of the stars while the Et Lunam fought not far from them. With their feet bare, they were able to run faster than the humans and their dog-like ears allowed them to hear the faint swish of Crater Fairies wings making them strong allies.

Just as Claretta finished fighting another fairy, she saw something white falling from the sky towards her. It hit the ground before her with a sound like lightning cracking in the sky. Claretta shielded her eyes wondering what it could have been. When she lowered her arms, a man whose wings were the same shade of white as her mother's fake Christmas tree, stood before her. Black armor with intricate white patterns covered his torso and in his hands were a chakram. It was round like a Frisbee but smaller. The entire outside was a glowing white blade with hints of blue and on the inside was a

281

handle shaped like an unfinished sword. Claretta stepped back as he separated the handle in two cutting the weapon in half.

"Do not be afraid. I am the North Star, ruler of the night sky and we have come to keep our promise to the late Sun."

Claretta looked up as the Stars fell from the sky all around the field.

"Return to the dark side of the moon where you belong," the North Star ordered facing one of the Crater Fairies.

"We do not fear you!" A male Crater Fairy shouted raising his whip in the air, "and we will have the girl," he pointed to Paige.

"Then come take her if you think you can," the North Star said. His wings flapped lightly behind him as he faced the Crater Fair a piece of the Chakram in each hand. "Go," he told Claretta as he ros into the air weapons raised.

White now mixed with orange as the Stars fought the Crater Fairies. Though they were outnumbered three to one, the Stars continued to carry out their promise. All around the field, the Stars chakram cut down the Crater Fairies whips and sliced through their wings. Though human size and weaponless; they were not defenseles for they had some skill in hand to hand combat. Red fairy dust rained down on the field from the Crater Fairies that carried it. The Stars use their own wings to blow it away from themselves and back at their enemies. Even though it had no effect on the Crater Fairies, it'd be le: that could be used against them.

Audi, Claretta, and Kiki continued fighting their way to the

282

force field. Claretta wished now more than ever for it to rain but the sky didn't answer her. Halfway across, their way was blocked. Stars took care of two of the Crater Fairies while Audi and Kiki dealt with the other. Audi shot an arrow at its leg and Kiki made its wings look like Swiss cheese.

They could go no further though as more Crater Fairies came at them. The Stars held their own against the Crater Fairies but were too busy to help them. The girls continued fighting on their own when two fairies flew behind Paige. She squirmed and swung her shield as they lifted her in the air.

"No!" Claretta yelled as they dropped Paige into the arm of a waiting Crater Fairy.

She turned to tell Kiki and Audi they had to go after Paige and noticed Audi running for the force field. Thinking they had won, the Crater Fairies let her pass. *What is she doing,* Claretta thought?

"Finally, we've won!" The male Crater Fairy holding Paige shouted. "Earth now belongs to the dark!"

"No, you haven't!" Audi shouted from inside the force field the moment everyone got quiet. "You're the ones that have lost!"

Audi made pure light for the first time since she'd given her powers to Claretta. Putting her hands on the ground, she did something Claretta would never have been able to do. The ground beneath them shook but didn't break. Everyone looked around wondering what was happening when light shot up like roots from the ground. They wrapped themselves around the Crater Fairies that were standing and swatted down those that thought they could fly away. Paige ran to Claretta and Kiki as the Stars took hold of the Crater Fairies wrapped in pure light.

"How did this happen?" Claretta asked when they were all safely back in the force field with 20 minutes to spare. Behind them, stars could be seen returning to the sky with their captives.

"I'll tell you on the way," Audi said.

CHAPTER 29

In the future...

Paige stayed in the lead as she guided Claretta and the late Sun's Daughters towards freedom. Stopping, she turned to look at the group behind them.

"Can all of you swim?" She asked.

The girls all nodded.

"I'm not sure how you all were brought down here but this is the exit. We're going to have to swim out of the lake and I don't know if they're still fighting up there, if we won or if we lost. So, me and Audi will go first and the rest of you will follow afterwards."

Not sure of what awaited them in the park; Paige took a deep breath and swam for the surface.

"You defeated the leader," Mathis said running towards her.

"That was reckless," Master Linen said from behind him.

"Audi defeated the leader and what happened to the shadows and Shadow People?" Paige asked realizing the fighting had stopped.

"The shadows and Shadow People are all connected. The moment the leader was defeated they stopped fighting and fled," Master Linen said.

"Which is why we need to perform the ceremony before they chose a new leader and regroup," a man that shined brighter than the others said.

Master Linen and Mathis bowed and stepped aside. "Paige, this is the North Star, ruler of the night sky."

"I appear to have made the right choice," the North Star said looking at the young girl. He looked as though he was about to say more when Daijon ran towards them.

"You're all okay," Daijon said looking at his sisters.

"I'm sorry for all you have lost," the North Star said standing before the late Sun's children. He unfurled his wings and got down on one knee bowing before them. All around them, the Stars bowed as well showing their respect.

"Where's dad, and Cynthia?" Daijon asked noticing he wasn' with them.

"We looked everywhere but couldn't find him," Audi said.

"We stopped the Shadow People before they reached the parl and they've been safe since then," the North Star said. "It was a promise I personally assured the late Sun I would keep. No one else knew about it."

"Where are they now?" Audi asked.

"An old Star has taken them to your father's home. You will see him soon but first we must complete the ceremony," the North St said.

With the Stars standing guard, the North Star led them away from the pond and into the trees. They reached a small clearing that they hadn't noticed earlier. On the ground was a circle that had three stone paths leading away from it.

"Three days after the death of the late Sun," the North Star said once they were all gathered around the circle, "a ceremony should have been preformed transferring the children's powers to the new Sun. Now another route must be taken." He waved his hands and two Stars stepped forward, one was Emilan and the other Star who was only a few years older than Mathis. "In order for the new Sun to take her place in the sky, three sacrifices must be made. An Et Lunam and Star must give up their lives and become human forever, one with the gift of pure light must give up her powers."

The children watched as the Star and Et Lunam each took a place at the end of a stone path then they looked at each other.

"You can have my powers," Claretta said speaking for the first time since they left the pond. "If I had just done something, none of this would've happened."

"I shouldn't have forced my powers on you," Audi said. "I would've found another way had I known you were still afraid of the dark."

"We can't change what has been done but we can repair the future," the North Star said leading Claretta forward. "Now Paige, you stand in the middle. The powers of these three different beings will pass through the stones and into you."

"Will it hurt?" Paige asked.

"No."

With that, the ceremony began.

"On this night, we bring forth another to take the place of the late Sun," the North Star said, "like has been done before and will be done in the future. We also bring forth three sacrifices. The power of the Et Lunam, the Star, and pure light."

Master Linen brought forward a cup of blue liquid and handed it to Emilan.

"In this cup is the water from both sides of the moon and star dust. Once you drink it, your powers will travel along the stones and go into Paige."

Each of them drank from the cup and when the last power entered Paige, her entire body started to glow the golden color of pure light.

"To the daughters of the late Sun, I will say this," the North Star said as he stood by Paige. "Whatever the Shadow People injected you with will wear off and your powers will return to you. The day Paige has her first child; you will cease to have the power of pure light. Use your powers well."

With that, he took Paige's hand and they shot up into the sky. Moments later, the Stars followed them.

That night the Sun was returned to the Earth and the citizens of Quincy where left to wonder what really happened over the last several days. Some thought it was the government at work; others chose to act as though nothing happened. But for a small group of people that were in the heart of the battle, they will always remember how a young boy with a rare gift and the power of pure light saved them all.

CHAPTER 30

In the past…

While Claretta had been getting her arm re-bandaged in the culvert, Audi whispered to Paige that she would take her powers when everyone was asleep. She wasn't sure it would work and in fact had to try three times. Paige didn't want the powers and she always wanted to be just like her mother. Now she would be.

By the time, they reached the Cooper home; they only had 10 minutes left. Though they knew it wasn't goodbye forever, her family and Claretta were sad to see her go.

"For the first few days, you'll stay in the sky," Finian said. His torso was bandaged from being tortured by the first Crater Fairy Claretta had seen. The police found him lying on the side of the road, without a necklace, so they called Mr. Cooper, who took over from there. "Once there's enough light in the sky to light the other side of the world at night, then you can come down at night just like your mother did," he said to Audi. He led them out the back to where the ceremony would take place. Prima, with Finian's help, had made a circle of stone with six stone paths leading away from it.

"Audi, you stand in the middle," Finian said. "Kiki, Daijon, Kamyra, Klarissa, Prima, and Claretta, each of you stand at the end of a path. Your powers will pass through the stones and transfer to Audi."

"The shadows took our powers," Prima said.

"No, they just blocked them. Once Audi has your powers, the

North Star will go with her and teach her everything she needs to know."

When everyone was in place, they started.

"On this second night of the Sun's death, we bring forth another to take her place," Finian said, "Like has been done before and will be done in the future. We also bring forth those with the power of pure light."

Mr. Cooper brought forward a cup of blue liquid and handed to Daijon.

"In this cup is the water from both sides of the moon and star dust. Once you drink it, your powers will travel along the stones and go into Audi."

Each of the Cooper siblings drank from the cup and watched their powers traveled along the rocks and into their little sister. When was Claretta's turn, she held the cup thinking about everything that had happened. It was crazy, dangerous and while she liked having the powers, it was time to give them back. Holding the cup to her mouth, she drank the blue liquid that tasted like cool breeze and ocean air. When the last of the power entered her, Audi's entire body started to glow the golden color of pure light. The North Star came down from the sky once again and took Audi's hand.

"All will be okay," the North Star reassured her.

He stepped into the circle with her and with a final wave; they both turned into small balls of light, one white and one golden and shot up into the sky.

290

That night everyone slept outside under the stars and insisted Finian, who chose to stay up, wake them for sunrise.

"Everyone, it's time," Finian said several hours later.

For the first time in days, the Sun rose over the horizon once again. They stood there watching as Audi filled the world with light. Claretta had no idea what she would tell the reporters that were bound to come knocking at her door but she did know one thing. For now, they would all keep this to themselves, the secret of how the Sun's youngest daughter and an ordinary girl beat the darkness and saved the world.